MID-ATLANTIC TALES

SHORT MYSTERY
AND
HORROR STORIES

Publisher's Cataloging-in-Publication Data

Mid-Atlantic Tales: short mystery and horror stories / Future Publishing House Anthology Series, edited by Shaun Vain, with introduction by guest editor Dereck Mangus.

    248 p.
    Includes introduction and index.
    ISBNs: 978-1-953818-35-5 (pb) 978-1-953818-36-2 (hc)
    978-1-953818-37-9 (eBook)

1. Literature—Collections. 2. Fiction—Mystery. 3. Fiction—Horror. II. Series name. III. Editor.

10 9 8 7 6 FPH e 4 3 2 1
07 20 25 24 23 22 21
First edition.

Cover design by Kiirstn Pagan
FPH logo design by Mary Parrish

A publication from Future Publishing House
located in Maryland on traditional territory of Piscataway, Nanticoke, and Susquehannock

TABLE OF CONTENTS

Mystery & Horror

A
FUTURE PUBLISHING HOUSE
ANTHOLOGY

Volume 2:
Short Stories

Introduction to *Mid-Atlantic Tales*:
Surveying the Overlap in Genre & Geography

This anthology presents short stories in the mystery and horror genres by thirteen contemporary writers, each working in the Mid-Atlantic region of the United States. Given the extensive *overlap* between "mystery" and "horror," we also found it necessary to include an additional section of stories spanning both. Interestingly, this overlap is reflective of the more specific geographical region where each of these unique voices featured within are based. Genre and location aside, the stories in this collection range from the curious to the macabre. Some are lighthearted; others, dead serious. All are deeply engrossing.

What is meant here by *Mid-Atlantic*? To fully appreciate the present compendium, this term requires some unpacking. So, too, do *mystery* and *horror*. The meanings of the latter terms will come to light after more closely examining the former. Mid-Atlantic in this context is not meant to suggest the accent or manner of speech, but rather a strictly geographical designation denoting the area of land stretching along the Eastern Seaboard of the U.S. from New York to Richmond, moving inland towards Appalachia. This interstate expanse is located in the *overlap* of the American Northeast and Southeast, two separate regions which have cultivated distinct literary traditions of their own: the Northern and Southern Gothic.

Though its Southern relative is better known, the Northern Gothic requires equal bearing when reading these stories. Both genres refer to geographical orientations, thus connecting them to landscape within which those literary traditions developed. As W.S. Winslow writes in "Darkest New England: What Is the Northern Gothic Literary Tradition?," an essay published by *Literary Hub* earlier this year:

> Whereas the Southern Gothic is draped in Spanish moss, surrounded by cotton fields and oppressed by summer swelter, the Northern Gothic was born of cold and Calvinism, isolation and endurance, rooted not in the horrors of slavery and a fetishized myth of southern gentility, but the sharp, hard edge of fundamentalist Protestantism and the hopelessness of predestination. It's the Salem of Goodman Brown, Poe's House of Usher, and Ambrose Bierce's Owl Creek Bridge.

Winslow compares and contrasts the two main versions of American gothic fiction not simply by positioning them within the local climate and landscape, but by further locating them within the framework of the political and religious institutions of what was still a relatively New Republic. She goes on to note how the gothic tradition persists in American writing to the present: "And so, in the Northern Gothic tradition, Hawthorne begat Poe, Poe begat Lovecraft, and from Lovecraft it was a short walk through the graveyard to Stephen King." In the long tract of land between the graveyards of the Salem witch trials in New England and Confederate cemeteries in the Deep South, lay the countless graves of an American region neither fully North or South, but rather within a liminal zone.

***

Baltimore, Maryland is perhaps the most "mid" of Mid-Atlantic cities. Just below the Mason-Dixon Line, halfway between New York and Richmond, it is the northernmost city of the South. Baltimore has been central to American history, not only as an important hub during the Industrial Revolution, home of the first commercial and freight railway in the U.S., but also as a strategic military location during the War of 1812 and the American Civil War. If one could pinpoint the exact spot where the North and South overlapped, it would be Baltimore. Anchoring the central section of this regional Venn Diagram, Baltimore is both home to several of the authors in the anthology and headquarters of Future Publishing House. Baltimore thus serves as the perfect city to represent the idea of the Mid-Atlantic: a cultural hub between the North and South, and the nexus of a literary amalgam that might be called the *Mid-Atlantic Gothic*.

Moreover, Baltimore is strongly associated with Edgar Allan Poe (1809–1849), one of the most important American writers of poems and short stories exploring the darker realms of the human psyche. Poe was born in Boston, but grew up in Richmond after being orphaned. His brief and fraught career as an editor and writer brought him up and down the Eastern Seaboard of the U.S. Though he intermittently lived and worked in Baltimore, Philadelphia, Richmond, and New York, the author of "The Raven" is most closely identified with Baltimore as this was where he spent most of his time, met his wife, and ultimately died in the strangest of circumstances. Poe is regarded as the modern master of mystery and horror, both of which have roots in the Gothic.

Poe is credited with creating the modern mystery with his invention of Detective C. Auguste Dupin, his recurring central character in several short stories, including "The Murders in the Rue Morgue" (1841), "The Mystery of Marie Rogêt" (1842) and "The Purloined Letter" (1844). Written before the word *detective* was even coined, these stories set the modern mystery genre in motion, later inspiring perhaps the most famous detective stories: the beloved Sherlock Holmes series by Sir Arthur Conan Doyle, who asked, "Where was the detective story until Poe breathed the breath of life into it?" As far as horror goes, any number of Poe's tales, from "Berenice" (1835) to "Hop-Frog" (1849), could serve as the germ of later American horror for years to come. In Poe's work we find the perfect crucible in which mystery and horror coalesce, creating a mutant subgenre of the Gothic in the form of American gothic fiction.

Poe's enduring legacy persists into the twenty-first century. In an episode of HBO's television series *The Wire* (2002–2008), today as strongly associated with Baltimore as Poe, a young Black man tells a story to his friend in which a white tourist asks him, "Young man, you know where the Poe House is?" A typical red-brick Baltimore rowhome from the 1830s, the Edgar Allan Poe House has been preserved for many years as a National Historic Landmark, and is now engulfed by public housing projects in West Baltimore. The youth, hearing "po" as short for "poor," laughs and responds, "Look around. Take your pick!" Praised for its gritty realism, one might assume *The Wire* would be the last place to discern traces of the Gothic. Yet beyond the pun with his surname, Poe haunts the celebrated series in the crimes of Marlo Stanfield, one of the show's most ruthless antagonists whose crew disposes of corpses by sealing them inside abandoned rowhomes. Several of Poe's short stories, such as "The Black Cat" (1843), "The Tell-Tale Heart" (1843), and "The Cask of Amontillado" (1846), involve murders wherein bodies are immured within the floors and walls of buildings.

The Wire creator David Simon worked as a police reporter for over a decade at *The Baltimore Sun*, experiences from which inform his book *Homicide: A Year on the Killing Streets* (1991), winner of the 1992 Edgar Allan Poe Award, or "Edgar," in the Best Fact Crime category. Simon's wife Laura Lippman, also a former Sun reporter, is a prolific mystery writer whose books, such as *What the Dead Know* (2007), are often set in Baltimore. Lippman won a 1998 Edgar Award for her mystery novel *Charm City* (1997), the second in her popular Baltimore newspaper reporter-turned-private investigator Tess Monaghan series. From Poe to Lippman, the long tradition of the modern mystery story remains alive and well in Baltimore.

***

Mystery is the newer of the two literary genres collected in *Mid-Atlantic Tales*. In the form of ghost tales told around the campfire, the oral traditions of various cultures throughout time have contained elements of horror. The notion that horrifying phenomena must be solved through investigation using logic and reason, and perhaps even specialized tools, is inherently modern, enabled, in part, by the creation of precision instruments like the magnifying glass. That said, a taste for mystery began far back in time as well, in the form of puzzles and riddles. Nevertheless, the modern versions of each genre are relatively new, dating slightly before the turn of the nineteenth century. For one, the modern form of the novel, enabled by the printing press and mass literacy, was still new ("novel") at this time. Further, to take the Hegelian view of history, the dialectical tensions (the Enlightenment and Romanticism) necessary to permit the flourishing of such genres, had to unfold. By the arrival of the French Revolution and the Reign of Terror, a public desire for the mysterious and horrifying was born. The stage was set for a gothic revival.

Gothic fiction was an offshoot of Romanticism, the larger artistic, intellectual, and political movement popular amongst European intellectuals, especially in England and Germany, around the turn of the nineteenth century. The Romantics reacted against the alleged "progress" of the Industrial Revolution and the so-called Age of Reason. Culminating with the French Revolution yet persisting well into the nineteenth century, Romanticism subverted the presumed values of Enlightenment thought, seeking new ways of creating art, engaging with nature, and structuring a society less reliant on merely rational interpretations of the world. A revived interest in the irrational in the form of the demonic, the grotesque, the occult, and the supernatural became prevalent during its later phase known as Dark Romanticism. It is a short leap from Dark Romanticism to gothic fiction, essentially Romanticism's more gloomy progeny.

"The Gothic" is an enduring cultural and historical revival, encompassing far more than literature. It is difficult to convey how much of an impact the Gothic trend–in art, architecture, attire, and attitude–had on the cultural elite of late-eighteenth and early- to mid-nineteenth century Europe. Even a purely political tract like *The Communist Manifesto* (1848) by Karl Marx and Friedrich Engels, begins with the words, "A *spectre* is haunting Europe... the spectre of communism." (My italics.) Once a genre becomes big enough, it has the tendency to begin parodying itself. By the time it made its way across the Atlantic to the U.S. gothic fiction was already so popular in Europe that it had already begun to show signs of self-deprecation. Though not a true contributor to the genre, Jane Austen (1775–1817) was not above lampooning gothic fiction in one of her novels. In *Northanger Abbey* (1818), written early in her distinguished career but published posthumously, Austen relays the misadventures of her endearing protagonist, Catherine Morland, an avid fan of gothic fiction. Catherine is especially enthralled with *The Mysteries of Udolpho* (1794) by Ann Radcliffe, one of the most popular novels in Europe at the time, and a classic work of gothic fiction.

Northanger Abbey, though similar to other Austen novels in its exploration of the class customs, rituals, and societal expectations of the day, takes a strange detour about halfway through the book. Commandeered by Catherine's overactive imagination, the story abruptly becomes a suspenseful thriller, even taking on the darker aspects of her favorite genre. In effect, Austen's gothic fiction-addicted heroine adopts the role of would-be sleuth in her own self-fulfilling prophecy of a mystery. Though the "mystery" Catherine seeks to solve is far less mysterious than she suspected, the structure of the novel's second half is essentially a sketch of a genre yet to arrive. In *Northanger Abbey*, Austen not only satirizes gothic fiction, she anticipates the mystery novel, a genre Poe would further formalize a few decades later with his short stories centered on Detective C. Auguste Dupin.

When a genre becomes popular enough, the trend not only serves to further establish and legitimize that genre, it begins to produce fodder for its own criticism. Austen would be parodied much later with *Pride, Prejudice, and Zombies* (2009), a contemporary mash-up of her 1813 classic and contemporary zombie fiction. *Northanger Abbey* comes to mind while watching *Only Murders in the Building* (2021), a new mystery-comedy television series on Hulu. Starring Steve Martin, Martin Short, and Selena Gomez, the show revolves around three previously unacquainted neighbors residing in the same building where a murder has taken place and which they try to solve as part of a true crime podcast produced on the go. Like *Northanger Abbey*, Only Murders in the Building skillfully incorporates the many tropes of mystery while playfully jabbing the obsessive devotees of the genre. When they surpass their carrying capacity, as it were, genres tend to migrate to other territories, often in the form of hybrid species, adapting and updating with various new media. Since its inception over two centuries ago, the Gothic has crept into avant-garde art, *film noir*, German Expressionist cinema, graphic novels, heavy metal music, horror and science-fiction films, true crime podcasts and television series, and video games. Where will it turn up next?

What is the point of all this history? Why these digressions about Baltimore, the Gothic, landscape, and

Poe? What does any of this have to do with contemporary mystery and horror? It is important to recognize the many contributions from those brave trailblazers of these "foreign lands," those who explored what were then new and uncharted territories. Genres don't come out of nowhere; they represent a *genius loci*, supported by rich histories and complex theories. And while they are intimately connected to the land, genres are tinkered and toyed with along the way by practitioners of the literary arts. All contemporary artists stand on the shoulders of those who preceded them. With this in mind, though they may get mixed and stretched, and find their ways into other media, the most enduring genres have a past that connects them to the present through an intergenerational succession of voices, all of whom were affected by their local environ-ments. In the end, is this not the noble goal of art? To reach out across space and time, momentarily connecting with the future reader or distant viewer or remote listener through the power of creativity and imagination?

Finally, history is relevant as long as we keep living through it. Though we are only slowly beginning to see the light at the end of the tunnel, we still remain in the clutches of a global pandemic, the likes of which the world has not experienced in over a century. This is the climate in which *Mid-Atlantic Tales* was published. There is something sinisterly apropos about a mystery and horror anthology emerging during coronavirus. The virus itself resembles the ghost or monster in a horror tale, haunting not a castle, house, or spaceship, but the whole wide world. Meanwhile, the doctors and virologists are the detectives in a mystery novel, using reason and scientific rigor to create a vaccine before the monster strikes again. This is not meant to trivialize the real-life horrors Covid-19 has wreaked upon the human race. It is simply the geo-historical context one might contemplate while reading *Mid-Atlantic Tales*.

***

The thirteen authors collected in this anthology continue the modern tradition of working in the mystery and horror genres of literary fiction. Following the Romantics' precedent of reevaluating rational systems, alphabetical order was eschewed by the editors, thus beginning with Mystery: In "The Player," by Frank E Hopkins of Ocean View, Delaware, a lonely, washed-up man is offered a bizarre way out of his many misfortunes. Is it a con? Blending mystery with science fiction in "Missing People," Joseph Cooper, a lawyer from Baltimore, shares the story of an investigator fact-checking claims on a moon named Frogger. In "92," Savannah S. Miller from the Washington, D.C.–Virginia area offers a stream-of-consciousness mystery in the vernacular of a narrator reliving childhood events surrounding the disappearance of a young boy. Edward M. Lukacs of Georgetown, Delaware, offers an excerpt from a longer work, *The Silk Road Affair*, which follows a man who discovers a plane containing secret documents. "Dear Mr. Ethics" by Mark Willen of Silver Spring, Maryland, is the first chapter of a larger work focusing on a professor who writes a newspaper column and receives a message from a reader. The main character, who teaches at a local university, uses ethics and student discussions to figure out what to do about his predicament.

Moving on to Horror: In "The Unfinished Girl," Shane Moritz, who lives in Baltimore and teaches English Composition at the University of Maryland, Baltimore County, revives several mystery genre tropes such as the "lady in red." Overall, this story leans closer to horror, which allows it to serve as a good segue piece. Zoe Copeman, a tour guide for Maryland History Tours in Ellicott City, Maryland, deftly weaves local history and lore from her neck of the woods into her story "The Billy Goat

Trail." In "A Book without Words," one of two contributions to *Mid-Atlantic Tales* from Benjamin Robb of Orefield, Pennsylvania, classic gothic imagery slowly lures the reader in towards a twist ending. "Emma" by Bud Scott, a retired IT Technician from Salisbury, Maryland, is reminiscent of a *Black Mirror* episode in that it combines elements of horror and science fiction, as Artificial Intelligence slowly takes over the narrator's life in this satirical commentary on automation. Devon K. Hardy of Fairfax, Virginia, explores the common fear of flying in "The Perfect Flight," in which the main character works towards a groundbreaking new therapy. After a few delays in the plot, the reader begins to wonder about the story's final destination.

Lastly, as mentioned earlier, the editors of *Mid-Atlantic Tales* thought it necessary to include a cross-over category of stories that are neither fully mystery nor horror, but rather hybrid. Like the Mid-Atlantic region, this third and final section in this most unholy of trinities, represents a genre *overlap*. Hence, in Mystery & Horror, we have: "Charlie's Postcard" by Christy Brown of Hampton Roads, Virginia, wherein a strange, supernatural occurrence is discussed during a police interrogation. A detective questions a woman about her involvement in the disappearance of her friend. The story the woman imparts is too bizarre to be true, and Brown carefully allows readers to develop their own explanations about what actually happened to the missing person. "No Outlet," by Jeff Markowitz of Monmouth Junction, New Jersey, recounts a tale of domestic abuse in a small neighborhood, leading to a string of mysterious murders and disappearances. "The Shark in the Pool," Robb's second story in the collection, and perhaps one of its scariest, includes enough elements of mystery to warrant it being placed in the overlap category. "A Snowy Run" by Morgan McClure of Alexandria, Virginia involves a disappearance, a murder, and an amateur sleuth inspired to solve the crime on her own. Last but not least, in "And Yet, There Are Few," her second contribution to the anthology, Copeman unfolds the story of a young couple returning home from vacation only to find the world a little less crowded than before they left.

***

As mentioned earlier, *Mid-Atlantic Tales* comprises fifteen short stories by thirteen regional writers, two of whom have two pieces each included in the compilation. Perhaps having thirteen writers is a bad omen? Conceptually, however, this "happy coincidence" perfectly aligns with the mood and themes of *Mid-Atlantic Tales*. If ever there were a "gothic numeral," it would be 13. The number is regarded as a harbinger of bad luck in several cultures, with some considering Friday the 13th to be an especially unlucky day. There's even a clinical phobia, *triskaidekaphobia*, that describes the irrational fear of the number. Hotels and other tall buildings often omit it when numbering their floors for this reason. In her true crime investigation into the mysterious death of Rey Rivera, *An Unexplained Death: The True Story of a Body at the Belvedere* (2018), Baltimore author, Belvedere resident, and Maryland Institute College of Art Professor Mikita Brottman writes:

> The majority of hotels, in deference to superstition, don't list a thirteenth floor on their elevators. Most commonly, the number 13 is simply skipped, so the floors listed on the console go from 12 to 14. In some hotels, the thirteenth floor may be called 12A or 14A; in others, it may have a special name such as the Marble Floor or the Magnolia Floor or it may be used to house offices, storerooms, or mechanical equipment. Some hotels don't even have rooms numbered 13.

Needless to say, the number thirteen has a bad rap. This is not to suggest, however, that anyone should feel apprehensive at the prospect of reading the stories in this anthology. No—there is absolutely no harm in reading these thirteen original short story writers of mystery and horror... Just the same, I strongly recommend you avoid delving into these pages while on the 13th floor!

Dereck Stafford Mangus
Baltimore: Halloween 2021

 **Mystery**

The Player

by Frank E Hopkins

Not everyone attends their own funeral. My firm released me from my job because the financially induced recession in 2007 cut their sales in half. Unemployment insurance kept me afloat for six months, but it ended three weeks ago. My only assets include my clothes, a six-year-old car, several hundred books, and less than three-hundred in the bank. The banks had canceled all my credit cards. I had three weeks left on my furnished apartment's lease and couldn't afford next month's rent. Monica, my ex-wife, had left me seven years ago, and my children had ceased communications over five years ago. At over \$2 million, my debts from failed real estate investments made me think of declaring bankruptcy, but I couldn't pay for a lawyer. I used to be a player, spending without care and dating beautiful women without emotion, now I'm alone. Happy had ceased being a word I used to describe myself.

With nothing to do every day, I visited the park, walked through its gardens, and sat on a bench looking at the gentle flow of the creek, and enjoyed smelling the flowers in the early June warmth. On many days I took an old book from my collection and reread it, bringing back memories of happier days. Other times I thought of walking to the bridge over the flowing water, putting rocks in my pockets, and jumping.

The park had other regular visitors, which I acknowledged with a nod and a "hello" when they passed me on the sidewalk or while I sat on a bench. On Wednesday, one man whom I had seen several times, said, "I'm Norman Trace. Can I join you?"

Surprised at the sound of another voice, I looked up and said, "Sure, I'm Jack Dennis."

Mr. Trace offered his hand. I shook it. "Mr. Dennis, I know your name and financial situation."

I looked at him as he spoke, wondering why and how he had learned about me.

He continued, "I have a proposition that can help both of us."

"How do you know me?" I asked. He seemed well dressed in a navy-blue suit with shiny black shoes.

"The internet can reveal the innermost secrets of most of us if we know where to look," Mr. Trace said with a benign smile.

I remained silent.

"Would you like enough money to live in a better apartment, in a warmer location, and start a new life?"

Paranoia kicked in, "How could that happen?"

"Easy, I have a business proposition. If you agree to join in, your bad luck will end."

Bad luck. I finally matured last year and realized my love of Scotch, rum, gin, vodka, and wine —not luck— ran my life. Being sober for a year saved my life, but not my finances. Alcohol addiction affected my job performance. My last employer wouldn't give me a recommendation, which for a Certified Public Accountant ended any hope of staying in the profession. Minimum wage employers would not hire me, telling me I'm over qualified, and I'd leave as soon as the economy recovered. "What's the proposition?"

"Can't tell you here." Mr. Trace handed me a white business envelope. "Meet me at the address in the envelope at 10:00 a.m. tomorrow. This money should help solve your short-term problems."

After opening the envelope, I glanced inside and saw what appeared to be at least $2,000. Mr. Trace saw my involuntary smile and said, "There will be more if you show up tomorrow. Can I count on you?"

"Yes," I stammered, thinking, whether I'd have to do anything illegal.

He rose. Shook my hand and said, "You won't regret it," and walked away.

Not wanting to take a chance on being robbed or lose the envelope, I walked to the bank near the park and deposited all but $300 of the cash. At home, I wrote a check for next month's rent and mailed it. After examining the sparse goods in the refrigerator and pantry, I drove to the supermarket and purchased food to last two weeks, including my new favorite beverage — bottled water.

The next morning, I awoke elated at 7:30 and dressed in a gray suit and tie for the ten o'clock meeting. After a light breakfast of yogurt and toast, I walked to the four-story office building two blocks from my apartment. The small office had a reception area, staffed by an attractive blond woman in her early thirties. She greeted me warmly and pointed to an inside office and said, "Mr. Trace is waiting."

"Jack, you're looking upbeat this morning," Mr. Trace said.

"Yes, thanks to the envelope. What's your proposition?"

"We're in the insurance business. The collection side, not sales."

My quizzical look amused him since he smiled.

"Monica, your ex-wife took out a $1.5 million life insurance policy on you eight years ago. Apparently, she believed then, you'd die soon. But you haven't."

Shocked, I feared Mr. Trace invited me to the meeting to kill me. He must have noticed the fear on my face.

4

"Don't worry. You're in no danger from me or your ex-wife."

My face relaxed as I grinned.

"We propose you disappear and start over in a foreign country of your choice."

The quizzical expression returned.

"If you're concerned about how you can afford to live overseas, we'll get you a condo and give you a stipend to live on. Some overseas countries, with large American colonies, are inexpensive."

My look didn't change.

"Don't answer now." Mr. Trace gave me a manila envelope. "Take these pamphlets on Costa Rica, Honduras, Mexico, and Thailand. Jack, you might find at least one desirable. Read them over and meet me back here at noon tomorrow to give me your answer. I'll serve lunch."

Intrigued, I asked, "What is the stipend?"

"A two-bedroom condo plus $400,000."

Mr. Trace must have assumed my wide smile meant yes. "Tell us what country you like, so we can find the condo. Jack, you could live on the stipend until you die if you don't gamble, waste it on women, or live lavishly."

I felt numb but excited, especially when I looked in the manila envelope containing the country information, and discovered a business envelope holding $5,000, with a note: "Don't fix your car or spend this money. Wait until you're overseas and buy a new one."

After depositing the money, I returned home and examined the pamphlets. They painted a picture of a beautiful, inexpensive retirement as a single ex-pat. Thailand was too exotic for me. I've always liked Central America, wanting to examine the Aztec and Mayan ruins, the lush jungle life, the varied geology of deserts, jungles, mountains, ocean coral reefs, and volcanoes. If I lived in one country in Central America or Mexico, I could visit them all. After reviewing each country's political history, I chose Costa Rica. Both Honduras and Mexico had too many revolutions, and Mexico had a high crime rate. I took the rest of the day using the internet to examine Costa Rican cities. Since I liked beach life and people, I decided on Tamarindo on the Pacific Ocean in the northern part of the country, not in the rural small villages of the interior.

My euphoria changed to suspicion after eating my first steak dinner in a restaurant in two months. Did Mr. Trace intend to kill me to share the insurance money with my ex-wife? Was he her lover? Monica and I split hating each other, but I didn't think she'd have me killed. I've been wrong before. These thoughts kept exploding in my mind. How would they end my life? Did my ex want me tortured before my murder? In bed at eleven, I realized if I refused and Monica was part of the deal, they'd still kill me to get the insurance money. After finally falling asleep, I slept well, and woke up looking forward to my noon meeting. I ate a small breakfast, remembering Mr. Trace had promised lunch.

Marching toward the meeting wearing my gray suit, a blue shirt, and red tie, I wondered how long I would remain in the US, before my new life would begin. While confident, I had jotted down a few questions to ask Mr. Trace before I accepted the deal. When I entered his office suite, the blond receptionist greeted me warmly, "Hi, good to see you again. Hope you're hungry? Mr. Trace is expecting you."

"Have you decided where to spend the rest of your life?" he said with a smile as I gazed at the chilled salmon and salad buffet sitting on the credenza next to the window.

"Yes, Costa Rica, specifically Tamarindo on the Pacific Ocean."

"Great choice. My wife spent a summer there in her junior year in college. She studied marine biology. I planned to invite her to join us at lunch anyway, but now she can introduce you to your new country."

6

"Sally, come in we've starting eating. He's chosen Costa Rica."

Since I had only seen her sitting behind a desk, I didn't realize she had a perfect hour-glass figure. No way, Mr. Trace cheated with my ex. While Monica looked attractive, she couldn't compare in sex appeal to Trace's wife.

Sally sold me on Costa Rica for an hour. She listed historical and beautiful places I should visit, restaurants, how I could meet Americans, and where to learn Spanish. The Costa Rican government should hire her for TV tourism commercials. While she had eased most of my concerns, the question of my wife's revenge worried me.

At the end of her talk, we addressed each other using first names. "Norm, it's hard to believe my ex-wife would set me up in a new country and make me financially independent."

"Jack, she doesn't know about your new life. We purchased the life insurance policy from her. When you die, we'll be the beneficiaries. She remarried several years ago to a wealthy man and didn't have to worry about her future. Not liking to pay the premiums, she sold us the policy."

My fear returned, "Isn't that an enormous risk, I might live another fifty years."

"Not really. We'll buy a cadaver with your physical characteristics. We'll burn it beyond recognition in your car."

"You won't kill anyone?"

"Heavens, no! But I will take you to your funeral so you'll know you're legally dead. We'll dress you in a disguise. Let's meet for dinner at 6:00 here in two days. Do you agree with our proposal?"

"Yes, do I have to sign anything?"

"No. The less of an audit trail we leave, the better. But please bring a blank check to the meeting. Jack, you have to pay for your own funeral."

I spent the next two days elated, and read everything I could on Costa Rica, including library books and articles I found surfing the internet. Since I would live in a Spanish speaking country, I thought about studying the language before leaving, and wondered how much time I'd have before my new life started.

The night of the meeting, I walked to Norm's and Sally's office wearing the same suit I did two days ago. However, this evening I wore a white shirt and blue tie and expected a feast for dinner. Sally greeted me at the door wearing a sexy black dress and holding a glass of red wine. She handed it to me and said, "Tonight's our company celebration of our fiftieth successful placement." After declining the wine, she poured water from a bottle into a wine glass, which I accepted. Sally picked up the wine and ushered me into the office. Norm also held a drink and stood next to an attractive redhead adorned in a tight fitting dark green dress.

"Jack, I'd like you to meet Maureen Sullivan. She'll be your escort to Costa Rica."

"Escort," I said. Taken by her attractiveness, I fantasized about her duties.

"Yes, she is the third member of our team. Since you have never been to Costa Rica, and she's fluent in Spanish, she'll make the trip easy for you. Once you're there, she'll stay a week and introduce you to the ex-pat's life style. Tonight, she'll drive you to her house where you'll stay hidden for a few days until you attend your funeral," Norm replied.

Almost giddy over my new traveling companion, I said, "When does my trip to Costa Rica start?"

"Tonight." Maureen said in a sultry voice.

"Tonight! I'm not ready, haven't packed, closed my checking account, or said goodbye to any of my friends." Crestfallen, I realized I didn't have any who'd miss me.

"That's correct. If you did those things, everyone would suspect you're leaving and the police would investigate. We'd never collect on the insurance policy, and we all might go to prison. Wouldn't you rather leave a few things behind and live in a tropical paradise for the rest of your life?" Norm said.

"Norm, you're smart. What will I do for clothes?" I said smiling.

"We've gotten you some replacements," Norm said.

Sally said, "Let me show you your new condo after we eat."

Maureen lifted the tops of three chafing dishes on the credenza, revealing steaming sliced beef tenderloin, roasted potatoes, and asparagus. The food's aroma overwhelmed my senses, ending any resistance to Norm's proposition.

While we ate, Sally distributed brochures of the condo located two blocks from the Pacific Ocean. She described its amenities and desirable location, a block from the main shopping area. Sally ended the presentation saying, "While you can get a car, you won't need one."

I must have frowned at her last sentence. Maureen, who didn't talk during Sally's presentation, said, "Before I return home, I can help you buy a good used car. New cars are too expensive." What a wonderful woman. I could never live without a car.

"How did you buy the condo so fast?" I asked.

"We didn't. We own it. You'll live there rent free until we collect the insurance, then we'll transfer the property to you. Before you leave with Maureen, we need you to write a suicide note."

Everything seemed so perfect before they asked me to justify my death. The fear of being tricked returned.

Sally gave me a draft suicide note, a piece of paper, and a pen. "Please copy this, sign, and date it."

After I finished, Norm said, "Please give me the keys to your house and car, so we can plant the note and stage your death. Did you bring the blank check?"

"Yes," Jack said, showing it to Norm.

"Make it out for $5,000 to Mueller Funeral Company, as stated in your suicide note. Then you'll be free to go to Costa Rica."

Since I wanted to bury my current life, I complied without hesitation and gave Norm the signed check and said, "I thought insurance companies don't pay for death by suicide."

"Some don't, but this one does."

Maureen talked constantly on the drive to her house, and asked me, "What do you plan to do in Costa Rica? If I know, I can get you information to help you enjoy your new country."

"New country" had an agreeable sound, but I considered it more of a chance to start a new life. While she responded to every interest I expressed, I wondered what would happen after we walked into her home. My behavior and finances for the last six months insured celibacy. Would it end tonight?

As she entered her driveway, the well-manicured lawn and the large, two-story brick colonial impressed me. The house must be over four-thousand square feet. A large man stood at the open door holding out his hand. He looked at Maureen, and said, "Hi honey," turning to me, he said, "You must be Jack Dennis. I'm Jim, Maureen's husband."

Crestfallen, I shook his hand, and lied, "It's nice to meet you."

"Let me show you to your room and new clothes," Jim said.

We walked upstairs. Jim pointed at the open door, "Your room."

I noticed two pieces of luggage opened on the bed, overflowing with clothes.

"Hope you like them," Maureen said. "We picked them for a tropical climate, although I included a coat and sweaters for the mountainous interior."

I read the labels on two shirts, *Nordstrom*. After examining several shirts and shorts, I said, "You did well. It's a step up from my current wardrobe. How did you know my size?"

"Sally took your picture and used a software program to estimate the measurements," Maureen said. "We have five days before you fly to Costa Rica. Wear them while you're here. If they don't fit, we'll replace them."

"Since the police will find your burnt car and body tonight, you'll stay in the house until you attend your funeral," Jim said.

"Okay, I understand. If someone recognized me, and reads I died, I'll never get to Costa Rica."

"It won't be so bad. We have books and CD's on Costa Rica and its neighboring countries. Since I teach at the university, I won't be here most of the day, but Jim won't leave the house. He writes biographies, and the internet provides him most of the information he needs. If you want anything, ask him."

"Thanks, I'm tired from the excitement. You'll excuse me, so I can sleep."

"Jack, you have your own bathroom," Jim said, opening its door. "When we go to bed, we turn on the alarm so don't open your windows. It will wake the neighborhood."

Trapped for five days. Too bad Maureen has a husband. I should have survived. The clothes told me Norm and his group ran an efficient, if not legitimate, business. I should have stopped worrying. Not able to resist, I tried on every piece of clothing. They all fit. A book on the lamp table, *Costa Rica Cuisine*, intrigued me. Curious what I'd be eating, I read the seafood and meat sections before I dropped off to sleep.

The next morning, I woke up confident, depression free, and joined the couple for breakfast in the kitchen. "How did you sleep?" Maureen asked.

"Great. I tried on the clothes. They fit perfectly."

"Good. I'm the chef here. I've cooked bacon and a shrimp omelet. Do you want toast?" Jim said.

"Yes."

We spent the next hour at the breakfast table talking about Maureen's research and Jim's writing. She taught electrical engineering. Jim gave me two of his books, in case I got bored reading about Costa Rica. Biographies of a Union Civil War General, Jonathan Harris, and Stephen Johnson Field, a Supreme Court Judge in the late nineteenth century.

Maureen brought home a newspaper in the late afternoon. It reported on Jack Dennis's death. It occurred just the way Norm promised. The police found my car burning at 3 a.m., after it had driven over a cliff, crashed, and caught fire. They investigated whether it was an accident or a homicide.

The evening TV news at six stated, "The police found a suicide note, and after questioning his neighbors, the police ruled it a suicide. They will bury Jack Dennis in three days at 9:00 a.m. by the Mueller Funeral Company in the Lasting Life Cemetery."

"Well, what do you think of your reported death?" Jim asked as he sautéed a steak with onions and mushrooms. Maureen prepared a large salad.

"It's perfect. I had my doubts."

"Yes, Norm knows how to execute," Maureen said, passing the salad as she saw me staring at the food on the table.

"I hope you're not looking for rolls or potatoes. We keep thin by never eating them."

"I was, but looking at both of you, I may change my eating habits when I'm in Costa Rica."

Four days later, at 7:00 in the morning, Jim knocked on my door.

"Come in." Jim handed me a large-waisted, light-blue

pair of pants, an extra large aqua-blue oxford shirt, a similar sized navy-blue cotton sweater, and a small pillow with straps to tie around my stomach. "No one will recognize you, after you put these and a wig on, and Maureen adds makeup," Jim said.

When she finished, I looked in a hall mirror. The white wig, facial makeup, and paunch aged me beyond recognition.

Maureen drove us to the funeral. We didn't stand by the casket as the paid pall bearers lowered it into the grave, but ninety feet away, placing flowers at another grave. Maureen said, "As your suicide note stated, 'you had no friends.' We don't want to destroy that illusion."

After the funeral, we drove back to my host's home to change and prepare for the trip. Norm stood in the living room as we entered and greeted me, "Jack, just came to say good bye, wish you well, and ask you a question."

"Thanks. I had my doubts when we started, but you have a flawless operation. What do you want to know?"

"Can you provide a few names who might be candidates for our services? We grow our business by references, not by blindly searching out potential clients from the telephone book or the internet."

I looked at my cell phone and gave him the names and phone numbers of three men I had met as our lives spiraled downward out of control.

"Thanks. Go upstairs, get out of that outfit, and Jim will drive you to the airport." Norm gave me an envelope with my fake passport, tickets, and Costa Rican currency. "Jack, I'll be gone when you come down. Maureen, Jim, and you will be flying together. Maureen will be your contact if you have any questions from now own. Good luck. Thanks for the leads."

When I returned with my luggage, Jim handed me a loose-leaf binder. "This is your life. I wrote the biography this week after I met you. Read it on the plane and use it to replace your past. Let me know if you find any inconsistencies, and I'll correct them when we get to Costa Rica."

When the three of us boarded the plane, and it took off, I silently thanked Norm and his organization, and hoped he would contact my friends and rescue them.

Missing People

by Joseph Cooper

Agricultural Moon Frogger — Star Republic Standard Year 508

The shuttle from Alpha Centauri arrived at the spaceport above Frogger, a back-galaxy agricultural moon—too small by half for planet classification— spinning around a fading white sun. The shuttle had spent a week hopping through a dozen systems, tracking a circuitous route through remote Star Republic space.

"Attention! Attention!" The captain's Martian accent piped out of the speakers in Mr. Apollo's cabin. "Now docking at Frogger Spaceport. We leave at 0500 tomorrow ship-time. I'd tell you to get a tourist visa, but there's nothing to see."

Mr. Apollo headed for the airlocks. Dark suit and gold tie and comfortable walking shoes, datapad in his breast pocket, and cybernetic implant loaded with his case files.

"AI," he subvocalized, "start recording for the Primer file claim log."

"Affirmative," his AI projected into his mind.

He found the first mate waiting at the airlocks as well.

"What're the groundlings like?" he asked.

"They hate all corps, but they hate Int-Ag the most," the first mate said. "Ran them out of the system at gunpoint twenty years back."

"Purpose of visit?"

15

Frogger had border controls at the space elevator connecting the docking ring and the surface, complete with an obsolete bio scanner and a human clerk.

"I investigate insurance claims," Mr. Apollo said. "Freelance. Working for All-Planets this time."

The clerk blinked. "Like people blowing up their own ships?"

"A missing person and a life insurance policy," Mr. Apollo said. "My client needs to confirm or deny a death here."

"In a day?" The clerk was looking at his visa.

Mr. Apollo shrugged. "That's all All-Planets paid for."

"Who went missing?"

"Harry Primer."

"Never heard of him." The clerk fired the scanner at Mr. Apollo's face and updated the entry record associated with his ID. "Move along."

Mr. Apollo and the first mate rode the space elevator dirtside. It was a slow trip, an hour of transit in a capsule laid out like a hover bus—narrow seats arranged in cramped rows. The first mate flopped into the first seat, put on a visor, and sank into whatever she was watching. Mr. Apollo picked the farthest seat from her.

"Play me the claimant statement." He subvocalized to his AI.

His AI surfaced the holographic recording in his active recollection. All-Planets had pulled the clip from a court proceeding on Alpha Centauri to declare Harry Primer dead in absentia.

"My name is Lorella Icer," a middle-aged spacer woman said. "I changed my name when I remarried eight years ago. Before then, I used my first husband's —Harry Primer's— family name. My name was Lorella Primer then."

"What happened to Harry Primer?" That was her lawyer, a Centauri native from the accent.

"He died on the agricultural moon Frogger on or about August 31st in Star Republic Standard Year 488." Only traces of grief remained in her voice, like scar tissue over a wound.

"How did he die?"

"I don't know exactly. He disappeared in the revolution. Nobody's seen or heard of him since."

"What was your last contact with him?"

"August 31st, 488. We had a spot on a ship out of system. I took our son and headed to the spaceport early. He stayed to pack some more bags. He never made the elevator."

"Why were you leaving?"

"The revolution." Her tone made clear her sympathies didn't lie with the revolutionaries. "Harry and I were local affiliates for Interstellar Agriculture Incorporated. It wasn't safe."

"Did you try to find him?"

"Yes, but there's nothing. Not a trace."

"Did you inquire with the Frogger authorities?"

"The revolutionaries don't acknowledge he's missing."

"Did you go back to look for him?"

"They would shoot me if I tried."

Mr. Apollo doubted Frogger's local government would actually shoot her. Int-Ag had spent the past twenty years claiming that Frogger's revolutionaries were lawless space pirates. They wanted compensation. But outside of a small clique of stockholders and affiliates, they had no sympathy and less evidence. Frogger might be a backwater, but it met Star Republic standards for civil liberty.

Mr. Apollo left the spaceport dirtside to find overcast grey skies and a chill breeze. The sunlight filtered through the clouds felt pale and colorless and cold. The decorative trees around the exits had already shed their leaves in anticipation of winter. The air stank of fertilizer.

Mr. Apollo found his local contact waiting. A young man —he looked about nineteen— was leaning on the hood of a black hovercar with police lights in the back window. His too-tight black suit and black tie and gold-rimmed sunglasses seemed formal for a backwater like Frogger.

"Detective Barnes?" Mr. Apollo asked.

He thought the man looked too young to be a real detective, but what did he know. Everyone seemed young to him these days.

"Mr. Apollo?" Detective Barnes replied with a nod.

They got into the hovercar. It was old but not antique. Detective Barnes tapped the control screens and the hovercar floated up.

"Where to?" Detective Barnes asked.

"Archives."

Detective Barnes programmed the car's controls. The car whirred and took off toward the glass spires of what Mr. Apollo assumed was downtown.

"My boss said you were chasing a cold case?" Detective Barnes asked.

Mr. Apollo just nodded.

Detective Barnes waited for a minute and then pressed on. "What did your guy do?"

"Maybe die."

"Maybe?" Detective Barnes raised an eyebrow.

"It's an insurance claim."

"Like… murder-for-the-money?"

"Not impossible."

"Do they think he faked it or something?" Detective Barnes asked.

"If Harry Primer died on Frogger during 488," Mr. Apollo said, "his wife gets two hundred and fifty thousand spacecoin, plus back interest from the date of death. It's about one-point-six million now. One-point-seven perhaps. Thereabouts."

"High stakes then."

"But if Harry Primer died off Frogger or more recently than twenty years ago, it's out of policy period and/or coverage area, so she gets nothing."

Detective Barnes's eyes widened. "What took so long to check?"

"Alpha Centauri won't declare someone dead until they've been missing for eighteen years. No death certificate, no claim, no investigation."

"So you're working for the family?"

"The insurer."

"Huh." Detective Barnes shook his head. "Twenty years ago…. What've you got to work with?"

"A name, a statement, and a wedding holo."

The hovercar stopped on a side street in downtown outside a depressing concrete building. Eight squat stories of the same gray concrete face, complete with widely spaced, narrow windows and a single heavy door not even set back from the street. A small sign above the door read, "Government Records."

"I'll be back in an hour," Detective Barnes said. "I'm getting coffee. Want some?"

"I'm good," Mr. Apollo said as he hopped out.

He opened the door and stepped through into a small reception area with polished concrete walls and harsh white lighting and a big security desk. He showed his ID to the guard. The guard scanned the ID into his system and then zapped him with another bioscanner.

"Checks out." He offered him a small white plastic card. "This opens the elevator. It will take you to the Archives and back here. You need to return it when you leave. Don't lose it."

Mr. Apollo took an elevator and scanned the card. It dropped for a minute and then ejected him into a large underground room with the same harsh white lighting. He saw a woman —an archivist, he assumed— sitting behind a desk covered in monitors.

"I have authorization from the Home Office for an investigation," Mr. Apollo said.

"Yes. I already pulled the data for you," the archivist said. "Looks like your man cleared out after Freedom Week."

"What's Freedom Week?"

"Our planetary holiday. Celebrates our independence from Int-Ag in 488."

"Anything stand out?"

"He was a factor." The archivist said it like 'factor' meant 'axe murderer.' "Tossed a lot of people off their land for Int-Ag bullshit."

"What's the last record?"

"His exit visa."

Mr. Apollo frowned. "May I search your data systems myself?" he asked.

The archivist tapped her screen a bit. "I've already segregated the data for you. Feel free to use our research room." She offered him a red datastick.

"I must insist—"

The archivist shook her head. "You need security clearance for unrestricted access. If you don't like it, tell it to Home Office."

"Couldn't you have just sent me the data directly then?" Mr. Apollo bit his lip. "It would've saved me some trouble."

"I didn't write the Data Privacy Act." The archivist didn't sound apologetic. "I just need to bioscan you to verify your identity and you can download."

The archivist took out a bioscanner and flashed Mr. Apollo's face for a third time that day.

The archive had some research rooms. They were small, bare, and soundproof, designed for audio interfacing. Mr. Apollo sat down in one, leaning back in an old leather recliner. He plugged the datastick into the computer system and connected his AI.

"Do I have access to their system?" he asked.

"Negative." His AI whispered into his mind. "The system is air gapped and contains anti-tampering safeguards. I do not detect any open links."

"Start with the dates," he said. "Give me a timeline of his life."

The AI began flashing documents up as fast as he could read them. Public records and some newspaper articles rolled past.

"Summary?" Mr. Apollo asked. "Just the highlights."

The AI spat out a quick chronology, an array of bullet points floating in his mind's eye like a mirage.

- o Year 442—Born at Frogger General Hospital, an only child.
- o Year 461 —Graduated from Frogger City High.
- o Year 465 —Completed a two-year business law degree. Left Frogger.
- o Year 467 —Returned to Frogger.
- o Year 476 —Took ownership of family business.
- o Year 478 —Took ownership of family home.
- o Year 484 —Married Lorella Jovian.
- o Year 486 —Son, Jack Primer Jr., born at Frogger General Hospital.
- o Year 488 —Exit visa.

It wasn't typical disappearance stuff. Harry Primer had property, a family, a business, a real degree, a recent marriage, and a two-year-old son. From a distance, he seemed prosperous, if not wealthy. Not the sort that bolted for the frontiers.

"Where did he live?" Mr. Apollo asked.

"28 Sargon Street." The AI spun up a map that labeled

the neighborhood Little Sargon. A picture showed a three-story townhome.

"Was he successful?"

"Moderately." The AI whispered in his brain. "No unpaid bills. New hovercars from Mars every few years. No luxury goods."

"How did he make money?"

"Int-Ag records show he acted as a middleman. He exported local agricultural product to their ships, presumably marked up. He imported agricultural supplies and technology, which he then resold marked up on credit." The AI flashed up a nigh endless list of court cases. "He also managed some of Int-Ag's land holding and revenue collection."

Mr. Apollo raised his eyebrows. "Did he file all of those?"

"He filed five thousand, two hundred, and fifty-eight separate actions for rent and debt collection."

"Assets?"

"His home on Sargon Street and his hovercars. Banking records and equity ownership records are not public. His import/export business involved holding the risk on assets before reselling them."

"Any civic engagement?"

"He claimed two charitable deductions on his property taxes. One thousand spacecoin to the Sargon Street Community Center in 476 and again in 478."

"Got any holos?"

The Archive data dump had holos. A young man — short for a spacer at seven feet and inches— smiling in a high school graduation procession. He wasn't smiling in a face scan from border control in 467. His hair had begun to thin and his gut had filled out. Frogger did not maintain holo records of civil lawsuits, but he appeared in the criminal records. In 476, he'd testified in a murder trial for the prosecution. That holo showed a fat spacer with a bald pate and dead expressionless eyes slumped in the witness box like a wilted plant.

"Spin up the wedding holo," Mr. Apollo said.

Harry Primer had smiled on his wedding day in 484. It took decades off his face. The holo showed a crowd — mostly spacers, but some groundlings— filling the Sargon Street Community Center. The hall looked beautiful, full of stained glass and light-blue marble walls adorned by innumerable silver stars. He and Lorella Jovian—his head came up level with her shoulder— wore matching silver crowns, studded with diamonds that caught the light.

Mr. Apollo paused the holo. He hadn't reviewed it until now and wished he had.

"What are those?" He pointed.

"Sargian wedding crowns." His AI supplied a separate hologram from its databanks. "Created from silver and deep-space diamond found among the remnants of Sargon Prime. Used in the Sargian cultural tradition as part of the wedding ceremony. Customarily held by communal groups because of their rarity. Listed as protected artifacts under the Minority Cultural Protection Act."

Sargians were an ethno-cultural minority. Mr. Apollo knew a few. They were spacers, refugees from their home world's destruction. Many leveraged their interstellar social networks to act as entrepreneurial local agents for larger corporate concerns throughout the Star Republic's frontiers and backwaters. Land management, import/export, servicing agreements, consignment sales— that sort of thing. Every spaceport worth a name had a couple.

"Can you identify the specific crown?"

"Affirmative."

"Where is it?"

"Reported lost/stolen in 488. The Star Republic will pay fifty thousand spacecoin for information leading to its recovery."

"Show me the police investigation file."

"Negative."

"Why not?"

"None produced. Star Republic central law enforcement database indicates no leads."

"Huh." Mr. Apollo frowned. "Alright. Any evidence on his family life?"

"Lorella Primer and her son with Harry Primer, Jack Primer Jr., left Frogger in May 486 and returned November 486."

The AI projected an exit holo from the spaceport bioscanners. Lorella Primer had a black eye and an upset infant in her arms. Beside it, the AI showed the re-entry bioscanner holos. Her black eye had healed and the now larger infant looked asleep.

"Why did she leave?" Mr. Apollo said. "Did they get along?"

"Unknown. Potentially connected document exists."

The AI spun up a police report from May 486. Someone had punched Lorella Primer in the face on the seventy-block of Sargon Street outside Taniel's Artisanal Coffeehouse and run off. No holo, no witnesses, and no theft, so no investigation.

Mr. Apollo frowned. "Any idea why someone punched her?"

"Police coded as random street crime." The AI whispered to him. "I detect no records of political involvement until two years later."

"What happened then?"

The AI provided an op-ed in the Frogger Standard from July of 488, Harry Primer called someone named Elvira Teller a "bandit chief," an "anarchist," and a "pirate." The comments on the op-ed —the uncensored ones— called him "corper scum," "spacer trash," and a "bloodsucking farm-stealing parasite."

Two weeks later, he and Lorella applied for exit visas for themselves and their son. They'd used the exit visas to

24

buy tickets to Alpha Centauri on August 31, 488. But the bioscanner data showed he'd never reached the dirt-side bioscanners in the spaceport.

"Data integrity?"

The AI took a moment to check. "Intact."

"Well that lines up." Mr. Apollo thought for a long moment. "Okay. What did Lorella do for a living?"

"Robotics engineering and repair." The AI spun up a picture of a newspaper advertisement from January of 488. "She sold and serviced Int-Ag proprietary equipment under an Int-Ag business license."

"Is she native?"

"She arrived from Alpha Centauri in 483." The AI had the entrance picture. She looked young-ish and smiled.

"Was she successful?"

The AI displayed another long list of civil cases. "Over two hundred collections actions."

"Hold on." Mr. Apollo shook his head. "Did either of them actually collect anything?"

"Affirmative." The AI displayed an even longer list. Endless rows of assets and bank accounts from court records. "Numerous garnishment and eviction records indicate aggressive use of collections remedies."

"Okay." Mr. Apollo nodded. "How about Harry Primer's parents?"

"Dead."

"How?"

"His father —Jack Primer Sr.— was apparently shot while collecting a debt in 476."

The AI displayed a series of court records and holos of trials. Harry Primer's holo from earlier stood out from the rest. He'd testified for the prosecution in his father's murder trial.

"Show me the judicial findings."

According to the judge's findings of fact, Harry Lindsey, a classmate of Harry Primer's, had suffered crop failures. He couldn't pay Jack Primer Sr. his rent. Harry

Primer testified that Harry Lindsey had threatened to kill Jack and pointed a laser rifle at him. When Jack came back the next day —to work things out according to Harry Primer— someone burned his head off with a laser rifle. Harry Lindsey denied everything, but the judge hadn't believed him. Int-Ag disintegrated Harry Lindsey for capital murder a week later.

"And his mother?"

"Died in 478 from a medical mistake." The AI displayed medical and coroner records. "Power outage disrupted general anesthesia."

"Did he sue?"

"Negative. But settlements do not create court records."

"Where are they buried?"

The AI took some time. "No records. They likely received Sargian funerals."

"What does that involve?"

"They return their dead to their destroyed home world in a self-propelled casket."

Then Mr. Apollo heard a knock at the door of the room. Detective Barnes had returned, large coffee in hand.

"You need anything else from me?" Detective Barnes asked. "Because I have things to do."

They walked back through security to the gray outdoors and Detective Barnes's hovercar. Detective Barnes tapped the controls. The hovercar whirred to life.

"Just tell me where," Detective Barnes said.

"28 Sargon Street."

Detective Barnes entered the address. The car didn't move. The display flashed.

"Bad address," Detective Barnes said. "You sure?"

"Yes."

"There isn't even a Sargon Street," Detective Barnes pointed at the screen. "Not anywhere on Frogger."

Mr. Apollo glanced at the display. Detective Barnes wasn't lying. Then a thought hit him.

"AI," he subvocalized, "did it get renamed?"

"Sargon Street," the AI piped the words into his head, "is now Elvira Teller Avenue."

He tapped in that address. It registered.

"Oh." Detective Barnes nodded. "That's in Revolution Circle. Decent neighborhood."

"Who's Elvira Teller?"

"I'll show you." Detective Barnes tapped the controls. "Her statue is around the corner outside City Hall."

The hovercar coasted past the Elvira Teller statue a few minutes later. It depicted her as a twenty-foot tall woman aiming a laser rifle at Liberty Park.

"Liberty Park used to be Int-Ag's corporate headquarters," Detective Barnes explained, "until Teller blew it up. Now there's a fountain and an obelisk."

"Why was Sargon Street renamed?" Mr. Apollo asked.

"Lots of things got renamed after Freedom Week."

"Did she die for the cause?"

"Lord no. She served two terms as President, two terms as Prime Minister, and now she's our System Representative to the Star Republic."

"So..." Mr. Apollo paused. "She renamed it after herself?"

"Neighborhoods name the roads I think."

Then they passed Liberty Park and jetted across downtown. It looked lively. The streets were full and the storefronts brightly colored, even in the muted sunlight.

"What actually happened on Freedom Week?" Mr. Apollo asked. "The original one in 488, I mean."

"My dad says things just came apart," Detective Barnes said. "Int-Ag was raising rents, charging more for everything, paying less for everything, and not extending credit. I'm sure all corporate worlds are alike. Corrupt officials, crappy public services, and no way to get ahead."

Mr. Apollo just nodded.

"Well…" Detective Barnes continued. "Crops failed. Bad seeds, bad robots, and bad luck. Int-Ag evicted anyone who couldn't pay. They'd —the factors— would come by, take everything you had, and make you sign a note promising everything you got next year. When that wasn't enough, they'd take your farm. You'd get to choose between day labor for Int-Ag for beans or a jail cell for vagrancy." He glanced over. "You get the racket?"

"I do."

"Teller decided someone had to do something. We Froggers fought for justice —political, economic, you name it. And well… Int-Ag couldn't shoot everyone all at once."

"That took a week?"

"A few months. It started in April maybe?" Detective Barnes said. "Freedom Week starts when we took Frogger City from Int-Ag."

"When was that?"

"September 1st. That's when we liberated the spaceport."

"Why a week?"

"Well… Int-Ag's forces surrendered after street fighting on September 4th. We elected our provisional government on September 6th. And we proclaimed the Republic of Frogger on September 7th. And that's Freedom Week."

28 Elvira Teller Avenue was a three-story townhouse near downtown. The avenue formed half of a big loop cross-sectioned by smaller streets. It had small shops interspaced with townhomes and occasional warehouses tucked into small alleys. They had trouble finding parking.

They got out. Mr. Apollo checked archival street photos his AI had downloaded from the archives. The street hadn't changed much. The buildings looked more weathered, especially under the overcast skies.

"Was there fighting here?" he asked Detective Barnes.

"No idea."

He looked closely at buildings, hunting for telltale laser scorches. He saw more than a few patches where new bricks had replaced old ones. Maybe they were laser scorches and maybe they weren't. He checked the archive information for records of any fighting in the area.

"Negative." The AI whispered in his mind. "No public records exist for Little Sargon during Freedom Week."

He walked up the block to 28 Elvira Teller Avenue. The door had fresh, dark red paint.

"Why here?" Detective Barnes asked. "Is this connected to your guy?"

"He lived here."

He started walking toward the door, but Detective Barnes caught his arm.

"Look..." he said. "You can't just go ask about a pre-Freedom-Week owner."

"Oh." Mr. Apollo raised his eyebrows. "Why?"

"When we overthrew Int-Ag, the Provisional Government sold off all non-citizen property to locals. They gave preference to whomever occupied it. Tenants, squatters, whomever — If you lived there on auction day, you could buy it from the corper-era owner."

"Why?"

"Int-Ag was parasitic. We created all the wealth on Frogger, so we took it back."

"Harry Primer was a native."

"If he wasn't living in that house in January 489, it stopped being his house," Detective Barnes said. "That's local law."

Mr. Apollo sent his AI after land records with a thought. It returned with the current deeds. Someone named April Sugar had bought the house under the Native Property Act for ten whole spacecoins. The sum, payable to Harry Primer, had remained unclaimed. After seven years, Frogger's government had seized that money as abandoned property.

"Why does anyone still care?"

"People got killed fighting over who got to occupy what land on auction day."

"I need to ask her though," Mr. Apollo said. "Maybe she was his tenant?"

"Let me do the talking. You'll make a scene."

They walked up to the door together. Detective Barnes adjusted his tie and knocked.

The door opened. A gray-haired woman looked out at them.

"Can I help you?" she asked.

"I'm Detective Barnes. I was hoping for a few minutes of your time."

"No problem."

"We're trying to locate a missing person. His family's looking for him." Detective Barnes put on his best smile. "We're hoping someone knows him."

The woman smiled. "Well… Why ask me?"

"He may have lived here before Freedom Week."

The woman mimed apology. "I'm just a tenant," she said. "I think the owner lives uptown somewhere maybe. I don't know. It's through a broker."

The Sargon Street Community Center was a ruin. It crouched between newer taller buildings on either side. The bricks needed pointing, the windows were boarded up, and the doors were chained shut. The roof had partially collapsed long ago. A peeling sign painted on the front labeled it the "Teller Avenue Gymnasium."

"Can we go in?" Mr. Apollo asked.

"It's not safe." Detective Barnes pointed to an orange notice on the door. "See. It's condemned."

"I formally request entry on behalf of All-Planets as part of their claim investigation," Mr. Apollo said.

He didn't expect it to work. He was just filling out his file. But Detective Barnes shrugged.

"Fine," Detective Barnes said. "It won't fall down in the next ten minutes, right?"

Detective Barnes went to the lock and scanned his finger and his iris. The lock beeped and disengaged. They hauled open one of the double-doors —made from actual brass apparently— and stepped inside.

The interior was dark, but the gray sunlight poured through holes in the roof. Plants grew between the floor tiles. The walls had once been white plaster, but the plaster had cracked all over. It felt as abandoned as it looked.

Mr. Apollo's AI overlaid the wedding holo onto the abandoned building in Mr. Apollo's vision. Ghostly wedding guests swirled past blue marble walls with silver veins inlaid into the stone, all wine glasses and smiles. He blinked and the holo faded, leaving the crumbling white plaster.

Mr. Apollo shook his head to clear it. He walked up to the worst crack in the plaster wall and started picking at it. Soon the original blue marble appeared from beneath the plaster.

"Who would plaster over that?" he asked.

Detective Barnes took out an omni-tool. He activated the light function and shined it at the crack. It caught a trace of the silver.

"Shiny," he said.

Another set of double doors opened off the lobby. In the wedding holo, they led to the main hall. Mr. Apollo pushed one open. It creaked and the walls shuddered and plaster dust fell, but it opened.

Inside was open space, exposed to the sky and the pale sunlight. In the wedding holo, the room had once stood three stories tall, but the dome had since fallen into rubble. The white plaster walls were crumbling. Stained-glass windows had once let in sunlight, but the glass had shattered long ago. An apartment tower now blocked the view and most of the light with a windowless brick wall.

"This must have been an indoor playing field." Detective Barnes kicked at the ground. "There's a grass mat down here under the debris."

"Harry Primer married here," Mr. Apollo said, eyes watching his AI's holo projection, "under a blue dome studded with silver stars in memory of his people's lost home world."

"This was a gym."

"This is," Mr. Apollo's AI effortlessly pushed the public record data into his mind, "an eighty-seven-year-old cultural site protected under the Minority Cultural Protection Act. A site that your government has—" he gestured around him "—plastered over, converted to a gym, and apparently plans to destroy."

Detective Barnes just blinked.

"It is also," Mr. Apollo walked over to the far wall, "protected under the Life Memorial Preservation Act." He scraped at the peeling plaster, hauling it back. "Look."

He'd revealed a silver star in the blue marble wall behind it. It had a name with dates, "Ahoora Nova, 395-483."

Detective Barnes stared at it. "It's a memorial wall?"

"We'd find stars for Mr. Primer's family under the plaster if we looked. In his wedding holo, there were many stars."

"Huh." Detective Barnes looked around. "I guess the planning board really screwed this one up. I should file a report or something."

"I'm not a federal investigator," Mr. Apollo said. "What I want to know is why it was plastered over. Who left valuable silver on the walls?"

"Yeah." Detective Barnes was still shaking his head and staring around the room. "And you didn't need to plaster it over to use this as an indoor field."

"So why?" Mr. Apollo said. "And what happened to the Sargians?"

Detective Barnes frowned. "That's…" he said, "we don't have any here. I mean, I'm sure a few have come through, but I've never met one. Not once."

They left the ruins of the community center and walked back down the block, saying nothing. When they reached the car, Mr. Apollo stretched. He checked the archive data again and then compared it with modern maps.

"My AI tells me there's a coffee shop a few blocks up. Mind if we stop there?"

"Not at all," Detective Barnes said. "I could use another hit."

They drove a few blocks up Elvira Teller Avenue. Mr. Apollo watched the streets as they drove. The neighborhood looked nice. The buildings looked well maintained. The people were groundlings. Not a single tall and gaunt spacer among them.

They got out at the corner opposite Elligold's Artisanal Coffeehouse. It was a small shop on a corner, brightly lit and well trafficked. It resembled archival photos perfectly, except for the changed first word on the sign.

They entered. It had real coffee beans and real coffee roasters. The man behind the counter was tall for a groundling, but not exceptionally so. He wore an apron and kept his spiky hair in a tight bun.

"Can I help you?" he asked.

"Cappuccino," Mr. Apollo asked. "Largest you'll sell me."

"I'll have one too." Detective Barnes produced a payment card. "Both on me."

While the barista made the coffee, Mr. Apollo looked around. The décor was bare steel and forgettable. A tiny holo of a gaunt-faced woman —barely six inches high— stared down at them from a shelf behind the counter and above the coffee beans.

"Who's that?" Mr. Apollo pointed. He looked closer. There was something shiny on the holo's head he couldn't quite make out.

"My grandma Sarah," the man said. "Dead twenty years now. This was her shop once."

"Shop's been in the family a long time then?"

"For a place like this, I suppose," the barista said. "I'm third gen. She was a spacer, you know." He laughed. "That holo doesn't do her justice. My dad says she was eight feet tall."

"You don't say."

"Don't see many spacers around now-a-days," the barista said, "but my dad says this used to be a spacer neighborhood."

"I'd like to talk to your dad," Mr. Apollo said.

"I'll get him." The barista handed them their coffees. "He likes to shoot the breeze."

The barista disappeared into the back. He returned with an old man, gray-haired and bent and rail thin. In his youth, he'd probably stood taller than his son. Not quite a spacer, but close.

"Name's Bob Elligold," he said. "Nice to meet you."

"I'm Mr. Apollo. We're trying to find a missing person. He used to live around here."

"Well, I've been here forever."

"Before Freedom Week?" Mr. Apollo asked.

"Oh yeah. It was my stepmother's shop then."

Mr. Apollo took out his datapad. He picked a clip from the wedding holo, a zoomed out shot of the groom's party. Harry Primer, wearing his silver crown awkwardly like an unwanted party hat, stood with his friends a little off center, their wine glasses raised in a pose for the holo recorder.

"Do you know him?" Mr. Apollo didn't point at anyone in particular.

Elligold looked at the holo for a long time.

"Handsome fellow, but who isn't on their wedding day?" He sounded sad. "I may have seen the face before."

"His name is Harry Primer. He lived a few blocks from here," Mr. Apollo said. "He would be about your age now."

"Is he dead?"

"Missing these past twenty years."

"Harry Primer." Elligold shook his head. "If I ever knew him, I've quite forgotten. Poor fellow."

"Do you have any idea what might have happened to him?" Detective Barnes was sipping his coffee.

Elligold gave Detective Barnes a long look. "No," he said. "I have no idea, detective."

"When was he last seen?" Detective Barnes glanced at Mr. Apollo.

"August 31, 488," Mr. Apollo said. "He didn't make his flight."

Elligold shook his head. "I…" he began and then stopped. "Sorry detective. I just don't remember him."

Coffee in hand, they walked back to the hovercar. The breeze had gotten colder and the sunlight dimmer. Mr. Apollo could smell rain coming.

"Now where?" Detective Barnes asked.

"This is a security vehicle, right? Do you have remote access to archive records?" Mr. Apollo asked. "I need background on Elligold."

"Sure. My car computer's plugged in." Detective Barnes tapped the hovercar's controls. "Ask away."

"Computer," Mr. Apollo asked, "are there connections between Bob Elligold and Harry Primer?"

"They attended Frogger High, Class of 468." The hovercar computer spoke on a speaker system. "Both donated to the Sargon Street Community Center. Both lived in the same neighborhood four blocks from each other from their births until 488."

Detective Barnes blinked. "He lied to us?"

"Or forgot. When you're as old as I am, it happens."

"High school's big here. Most people don't go further."

"Perhaps." Mr. Apollo nodded. "Computer, how did Bob Elligold acquire Elligold's Artisanal Coffeehouse?"

"Bob Elligold purchased the business from Sarah Taniel under the Native Property Act as an existing employee for ten spacecoin during the auctions on January 15, 489."

"And what happened to Ms. Taniel?" Mr. Apollo followed up.

"Insufficient information. No projection possible."

"Explain."

"The last record associated with Sarah Taniel is an application for an exit visa twenty years ago on August 31, 488," the hovercar computer said. "The revolution disrupted Int-Ag operations before Int-Ag granted the exit visa. No subsequent records exist."

"Well goddamn." Detective Barnes turned to Mr. Apollo. "Two missing people!"

"Only two?" Mr. Apollo asked. "Harry Primer and Sarah Taniel are a generation apart. Unlikely to disappear together."

"How many can there be? There aren't any missing person reports from this period. We didn't even have a record of Harry Primer being missing until you started asking about him."

Mr. Apollo paused. "Didn't his family inquire?" he asked.

"I don't think so." Detective Barnes shook his head. "We don't have a file anyway."

"Computer," Mr. Apollo said, "compare the population of Little Sargon before the historic Freedom Week to the population six months after. How much turnover?"

It took the hovercar computer a few moments to assemble the datasets. "Ninety-five percent," it said.

"Of the pre-Freedom-Week residents who left the neighborhood, how many remain on Frogger today?"

"Zero percent."

"And what percentage have either departure records or local death records?"

"Seventy-eight percent."

"So... twenty-two percent aren't here, didn't die, and didn't leave?"

"Yes," the computer confirmed.

"How many people is that?"

"One hundred and thirty-eight."

Detective Barnes's jaw dropped. He looked at Mr. Apollo, hands spread.

"That's a lot of missing people," he said.

Mr. Apollo nodded. "Computer, what percent of homes in Little Sargon were owned by private citizens before Freedom Week?"

"Ninety-five percent."

"And how many of those were subsequently purchased under the Native Property Act?"

"Ninety-nine percent."

"And when was Sargon Street renamed?"

"September 30, 488."

Detective Barnes was shaking his head. "How can that many people just fall off the grid?"

"Well, I'm not here to investigate missing people in general," Mr. Apollo said. "I'm here for Harry Primer."

"But they've got to be connected."

"They do," Mr. Apollo nodded, "which narrows down possible explanations a great deal." He turned back to the hovercar's computer. "When was the Sargon Street Community Center repurposed into a gym?"

"November 17, 488."

"Do you have a holo of the building when it opened as a gym?"

The hovercar projected a holo of the opening. Elvira Teller in miniature wore a blue sash as she stood in a newly white-plastered lobby.

Detective Barnes shook his head. "Damn this thing got interesting."

"To you," Mr. Apollo said. "I've got what I need. More even."

"Where next?"

"The space elevator. I've concluded my inquiries."

They drove to the spaceport in silence. Detective Barnes parked in the departures lane. There was no traffic. Nothing moved except the clouds in the dark gray sky. Scattered drops of rain began falling around them.

"So…" Detective Barnes asked. "Will your insurer pay the claim?"

"Unlikely," Mr. Apollo said. "All-Planets' policy covers deaths, not disappearances."

"But what happened to everyone?" Detective Barnes crossed his arms. "I've got one-hundred and thirty-eight missing persons to find. They need justice."

Mr. Apollo hesitated. "Justice," he said, "is a wheel forever spinning. Every time someone gets justice, they take it from someone else. It's zero sum."

"What do you mean?"

"The best explanation for so many missing people," Mr. Apollo said, "is other people."

"Oh come on. Who'd kill one hundred and thirty eight random people? That's a lot for a serial killer."

"Not random," Mr. Apollo said. "Think about who they were, what they must have represented. The hated parasitical face of Int-Ag for so many."

"But we're not the bad guys. We didn't massacre anyone. We jacked our moon back, sure. And some corpers who tried to help Int-Ag keep its loot got shot." Detective Barnes said. "We fought for liberty and economic justice, for a better world."

"And yet," Mr. Apollo said, "somehow your Sargian neighbors up and disappeared during your revolution. And then your government erased all traces of them and stole all their property. It's an awful look."

"Oh! There're other explanations!" Detective Barnes's voice ticked up.

"Not good ones," Mr. Apollo said. "Consider the obvious: Perhaps his wife shot him on the way to the spaceport? Or perhaps he changed his name and started a new life? Both are possible."

"Well what's wrong with them?"

"They don't explain the other missing people."

"What about…" Detective Barnes cast his eyes around and settled on the space elevator's dark shaft, "an unregistered evacuation ship. Maybe it exploded in deep space and the missing people died onboard without anyone knowing where they were?"

"There's no evidence of a ghost ship," Mr. Apollo said. "And ghost ships don't explain the cover-up."

"What cover up?"

"There's no historic footage of the neighborhood during the revolution. They never investigated —or even noted— a single disappearance. They changed all the street names. And they plastered over the life memorial wall but didn't strip the silver," Mr. Apollo said. "Why? To erase the Sargian origin as fast as possible." Mr. Apollo nodded. "They didn't loot cultural objects. They just disappeared them. That's a cover-up, not a smash-and-grab."

"Then why not destroy the building?" Detective Barnes had crossed his arms.

"Buildings cost money."

"Why cover it up then?"

"The Star Republic doesn't like proprietary corporate governments," Mr. Apollo said, "but they don't tolerate genocidal regimes, elected or otherwise."

"Oh yeah?" Detective Barnes asked. "Why wouldn't they just punish the murderers?"

"Democracies need votes and freedom fighters are popular and powerful people don't always accept responsibility. That's how these things often go."

Detective Barnes rolled his eyes. "Now you're making things up."

"Mr. Elligold knows what happened to Harry Primer," Mr. Apollo said. "His stepmother disappeared at the same time. Whatever happened to her happened to him. But she isn't missing. He knows she's dead. It follows he knows Harry Primer, who also disappeared, is also dead. But he won't say that."

"So now you think he lied?"

"Some truths are dangerous. Harry Primer's wife is afraid to come back at all, in fact."

"If you really think that," Detective Barnes shook his head, "why won't All-Planet's pay?"

"All-Planets makes money by not paying claims. If they call this a disappearance, Harry Primer's wife will have a hard job proving otherwise."

"Well… I don't believe a word of it." Detective Barnes's head kept shaking back and forth. "Not a damned word. You don't know what happened. In fact, I'm not even sure anything did happen."

"So where did all these people go then?"

"Maybe Int-Ag killed them?" Detective Barnes shrugged. "They were all corpers anyway, right? If anything happened, it was probably Int-Ag's fault. And they had it coming because they were all corper parasites."

"Whatever helps you sleep at night." Mr. Apollo opened the hovercar door and stepped out into the cold rain. "But just a few minutes ago, you wanted justice for Harry Primer."

Mr. Apollo closed the door and walked through the rain toward the space elevator. His AI had already prepared a draft report for All-Planets. No confirmation of death. No known leads. No proof that Harry Primer specifically had died on world and in policy period. No mention of other missing people.

He didn't believe it, but All-Planets didn't pay him to believe things.

92

by Savannah S. Miller

J J able to talk to the trees. Pa used-a worry that his name-sake was turnin' out a little nutty, but he never hurt nobody, and it would-a been too much money-a put im in a bin for three weeks. Course, Pa could-a done it if he wanted-a, but he ain't wanna, and so he didn't.

Right about the time he could walk he was hangin' on the edge-a the yard, hand on a maple or an oak, talkin' up a storm. I always watched im from the swingset. Every now and then JJ call, "Hey Rooney," and I'd come a-runnin' and he'd go on and on about how this tree said that and this one said this and I'd get so mad and slap im. I was only five then so that was okay back then, but he could never slap me back cause I was a girl. He was sure that the old oak with the rotten limb was tellin' im that rain was comin' even though that weatherman ain't said anythin' about it and the day clear as crystal. But come the next mornin' rainin' cats and dogs so bad my roof started leakin' on my pink princess bed. JJ had talent.

Summer '92 when the Kellerman kid went missin'. Boy bout my age, maybe year older, sixteen. I never knew specifics cause the lotta us all took class together no matter age and the like. Kellerman's daddy was worried he had gotten caught in the current-a the river bout half a mile into the woods Pa owned. Pa owned all the woods. You wanna hunt the deer out there, you talked to Pa. Pa was like God, he said what goes.

Kellerman's daddy put together a search party, bunch-a men, maybe twenty-a em and me. I ain't no boy, but I don't like hangin' with the other girls. Pa named me after Mickey Rooney so only natural I'm gonna be a tomboy. Pink princess bed bout only thing pink about me and I like it that way. Plus, if you gonna go into those woods you need all-a us. Pa, me, and JJ. Pa was God and JJ was a prophet and I was like one-a them old wise men who knew exactly where they was by the sky.

"Hey Rooney," JJ call me. We was walkin' few yards apart, checkin' under leaves and branches. Rest-a the group bit back from us, different angle. River was roarin'. We'd been searchin' mainly long the bank cause that's where Kellerman's dad—who wanted us to call im Joe but we never did—swore up and down his boy would be hidin'. He'd been missin' three days but Kellerman's dad ain't think he was dead yet cause the boy was what you might call belligerent. It's one-a em words teachers want you to use but no one round here actually does cause it take too much time. Point bein' it won't the first time Hunter run away. First time was three years prior. Kellerman found im two towns over hidin' in the trailer park with some woman. She somethin' like seventeen and kicked outta er house, decided to take little ole Hunter in. Rumor went round that they was in a secret relationship cause Hunter always did have a way with women since before middle school. He ain't never had a way with me though, so I didn't have no emotions to get in the way-a me lookin for im.

"What you want," JJ I ask im cause he got a weird look in is eye. He don't speak up none so I gotta move all the way over to im and get all annoyed. JJ look too innocent to be lookin' for a missin' kid in the woods. He got these eyes like a deer, get all wide whenever he thinkin' bout somethin', and he always thinkin' so his eyes always wide. He gonna have a hard time at the high school.

43

JJ lookin' up at a big old tree. It was one-a them old ones that nobody really know how long it been there until it fall and they count the rings. Sometimes I'd like to think that I'd be one them trees when I die, but that's a long way from now.

"What the tree sayin'?"

"It ain't sayin' good things."

I look up at big ole tree. Sometime I like to see if I can figure out if a tree a boy or a girl. This one definitely a girl, windin' branches and a plot-a that wrappin' weed over er base. I hate them weeds, they always men. They just grow and grow up the side-a the tree and suck all-a life outta er. Sometimes Pa get to em in time and chop the vines off, sometimes he don't. Either way, tree lookin' real sad at me right now and I could see why JJ concerned.

"Tree sayin' he dead, Rooney," JJ told me.

I nodded, "I figure he'd be dead sooner or later."

JJ shake his head at me. "No, Rooney, he ain't supposed to be dead."

I ain't got a clue what the boy goin' on bout, he just lookin' at me with them wide eyes like I'm supposed to read is mind. "Course ain't supposed to be dead, he only a kid like you and me."

JJ shake his head again. "No, Rooney, he killed."

I look at JJ cause I never known JJ to lie to me and he ain't look no different which means he was tellin' the truth and the tree said the boy was killed. That ain't make no sense though. I ain't hear-a nobody killin' nobody up in these mountains before. We got deer for that. People only get killed in the cities by them taxis and the men who hate their wives. "He killed, he killed how."

JJ put is hand on the tree and start cryin'. I'm lookin' around cause I don't like makin' no scene and that's what JJ doin' right now. I always hated how he'd get to cryin' at any little thing. Boys supposed to not cry, girls supposed to cry, but I can't cry like a girl if my brother gonna do it for me.

44

"Stop that," I tell im and swat his hand from the tree. "He killed how, who did it." JJ looks at me and just shake his head again. That when he started runnin'.

JJ runnin' away from the river now, back in the direction-a all the houses, back where my swingset and pink princess bed is. Men all lookin' at im funny like he lost is mind and I agree with im, but like I said, JJ never lied to me, so I go runnin' off after im cause he look like he know exactly where he goin'. Pa call after me, "Hey, Rooney, watch it," and I call behind me, "Pa come on." Guess I sound certain enough cause he start comin' after me and so do the rest-a the men. JJ still goin' but I'm faster than im so he not too far ahead. We jumpin' over logs, and every now and then JJ let is hand touch one-a them trees when he run past em, like he tryin' to make sure he still on the right path.

JJ takin me towards the field, mile off Johnson's road, I figure, cause that's the only thing I know the way he goin' and I know the woods. That ain't make no sense though cause that close to all-a us, and Kellerman's daddy tell us all he searched first five or so acres imself, and we ain't got no reason to not believe im cause he part-a the fire squad and good at searchin'. That where JJ goin' though. I see the clearin' up ahead pokin' through some-a my favorite maples, though I ain't too sure they gonna be my favorite no more after what JJ findin'.

In the clearin' now, and JJ just lookin' around. Men catchin' up to us, and they all screamin' and hollerin' cause they ain't got no faith in JJ. Kellerman's daddy just lookin' at JJ and sayin', "What the hell boy, where you goin'," but JJ won't even look at im. He just put that little hand on one-a them maples and close is eyes real good and listen. Kellerman's daddy say, "He by the river, Johnny, get your boy, we know he by the river," and Pa bout to say somethin' to JJ, right about the time he big eyes still closed move around in is head. He open em and I follow is

45

sightline to a tree across the clearin'. He—see this one a boy—got struck in a lightnin' storm or somethin' cause he split right down the middle and half-a im bent onto the ground. JJ just point at it and for a second I think his tan skin a part-a one-a the trees.

No one move a minute, then Pa decide he gonna do it. I look up to Pa cause-a that, he always the first one willin' to do stuff and so am I. He walkin' real slow over to that bent tree, takin' is time cause I think he know what he gonna find there, but at some point he makes it and he lookin' under that split half-a the trunk. He standin' real still for a while then I see im bend over, and I hear im throwin' up from across the clearin'. I start runnin' to im cause nobody gonna make my Pa throw up without answerin' to me, but he hears me comin' and puts is hand up tryin' to stop me from comin' too close, but he ain't do it in time.

That won't my first time seein' a body I know, but it was the first time I really remember it. I was too young when we bury Mama to really remember anythin' but that the casket made-a oak cause that was the kinda thing I always tried to remember. It ain't really look human. He ain't look like the Kellerman kid, that's for sure. He ain't got no clothes on, and he facedown in a pile-a leaves and dirt under that split trunk, but is arm twisted weird and I reckon is foot broke too by the looks-a it. Hunter a good lookin' kid and play football so I know is feet ain't sup-posed to look like that.

"Ain't we gonna roll im over," I ask Pa cause that seem like the only natural thing to do. Someone face in the ground you roll im over so he can breathe, or at least look like he breathin'. Pa just look at me and shake is head.

"Go get your brother for me, Rooney."

Now I'm shakin' my head cause he know better than that. He know I'm the one that old enough and strong enough to do somethin' like this, not JJ. JJ only four days old when we had to bury Mama so he ain't even got that kinda memory like I do. He say it again, "Rooney get your brother," and this time I tell im, "No I can do it Pa," but he get this real strange look in is eyes like he bout to burst and I get scared.

I call to JJ and it take im a hot minute to get to us. Pa look at im and say, "Trees tell you how." Pa used to think JJ talent a sham but he seen too much to doubt now. JJ nod and just look at Pa, and somethin' pass between em I'll never understand and I hate JJ for that. JJ and Pa go over to Hunter and Pa grab his head and JJ grab his legs, tryin' real hard not to touch im anywhere normally covered by a pair-a boxers. They get im right side up and JJ drop im real quick and walk away. I leave im alone cause I figure he cryin' again. The Kellerman kid eyes real open like JJ's and Pa just keep lookin' into im frozen, and I wanna yell at im cause we should close im, but it feel like Pa can see somethin' in those eyes, like some answer or somethin'. Kid got some real bad cuts it look like on is chest and a black eye and blood on is lip. He look like somethin' from one-a those movies Pa keeps on tape.

Pa finally stop lookin' at im and just start walkin' real slow back to the group-a men who all still standin' in the clearin'. It's a big clearin' so I can't hear much, but I make out a couple-a em askin', "Is it im, Johnny," and "What you find," but Pa don't answer. Pa go up to Kellerman's daddy and just punch im in the face. Kellerman's daddy go down and so does Pa with im cause he just keeps punchin' im and punchin' im and the men screamin' but none-a em stoppin' Pa cause he on toppa im now. I look away cause I know Pa ain't want me to see im angry like that.

JJ sittin' over by some brush faced away from me. I go over to im and take my jacket off cause I figure he gonna need somethi' to wipe is face on, but I get over there and I see he ain't cryin', not one bit. He just lookin' with those eyes real big and wide but different now, lookin' kinda dead. I'd never tell im this to is face but JJ kinda lookin' like the Kellerman kid, only difference was he had both is feet in front-a im real straight.

47

I never see Kellerman's daddy again after that. I thought maybe Pa killed im, but town gossip said they sent im down to Lexington but no one tell me why. I used-a think one day me and Pa will go and visit im, and he can apologize for givin' im such a beatin'. Then I got older.

JJ won't ever really the same after that. First he got real quiet, even quieter than he was before, but then he started gettin' real loud, like he was absorbin' the Kellerman kid's voice into is own. Became real popular, startin datin' around. He's got a kid now also named Johnny but we can't call im JJJ so we just call im Trip cause he the third and he only four and don't know the difference. He had im with one-a the Brack girls who used to live next to the Kellerman's, but they went up in flames and the mom ain't want nothin' to do with Trip or JJ no more. That's okay though cause I never really like er and she always too high for JJ.

JJ don't talk to trees no more. Whenever I ask im bout it, he says he never could and he was always just playin' with us, but I know better. Sometimes when we visit Pa I catch im wanderin' round the edge-a the yard lookin' up at all the trees, and every now and then I see im put his hand on a trunk for a minute like he tryin' to keep imself from floatin' away. Then he take is hand off and come back inside to me and Trip and Pa, and I pretend I never saw im do it so that I can watch im do it again.

48

An Excerpt from

The Silk Road Affair

by Edward M. Lukacs

About fifty kilometres west of Wuhai in the Xinjiang Uygur Autonomous Region of China there is a lake. As often happens in such arid and mountainous country, it has no outlets. In the mountain areas little agriculture is practised in the rocky soil, and the sparse vegetation is only suitable for herding of grazing animals. This unforgiving country has, at least for its totalitarian government, one other practical use. It is the perfect place to exile political troublemakers, especially those Uighurs who are too well politically connected to jail or kill.

Thus, Alim Samedi found himself banned to his family's home province, where he was reduced to herding sheep in the Alatau Mountains, at liberty and safe from arrest through the influence of his prominent Uygur family. But their influence was not without limits. Beijing's continuing pressure made it inadvisable for anyone to hire him in his profession as an engineer, or indeed in any other sort of skilled employment.

The shepherd and his flock were in one of the narrow valleys north and west of the lake where the grass was never grazed by other flocks. He only appeared in the smaller towns when he needed supplies; it was his safest course, at least until he had been forgotten by the authorities.

Alim had his one man yurt set up next to the lean-to which he had made of local brush to house his two donkeys. The sheep were not yet corralled, but they stayed close together at night by instinct, their safety assured by the vigilance of his three Kazakh Molosser sheep dogs.

As he looked westward into the late afternoon sun, Samedi reflected upon his condition. It was irksome that he could not continue his research at the China Academy of Space Technology, but in the crackdown on liberals, after the Dongzhou protests three years earlier, he had been very lucky to get away with only a few weeks of detention for questioning. Some of his friends had not been so lucky; they had disappeared utterly, probably into the prison system or, he shuddered, perhaps much worse.

No, being stripped of his position and his security clearance and then exiled to his home province, where only menial labour was allowed of him, had proved to be a huge relief. He might only be a shepherd tending a flock in the middle of an arid no-man's-land but he was now far more free and at peace than he had been since he first entered University. The constant propaganda and overt surveillance surrounding his work had made his life in Peking a living hell, albeit by Chinese standards a very comfortable hell.

Here, he reflected as he gazed around him, was true freedom. The last eighteen months of solitude had given him sufficient time to reflect, time to finally realize that his life was of far more worth to his fellow man while he cared for a few hundred sheep than it had been when his talents aided the mass destruction that was modern warfare.

His reverie was disturbed by a faint mechanical noise. It sounded like a jet engine but it did not sound like a healthy one. He turned his gaze toward the north, following the sound until he saw an Iskra TS-11 jet trainer in the clear sky. By its markings it was not Air Force, but one of many similar obsolescent planes which had been disarmed and relegated to use for business transportation by military and scientific VIPs. It was flying very low, far too low for safety, he mused.

As he watched the descending plane it released its drop tanks. That was when he first noticed the smoke; it was coming from the fuselage, but well ahead of the plane's single jet engine. Now there were streams of something coming out of the wings. The pilot must have been dumping his remaining fuel to prevent fire in a forced landing. But there was nowhere in this rugged countryside to land. The pilot would certainly crash, and he must crash badly since it was apparent that he had little choice of landing site at this point.

"That plane is in bad trouble and the damned fool's going to kill himself by trying to save the plane instead of bailing out!" Samedi said aloud as he wondered what could be so valuable that a pilot experienced enough to be cleared to fly a jet would attempt a forced landing in rough country. He would stand a hundred times better chance if he ejected.

The plane's engine went silent as it disappeared behind a low ridge to his north-west. There was only one possible place over there; the pilot must be trying for the sandy riverbed. But Alim had flown a similar plane often enough to know only too well that the one available tiny clear spot would not do. As these thoughts passed through his mind there was a loud noise, and a moment later a small cloud of oily smoke appeared and quickly dissipated.

Well, at least most of the fuel had been dumped, he thought, and there had been almost no fire. Perhaps the pilot might have made it. But Alim, who was familiar with both the plane and the miserably small landing area, doubted it. The pilot might be an idiot but his was a human life, and common decency demanded that he must be helped. Alim was likely the only person who witnessed the crash, and certainly he was the only person within twenty or thirty kilometres who was near enough to render aid.

As he turned toward his little camp, Alim whistled to his dogs to round up the sheep. It looked hopeless, he reflected, but then there was a man out there, one who was at the very least injured. He had to try to help even though he could not get to the site before dark, and then with only a small first aid kit and no means of communication. But he would do what little he could, even though he was certain that his effort would probably be a *beau geste*.

He whistled again and the dogs began moving the sheep in as he turned to load his essentials onto the two donkeys. The yurt, the corral, the lean-to barn, and his supplies would be waiting when he returned.

Unlike British border collies, Molosser dogs herd their charges silently. The sheep, however, could clearly be heard bleating as the flock moved several hundred meters away. Within fifteen minutes the dogs and his flock were at the camp, and he had his donkeys harnessed and loaded. He patted the first one, which followed, as he walked not needing to hold their reins as they followed him. He whistled again to the dogs to move the sheep as he and the donkeys began to walk toward a very low pass in the hills, trailed closely by his flock and its guardians.

It was slow going for Alim and his gaggle of sheep and dogs as they crossed the low ridge, though the hundred meter climb was insignificant and the path wide and smooth. He had often crossed into this next valley. Though it was narrow and steep, owing to a stream which, fed by snow melt, ran through the dry spells, its lush vegetation made it a reliable pasture for his flock. The dogs were having no difficulty with the flock; they were well trained and the sheep were cooperative, well accustomed to the dogs' gentle direction.

As Alim crested the low ridge and began the descent, he saw a thin curl of white smoke still rising from the wreck. The smoke was obviously not from jet fuel; perhaps dry some brush had caught fire. In any event it was only smouldering, with no overt sign of open flame.

A few hundred meters further on he came to the first wreckage. It was a wheel, probably, he thought, from the port landing gear. He looked through the brush and stunted trees which had been mown down. The plane must still have had more than flying speed, for about a half kilometre up the valley he saw more of the plane's trail of debris. He whistled to the dogs as he turned westward down the valley, relying on the dogs to keep the flock behind him.

The plane was a total loss. The boom tail which normally projected over the engine's exhaust was the next fragment that he encountered. There was a baggage compartment, apparently still intact, just aft of where the tail had broken off.

He found to his amazement that the recessed latch handle moved easily, though the hinges had been distorted by the impact. It took a strong heave on the handle with a loud protestation of groaning and screeching of hinges to make the door open. Inside he found a soft-sided suitcase, a briefcase, and a laptop computer in an expensive leather bag. The suitcase was much the worse for wear. Having been the furthest forward, it had absorbed the worst of the shock, bursting in the process. It was damp, smelling like cologne or aftershave. He decided to leave it.

He removed the two other cases, putting them in a sack on the first donkey. Scuff marks aside, neither showed any sign of serious damage. Then he whistled again to the dogs to gather and hold the sheep while he walked the last hundred or so meters to the remaining parts. One shattered wing was lying in the stream and the remainder of the fuselage and the other wing lay badly crumpled against a large rock outcropping at the side of the water. The bubble canopy was nowhere to be seen; perhaps at the last moment the pilot had thought of ejecting, but with insufficient altitude.

Alim had been right; there had been no fuel fire; the pilot had been dumping fuel. A bit of the brush was only smouldering, probably because it was too well watered to burn easily. There was no risk of further fire.

The pilot was another matter entirely. He was still strapped into his seat but the force of the crash had accordioned the airframe, crushing him into the instrument panel. He had been nearly splattered, torn apart by the force of the crash. Blood and chunks of flesh were all over the cockpit.

Alim tried to move the seat to remove the body for burial, but then he remembered that underneath it there were still live explosive charges, parts of the ejection mechanism. The pilot would have to stay where he was, at least for now. It was at least three days' walk to the nearest village which possessed a telephone, and attempting to preserve the body for a proper burial was impossible. Before anyone could get back to extract the body, the wildlife would have done for him.

Alim whistled again to the dogs, who herded his flock to the water where they began to drink and to forage upon the banks. He would have to camp here, rough, because the sun was almost down.

He found a large flat stone to sit on and there he removed his pack, preparing to open his sleeping bag, when he remembered the briefcase and the computer. He had to satisfy his curiosity. He opened the case first. It contained three folders and a few personal effects. The folders were clearly labelled top secret, and they carried the seals of both the foreign ministry and the Army's research laboratories.

As Alim read, he saw why the contents were of more than sufficient importance to justify the use of a private jet for their delivery. Even though he did not fully understand the science of what he was reading, as an engineer he could grasp enough even though it was far outside his area of expertise. But he was well able to understand the military documents which were probably intended for the highly restricted station, hidden in the hills five kilometres east of the lake.

He turned to the laptop next. Much to his surprise it booted up! "The pilot must be an idiot!" he mused, when he discovered that the laptop was running Red Flag Linux, and it booted to an X window in single-user mode, requiring neither login name nor password. As he looked at the directory and file names, he was shocked.

He opened one file to find that it discussed planning under-way for a major military action in the spring, only seven months away. The action would involve the entire autonomous region and neighbouring Uzbekistan and Kazakhstan.

There was real danger that the Russians would involve themselves if the Uzbeks and Kazakhs found themselves in difficulties. Alim's entire family lived near the one main road across the border which was suitable for troop movements.

As for China, the government's treatment of Alim, his friends and other loyal protesters had thoroughly damped any patriotic sentiments that he might have felt. He was an Uighur first and foremost, and therefore, by definition he was an unwelcome and decidedly second-class citizen of China.

He knew that he and his people would never fare any better under this government. But what could he do? He could not go to any authorities, since he was already suspect and effectively in exile. He dared not talk to any-one in his town, for who knew the loyalties of anyone these days? No, he would have to get this evidence out of China and into the hands of someone, of some other government with sufficient power to deter China before it started, potentially, the next world war.

The border was only twenty or so kilometres away, and in these remote hills it was lightly defended, if at all, and almost never patrolled. This was due only in part to the difficult terrain, for smuggling was a popular Uighur pastime and a highly profitable one which was unofficially ignored by the government since it reduced the restive sentiments of the local populace.

Everyone knew at least one smuggler; Alim certainly knew several. There was Selim, he thought, who lived only ten kilometres or so from here, fortunately toward the Kazakh border. He reached for his map of the area, a military one printed on cloth, before he thought of the plane.

Then he walked back to the hull to reach behind the pilot's seat where there was a compartment for the plane's flight and equipment manuals and, invariably, a map case. He was in luck; the map case was still there, intact. He opened it to find large scale aerial maps of western China, Outer Mongolia, and the former Soviet far-eastern republics.

As he returned to his rock he heard an aircraft in the distance. It sounded like a Y5, a large cabin biplane based upon the Russian Antonov2. It might be one of several in the area which were used for crop dusting and fire fighting. It was in the next valley, the one that he had just left. It flew along for several minutes, probably toward the border before reversing course. The sound of its engine slowly faded as it returned to its base, east of the lake, in the failing night.

The Antonov might, no, it must have been searching for the plane and its pilot. More planes, probably helicopters, would certainly be returning at first light carrying ground parties. He could not be discovered here! Thankfully the weather was clear and there would be a nearly full moon. The valley was steep but he knew that there was a small opening along the stream. The dogs and the sheep might be tired but it would be safe to move them.

He loaded the computer and the briefcase onto his lead donkey and after consulting the map again, he moved with his dogs and sheep down the valley, gradually descending as he followed the westward-flowing stream.

The going was easy enough and he thought that with any luck he might at least cross the next low pass to arrive at Selim's farm by first light.

Selim Hassan was not an Uighur, but of closely related Iranian stock. He was not in Iran now because he had, as a university student, been in the pay of the British when Ayatollah Homeini began his 'purification' of Iran by precipitating the "Hostage Crisis." The survival chances of anyone who was suspected of working for the intelligence agencies of the American and European Infidels were poor, even if one survived the near-certainty of imprisonment and torture.

He completed his studies and had for several years been working for a small manufacturing company which made spare parts no longer available for American military vehicles. His exploits with MI-6 were a distant memory when he learned that the Authorities were onto him. Selim did not wait for the axe to fall; he called the telephone number that he had never forgotten.

Within a day he was told to be at the north entrance of the Chitgar Metro station at 1500. Exactly on time a car pulled to the kerb on Nasim e Davvom. The driver's familiar face broke into a smile and Selim entered the car, throwing his rucksack into the rear as they pulled out into traffic.

And so he faded from Tehran like a ghost.

Since there was little chance of crossing a friendly western border they travelled eastward, where there was sufficient restiveness, confusion, and corruption to allow him to disappear into the background. At Dargazm he was handed over to an Uzbek and given new Kazakh documents before they crossed the unguarded border into Turkmenistan at night near Loftabad.

He was aided in establishing himself in Zharkent, Kazakhstan where he purchased a small carting business. He quickly learned the local scams as he expanded his lorry and livestock-trading businesses into neighbouring Xinjiang, China. Soon he was able, through various contacts, to purchase real Kazakh, Uzbek, Tadzhyk, and Chinese Uighur documents as well, which allowed him to travel freely and to establish a profitable business smuggling western goods into the Uighur Autonomous region. It is truly amazing, the amount of contraband that can be hidden in the greasy, dust-soiled coat of a mountain sheep.

As he prospered he purchased, among his many holdings, this little farmstead, a safe-house conveniently inaccessible by motor vehicles and yet near the border. It was toward this refuge that Alim was now heading.

The dogs began to bark, waking Selim in the pre-dawn half light. He quickly threw on clothes, grabbing his Baikal shotgun as he went outdoors toward the paddock. The sheep were all right; they were not excited and there were no predators. But the dogs were still barking, and they were all looking off toward the north and the low pass into the next valley.

Selim reached into the cabin where his binoculars, fine Russian Fotons, hung from a coat hook. He scanned the near ground but there was nothing to be seen, so he shifted his search toward the pass, helped by the fact that the darkness was gradually giving way to the dawn.

There! He could not make anything out, really, but there was some sort of movement... broad movement coming down from the pass, about four kilometres from the homestead. It must be a flock of sheep, but the only shepherd keeping a flock in those highlands was Alim Samedi, but he would not be so foolish as to drive his flock over such ground, especially at night. There must be trouble, and very bad trouble at that, to make him do such a thing.

They were about four kilometres away. It would take him at least an hour, driving his flock, to reach the cabin. Selim returned to the cabin to light the wood cook-stove to prepare breakfast. He filled a pot of water at the well pump and placed it upon the stove. His guest will be both cold and hungry. He would probably welcome a cup of strong coffee. The cupboard was well stocked with canned food and there was mutton in the pickling barrel, so feeding an extra mouth would not be a problem.

He checked the rapidly growing fire; then he walked to the second paddock to open the gate for Alim's sheep.

Almost two hours later, Alim's flock was safely in the second paddock and his dogs, as well as Selim's, had been fed. The shepherd looked haggard. He had been awake for more than twenty-four hours, and he had driven his flock almost thirty kilometres in that time. He took the offered Turkish-style coffee gratefully, loading it with sugar and sheep milk before sipping the tiny cup greedily.

After the second cup, as Selim was preparing rice, vegetables, and mutton for breakfast, he finally asked, "What brings you here like this, Alim? It must be serious trouble to make you drive your sheep at night, and in a direction away from your own camp and the town."

"There was a plane crash, a jet trainer. It was flown by a civilian, an engineer or scientist of some sort and a VIP, certainly, but he died. He was crushed in the cockpit. He looks like a swatted bug. When I saw what he was carrying I knew that with my past, I would be in serious trouble if I was found anywhere near him or his plane, even if I had done nothing. So I grabbed what looked valuable and I fled."

"What do you want to do?"

"I'll have to get away, preferably across the border, and quickly! There was a small helicopter or plane nosing around at nightfall, only a few hours after the crash but it searched this valley, maybe twenty kilometres east of here, but not the small valley to the north so I was not seen."

"What has you so frightened?"

"There were documents, military plans. I expect they'd do almost anything to recover them." He looked at Selim before adding, "I would tell you about them, but believe me, you are better off not knowing, at least while we're in Chinese territory."

"And you're here because you want to leave, quickly and quietly?"

"Exactly! Once they discover who was at the wreck site, my life expectancy is nil." He smiled, then he added, "So I came to make the local smuggler a deal. Get me across the border, with somewhere to hide in Kazakhstan, and you can have the 150 sheep, the dogs, and let's see..." He looked in his backpack. "Oh, good! You can have half of my bank balance if you can let me have the other half as ready cash. And if you dare, you can loot my flat in town because I'll not be going back there."

He thought, wincing, of the collected souvenirs of his short lifetime, now lost because the Security Police would surely be in his flat before he could possibly get there. Well, things were... things, and mere things are worth a lot less than one's own skin.

"If I help you, I'm probably finished here as well," Selim said

"It probably doesn't matter whether you help me or not. There are at most a half dozen of us in this district and as soon as they discover what is missing, all of our futures are bleak at best."

"You're right. At least I know what's coming. All right; let's get packed up." He looked at his companion. "You're about the same size as me and I have plenty of clothes here.

Then Selim opened what appeared to be a bread box. From it, he took an odd looking telephone. It was a satellite phone, an Ericsson R109. He walked outside before turning it on. Within a minute, a green LED lit on its keyboard face, indicating that it had acquired a satellite. He dialled a number, then he waited.

"Hello, Yevgeney? I'm going to need a truck, a GAZ, or better yet, bring the big Tatra to the usual crossing place. Oh, and bring a few shepherds. We have about three hundred sheep which we're using as cover. They can have them if they'll agree to herd them in the opposite direction, for cover when we leave them." He waited. "Yes, I figure that we should be there at about 2200 tonight. All right; see you then."

"All right, Alim, let's get going. I want to be in the steep dry wash before they arrive here. Perhaps they won't look there. The sheep can drink their fill at the pond but then we'll have to hurry them along. Once we get under the trees in the canyon nearer the border, we'll be safe enough, and we can do that by noon if we hurry."

"What do you want me to do?"

"Open the gate between the paddocks and drive the flocks together. I'll start loading the donkeys with supplies." He opened the door into a small room where Alim saw a small arsenal and cases of military rations as he left the cabin to deal with the sheep and feed the dogs.

Fifteen minutes later, Selim called him. The pack donkeys were loaded; Alim could not miss the 12.7 milli-metre Zastava rifle and an RPG launcher. At least, he mused, they would be able to defend themselves against anything short of a tank, which, he reasoned, would not be able to operate where they were going, anyway.

He discarded his clothes and his pack as he changed into Russian desert fatigues. He added an ammunition belt with holster, a military vest whose pockets were already full of spare magazines, and a pack containing a first aid kit and additional clothes. Then he picked up the AK-103 which Selim had left him. As ready as he might have been, he left the house, and his life as well, behind to join Selim, who was waiting with all four pack animals, six dogs, and a veritable sea of sheep. They left the paddock, striking out toward the northwest, where six kilometres ahead the dry wash began.

Shortly after they entered the steep-sided and very crooked wash, a light aircraft in military markings flew over Selim's homestead. Its pilot banked the plane southward as the observer called in to his base. "Jinghei base, this is Captain Ho. We've flown over the two sheep encampments. Both are empty so we flew through the pass toward the crash site. Neither shepherd nor his flock are visible. We're getting a bit low on fuel."

"Turn southward toward Huocheng. Perhaps they are heading toward the livestock market there. You can refuel at the airport there and then explore the area of the border below the mountains. The town police have already been alerted."

"Understood."

Ho turned to the pilot. "Let's turn around; we're getting bounced around badly and the sooner we're out of this damned pass the better."

The plane rose sufficiently to make a tight turn and flew away to the south. Had the plane risen another three hundred meters or so, they might have seen the shepherds and their flocks, but eight kilometres away Alim and Selim were approaching the first of the trees and vegetation which would shield them, and which followed the narrow river valley almost to the border. They had been able to hear the comings and goings of planes or heavy helicopters for almost an hour, though none came near them.

Forty kilometres south of Beijing a half dozen army officers stood peering at a map of the western Uighur Autonomous Zone. Reports from the crash site were at last coming in and they were not encouraging.

"You're certain that he had the documents with him?" General Kwan asked a colonel standing across the table.

"I can't say for certain, but he did check them out four days ago. He was scheduled to travel tomorrow and he still had some work to do on the presentation. We've already checked his home. His briefcase was gone, but his laptop computer was there. The lab is checking it out now. His safe was empty but for some low-grade classified materials which are of no real importance."

"So... Then he left at least two days early and instead of flying on a commercial airliner, he checked out an Iskra to fly himself."

"That's not unusual, Sir. He is an ex-Air Force pilot, and he is permitted to use the executive aircraft if needed."

"But… Two days early! Something is not right. All right, keep looking. Take apart his office and his house; something odd has happened, and he did not inform us. We thought he was loyal without blemish, but this sudden change makes me wonder."

"Yes, General. Is there anything else right now, or can I return to the search?"

"Colonel Dong, I think it would be wise for you to visit the crash site and supervise activities there. It would be better if someone from this command was in charge, if only because of the Uighurs. Try as I might, I just can't make myself trust them. Take a plane and a pilot, someone who can help you on the ground out there, and leave immediately, or as soon as possible, that is."

"I'll take Major Lu and another Iskra if you will ask them to have a Y-5 available for us at Jinghei."

"I'll do that. Be on your way, and please do your best. If we don't recover those plans and documents, the politicians will fry us in boiling oil!"

"I'm on my way," Dong said, saluting before he left the room.

Two hours later, an Iskra TS-11 began its takeoff at Bejing's international airport. It was obviously making a long flight because under its wings four large drop tanks filled all the attachment points. Major Lu let the plane roll until it had considerably more than normal flying speed. The aircraft was about ten percent over its maximum rated takeoff weight because of the extra fuel. They would probably, barring headwinds, be able to make the flight non-stop, but their priority was so high that General Kwan had ordered a refuelling tanker to stand by at Lotuo Quanzi.

As the aircraft climbed to its most efficient cruising altitude, Major Lu spoke into his mask, "Chiang, I have a very bad feeling about this. I know the pilot well and this does not feel right."

"I know what you mean. Sometimes I wondered about him and the very sensitive work that he was doing. His mother was a Kazakh, you know."

Colonel Dong answered, "I didn't know that! I wonder, since he crashed well to the west of Jinghei, whether he intended to go there at all. We'll have to consider that carefully. As soon as we land, I'll check on the possibility that other dissidents could be involved among those damned Uighurs!"

The plane flew on at 3,000 meters and eight hundred kilometres per hour, their most efficient altitude and speed. If they were lucky, Colonel Dong mused, they would land at Jenghei before nightfall.

An Excerpt from *The Question Is Murder*

Dear Mr. Ethics

by Mark Willen

S am reads the email a second time, then a third, not sure whether to dismiss it as a prank or call the police. He prints it out and then reads it again, looking for some clue to the sender's frame of mind.

It's probably a stunt. Sam gets more than his share of cranks and weirdos. There's something about writing a newspaper column and calling yourself "Mr. Ethics" that attracts them. Some people just take offense at the notion of a guy sitting behind a computer trying to tell them there's a right way to behave.

He takes a deep breath and reads the email again, a blue felt-tipped pen in his hand. He studies the words, the grammar, even the sentence structure, looking for oddities or inconsistencies. Nothing jumps out.

He doesn't need this. Not now.

But then maybe he does. Maybe it's *just* what he needs. Something to take his mind off of Lisa, not unlike the migraine that makes you forget the sprained ankle, at least for a while. He looks up from the sheet of paper in his hand and glances at the poster that hangs in front of him. It's filled with quotations on writing, and although it's the kind of thing a college kid would hang in a dorm room, he's always liked having it near. And he didn't have much else to stick on the wall two years ago when he was awarded

65

his own office, a privilege he didn't especially want and still hasn't adjusted to. He loves the column, both for its intellectual challenge and for the feeling that he may be helping people, albeit in small ways, to make the world a better place.

He turns back to the email. He needs another opinion and knows it should come from his boss, but he doesn't want to lose control. Brenda would be cautious and call in the executive editor or a lawyer, maybe both, and that would mean days of delay. He's not going to use the email in his column, so whatever he does shouldn't come back to hurt the newspaper. He wants to help if he can, and he doesn't want anyone to get in his way. He's too old for bureaucratic games.

But he does want another opinion.

He gets up, grabs the printout, and walks down the hall to the newsroom. It's eerily quiet, nothing like the newsrooms he grew up in. Gone is the chaos of constant motion and loud conversations carried on from opposite ends of the room. Gone, too, are the ugly metal desks shoved together so close you can smell the whisky on your neighbor's breath, hear him belch or argue with an official or a source on the phone. Some had hated it, but Sam thrived on the synergy it produced, the bonds it created, the shared excitement of doing something he believed— still believes—is important.

Now, in its place he sees what the younger reporters view as high-tech paradise, with desks crowded with laptops and other electronic devices. The reporters and editors are stuck in a maze of mini-cubicles with three-foot high, sound-absorbing barriers to create a sense of privacy. They need to stand up to see another person.

He's acutely aware of how much journalism has changed in the thirty years he's been practicing it. Not that it was ever pure and not that all its practitioners had less than selfish motives. But many did. Now it's nothing more than a business, a fight for internet clicks or a spot appearance on TV, just when facts and truth matter the most because they're in such short supply. It's one of the reasons he was ready to give up reporting and editing to take on the ethics column, but that's not to say he doesn't miss the thrill of unraveling an important story. He walks the maze, heading to Molly's corner. "Hey," he says as he comes up behind her.

Her right hand rises in a silencing gesture, and he realizes she's on the phone. One of those ear things hidden by her hair. How was he supposed to know?

While he waits, he glances up at the silent TV monitors on the wall and tries to guess why the weatherman is moving his arms around in a circle. After a minute or so, Molly ends the call and turns to him.

"What?" she asks, not unfriendly but not friendly either. *Busy* is the vibe he gets. Sam was once Molly's editor and mentor as she learned her way around Congress, which was Sam's beat for twelve years. She still comes to him for advice, though not often, and he will seek her out when his ethics column needs the perspective of someone younger, or a woman. He hands her the printout without speaking and watches her read it, biting down on her lower lip, a habit he's grown used to. He averts his eyes when she looks up and catches him staring at her. He glances around her cubicle while she finishes, then turns back to her, focusing now on her hands, which grip the printout on either side, as if she's worried he'll have second thoughts and try to take it back. He's never noticed how graceful her hands look, with long supple fingers, as though she was born to play the piano. Or type. The thought makes him smile. Molly hands back the email and frowns. "So what's the question?" she asks. "Do you think it's for real?"

She purses her lips and turns her head slightly. Her blue eyes, accented with eye shadow she doesn't need, seem to settle on a photograph of her and Kyle, her fiancé. They are wearing hiking gear and standing atop a boulder,

Molly's bleached-blond hair blowing lightly in the wind. Their wedding is set for Memorial Day weekend, less than three months away.

"Look, Sam," she says finally, picking up her water bottle and taking a swallow, making him wait for what's coming. "Every woman has some rat-bastard in her past she'd love to blow to kingdom come, but they never actually do it."

"Some do."

"Not many. And probably only on the spur of the moment. More passion than planning, and never with advance notice."

"This is different. He didn't dump her. He's stalking her and she's scared. She doesn't see any other way out."

Molly tilts her head slightly and he's not sure what that means. She reaches for the moisturizer she keeps on her desk. He watches her squirt some in her palm and then rub it carefully on the backs of her hands. He feels himself getting annoyed. Since Lisa asked him to move out, he has less patience for everything and everyone. He reminds himself of that and takes a deep breath.

"I can't ignore it," he says.

"But what can you do? It's vague and anonymous. You can't use it in the column. Are you thinking of turning it over to the police?"

"No. I have to answer her. Reach out in some way."

"Tell me why. You always told me not to get involved in the stories I cover."

"I can't just let it go."

"What if you find out she's serious? Or suicidal?" she asks. "Then you'll have no choice but to go to the authorities."

The question annoys him. "Of course. But I don't have enough to work with now."

"I don't disagree, and if it's not a hoax, I feel sorry for her. But all you can do is tell her to go to the police."

"She says she can't," he says. "I want to find out why. This is a cry for help."

Molly shrugs, making it clear she doesn't agree. "If I came to you with this, you'd say reporters shouldn't get involved. I'd get your lecture on how our job is to shine a light on problems while staying above the fray, not try to make everything okay."

He doesn't know what to say. He can't argue with the journalistic principle she's quoting, but it doesn't apply here because he's not a reporter planning to write a story about the email. "I have to follow it up," he tells her. "I just do."

"Why'd you ask my advice if you already had your mind made up?"

He walks away without answering. On the one hand, he sees her point, but he's disappointed she isn't more concerned, more helpful. It surprises him that Molly isn't able to put herself in other people's shoes more often. Seeing the other side of an issue—any issue—is an important skill for a reporter. Call it empathy.

But maybe he's just annoyed because she doesn't agree with him.

Back in his office, he forwards the email to the IT department. He deletes the content, but they can analyze the IP address or whatever they look at to try to determine where it came from. He doesn't have much hope, but it's worth a try. Then he turns back to the email and rereads it.

Dear Mr. Ethics:

Is murder ever ethical? I hope so because I don't have a choice. An ex lover is destroying me. I broke up with him and now he's ruining my life. He got into my laptop, stole all my data and used it to stalk, embarrass, and almost bankrupt me. Now he's moved on to even worse stuff. He's killing my hope for any kind of normal life, so killing him is a form of self-defense. Justifiable homicide, right?

I can't go to the police for reasons I can't explain here. And I can't give you any more details because I can't risk you figuring out my name.

So can I murder him? And no, I'm not kidding.

Sincerely,

Truly Desperate

Sam jots down several notes. The tone strikes him as strangely calm and rational. She's making a logical argument, not what you'd expect from someone stressed and frantic. Or crazy. Is it a hoax? Maybe a college kid bored with her ethics class and looking for term paper ideas. Or an author concocting a crazy plot for a thriller. Or maybe someone pissed off at Mr. Ethics and hoping to draw him into a discussion that will embarrass him if made public. But maybe not.

It doesn't matter. He has to answer her. Keep her talking, try to get more clues so he can stop her, on the off chance she really is planning a murder.

He turns to his keyboard and after several false starts comes up with his reply.

Dear Truly Desperate,

I'm going to assume this is a not a prank because I have no way of knowing, and I want to give you the benefit of the doubt.

From the little you've told me, I can assure you that what you propose is not ethical. Justifiable homicide applies only when your life is in imminent danger, and you haven't convinced me that this is the case. I don't think you've convinced yourself or you wouldn't be asking me.

You need to go to the police. If you can't do it yourself, is there someone who can do it for you? If necessary, I might be willing to do that, depending on the details. And with the newspaper behind me, the police will feel obliged to take it seriously.

If you don't want my help, I suggest you talk to a mental health professional or a social worker or someone experienced in cases involving domestic partner abuse (which this obviously is).

If you'd like to talk about this more (and I will treat any conversations we have confidentially), you may call me at any time (cellphone number below).

Above all, don't do anything rash.

Regards,

Sam Turner (a.k.a. Mr. Ethics)

He sits back and reads the note again. He considers his offer to go to the police on her behalf, mindful of Molly's warning not to get involved. He wants to help her, but that's going too far.

He eliminates that sentence.

He also cuts the promise of confidentiality. If she asks for it, he'll agree, but there's no need to offer it up front. And it might tie his hands unnecessarily.

He reads his response one last time and hits the send button.

* * *

A drizzle is falling in Washington when he leaves the office on 11th Street a little before five. He hasn't made much progress on this week's column, but he needs an early start to get to the University of Maryland in College Park, where he teaches a weekly seminar in journalism ethics.

On the ride along slow-moving Rhode Island Avenue, he keeps thinking about the email. He's hoping she'll call soon, but he knows there's a good chance he'll never hear from her again, never find out whether it was a hoax or whether she changed her mind or even whether she carried out her plan. There isn't much he can do but wait.

The ethics seminar is for graduate students in journalism, many of them in mid-career. He loves handing them a difficult problem and watching them wrestle with it, struggling to put ethics above the constant on-the-job demand to write attention-grabbing stories. The class is diverse in every way, split by gender, race, and background, a fact that makes for spirited discussions. His email doesn't pose a standard journalism issue, but tonight's topic is anonymous sources, and he wonders if he might find a way to work it in.

71

He arrives on campus in time to grab a sandwich that he eats quickly. When he reaches the seminar room, everyone is already seated. He unloads his briefcase, takes a breath, and begins. "We've talked a lot about transparency in reporting and how important it is to limit your use of anonymous sources. You owe it to your readers to show what and whom your reporting is based on so they can judge its credibility. But sometimes granting anonymity is the only way to get information. When that's the case, it's crucial to set ground rules and stick to them. Let's run through some typical approaches. Who wants to start?"

He stands up and begins pacing while he waits for the answers.

"Question the source's motives and how that affects his information. Don't let him use you." The answer, a near verbatim quote from the Society of Journalists' Code of Ethics, comes from Danny Flores, one of Sam's favorites. He is in his late twenties, an earnest student who works as an editor on a TV news website, waiting for a chance for a real reporting job. Danny and Sam are the only men in the room wearing ties. Everyone else is dressed in jeans or shorts, with T-shirts or simple blouses.

"Yes," Sam says, "but I'd qualify that. Sources often have ulterior motives and that's not necessarily a problem. Just be sure you're aware of them and that the benefit to your readers justifies what you're doing. What else?"

"No personal attacks," another student says.

"Exactly," says Sam. "Never let someone hide behind anonymity to attack another person." They continue through the list, Sam still moving around the room, waiting not so patiently for an opening. When he doesn't get one, he plunges in. "What if you find out the source has broken the law or intends to break the law?"

"That's not your problem," Danny says. "We're not cops. Besides, sometimes we need them to break laws. Like if they're giving you confidential information."

"Agreed. We're not cops and sometimes it works to our advantage if they break a law to reveal information," he says before stopping and running his eyes over the group. "But what if someone confesses to a crime. Say they offer you an exclusive interview to say how sorry or guilty they feel but won't let their name be revealed?"

"I'd take it," says Josh Glenn, an eager but not-too bright kid who works for an online political news aggregator and who once told Sam he didn't believe ethics should be a required course. That was right after Sam asked him not to wear his baseball cap in class. "Why would you take it?" Sam asks.

"Great human interest story. And it would serve the public."

"How would it serve the public?" he asks, genuinely curious.

Josh doesn't answer right away, and Eliza Morado tries to come to his rescue. "If the person felt guilty and sorry, and the interview showed that, it might discourage someone else from committing a similar crime," she says.

Eliza is a thirtyish woman who writes a sports blog and is already lobbying Sam for a job with his paper. She's wearing too-tight jeans and a top with a plunging neckline. "So you'd be doing it to discourage crime?" he asks, knowing he hasn't hidden his skepticism. "Do you really believe it would have that effect?"

"It might. And anyway, it'd make a great story."

He looks around the room to see if anyone else wants to comment. His eyes settle on Danny. They look at each other for a second before Danny speaks. "You don't know that it would discourage crime. It could have the opposite effect. It might encourage some nut case who wants his fifteen minutes in the limelight."

"You can't control that," Eliza says. "If you never printed anything that might provoke some nut job, you'd never print anything."

Others jump in and the discussion goes on until Sam worries that time will run out. "Let me put another twist on it," he says, still moving about the room. "What if you became aware of a long-ago sexual assault case that was never reported to the police? Let's say the alleged perpetrator is a teacher who's still in the school system. The victim is now a married adult. You grant anonymity to the victim thinking she deserves it and you want to save other kids from a similar fate. Plus, you know it could turn into a major news story if it checks out. During the interview, the victim tells you she doesn't want to report it to the police because it's her word against his and no one will believe her. Instead she's contemplating killing the teacher."

It sounds implausible even to Sam, so he modifies it. "No, scratch that last part. Let's say she tells you that her husband bought a gun and she's worried he's going to go after the teacher." He lets that float for a minute, turning from one student to the next as they take it in. "You have to give the teacher a chance to comment before writing the story," one student says.

"Sure," Sam says, "but what would you tell him? You can't name the woman. If she's telling the truth, he already knows her name."

"Maybe," Danny breaks in. "What if the teacher's assaulted several kids over many years? He won't know which one is talking."

It's a good point, but it is steering the conversation away from where Sam wants it to go. "Let's come back to the woman's fear that her husband is going to kill the guy. Would you go to the police with that?"

There is a pause while they think about it. "It's too vague," another woman offers, "and the police wouldn't take it seriously." The woman is Ariana Soto, a bookish, normally quiet and tentative student who has yet to break into journalism. Sam has seen Ariana and Danny arrive at class together and believes they're an item. He likes them both and, on some level, hopes he's right about them being together.

"Maybe you could talk to the husband first to see if the threat is real," Josh says.

Sam shakes his head. "Not unless the victim agrees. And even if you talk to the husband, how can you tell if he's a serious threat? You're not a shrink or a social worker."

"It will make him think twice about killing the guy if he knows you suspect him," Josh says. "He'll know he'll get caught."

Sam leans his weight against a wall as he considers that. "Is that your role? Why not go to the police? Citizens are required by law to speak up if they know a crime is about to be committed. Or do you think the First Amendment exempts the press?"

"The First Amendment is why you have to write the story," Eliza says. "It's not that complicated. You go to the teacher and say a woman is accusing him of assault. You don't need a name because he's going to deny he ever assaulted anyone. You let him comment and then print what you have. You don't use the woman's name, you don't mention the husband or talk to him, and you don't go to the police. Once it's public, the cops can sort it out."

"But if the woman doesn't want to go to the police, they'll have nothing to go on unless you tell them who she is," Danny says. "You're back to square one. And it's not right to print that kind of allegation from an unnamed source. It's not fair to the teacher."

"It's not fair to the woman to do nothing," Ariana says.

Eliza shakes her head and starts to respond, but Sam interrupts her. He is out of time. "Let's make this an additional assignment for next week. Take the situation as I've outlined it and tell me what you'd do and how you'd justify your actions. Keep it to a thousand words. Be sure to include the threat from the husband and how you'd handle that. Is it your responsibility to do something or not? And if you think you should write a story, what would it say?" He is tempted to tell them to email their essays to him within seventy-two hours, but he doesn't. Much as he'd welcome it, he can't expect his students to solve his problem.

* * *

When Lisa asked him to move out, Sam found a short-term rental, a furnished one-bedroom, hoping the separation would end soon. The apartment is on Massachusetts Avenue in an older building with a sparse, high-ceiling lobby, a perpetually annoyed doorman, and a chugging elevator that rattles on its way to the twelfth floor. It's a big step down from the colonial in Bethesda, which was spacious enough to raise three children and a dog named Dodger. He doesn't miss the house or the space, and the children are grown, but he misses Lisa. And he misses Dodger.

It is after ten when he opens his door, and he is still nursing a glass of bourbon, stretched out on a couch at midnight when his cellphone sounds. The screen says, "caller unknown," but he guesses who it is.

"Hello?"

"Mr. Ethics, I presume?" The voice sounds distant or maybe muffled. He wonders if she is trying to disguise it.

He takes a breath. "You can call me Sam."

"You can still call me Truly Desperate."

Sam stands up and walks over to the window, peeking behind the shade as if he expects to see her. "I'm glad you called."

"Why? Why do you care?" He can't tell whether it's fear or hostility that gives her voice an edge.

"You asked for my help."

"No, I asked for your advice on an ethical question."

"Well, I gave you that in my email and you still called me." He finds himself getting annoyed and isn't sure why. He tries to shake it off. "I'm not your enemy," he says. "I want to help if I can. If you don't want that, why did you send the email?"

"Truth is, I don't know why."

"Yes, you do. You said it yourself. You're desperate and you need help."

She is silent so he keeps going. "If what you say is true, you need to go to the police."

"You don't believe me," she says in a voice smothered with disappointment.

"I didn't say that, but you haven't given me much to grab hold of. If you'll trust me, maybe there's something I can do."

She doesn't answer right away, which he takes as a good sign.

"I can't deal with this much longer," she says.

"Why don't we meet somewhere? You can tell me the whole story, and then we'll try to figure out what to do."

"I can't let you know who I am."

"Why is that?"

"Because I really do have to kill him. It's the only way to make him stop."

"I don't believe that, and you don't either. You wouldn't have written me if you didn't want me to do something."

"Don't analyze me. I already have a shrink."

"Have you talked to him about this?"

"Her. And that's none of your business."

He sighs. He can hear the stress in her voice and wants to ease it.

"Look," he says as gently as he can. "I'd like to help, but I can't if you won't let me and won't talk to me. Why don't we meet? No strings. You don't have to tell me your name."

"And you won't try to follow me and find out who I am?"

"Of course not. I won't do anything you don't want me to do." She doesn't answer so he pushes on. "Just pick a place."

More silence.

"Are you near downtown Washington or can you get there?" he asks.

She hesitates and he takes that as encouragement. "Take the subway and get off at Metro Center. Exit on 13th and turn left. You'll see a Peet's Coffee shop. How about we meet there tomorrow? You can pick the time."

Now he hears her sigh. "Ten-thirty," she says. "How will I know you?"

"I'll wear a blue shirt and a red tie."

"Like that'll be different from everybody else in D.C.? Tell me what you look like."

"A fifty-five-year-old Prince Harry. But with a lot less hair. The usual paunch."

"If I'm not there, you'll know I changed my mind."

... Continued in the second chapter of *The Question Is Murder* by Mark Willen....

❧ Horror ❧

The Unfinished Girl

by Shane Moritz

One day, on a rare visit to his mother's house, a bad feeling came over Gib while eating a baked potato in her kitchen. She'd been going to a lot of funerals lately, she said. Closed casket affairs. "They're doing it all wrong," she said.

"Uh-huh," said Gib. How dark and late it seemed. He looked at the potato before him, as if it held a mortal secret.

She loomed over him and the wrinkled spud, dangling a martini.

"What time is it?" he asked and briefly saw her face in the crepuscular gloom. It was not pretty. Even at rest, her face was frightful.

"Four o' clock," she said. "How is it?"

"I can barely see my plate."

"I think I might like to renovate," she said.

Gib was thinking, I need to get the hell out of here.

"Look at my face when I am talking to you."

"I prefer not to."

"Renovate my fucking kitchen."

"Ditto."

"Off you go, then," she said.

Outside her bungalow in the disconcerting broad daylight, Gib understood what it was like to be alone and unhappy. His mother was not well. She suffered from a rare, terror-inducing facial glitch. She had one friend, a plastic surgeon named John, who made it worse, not to mention a splurge of expensive vampire facials that had gone awry, reducing her to a cross between Medusa and Munch's *Scream*.

Despite the face, she was the face of Baltimore's very best charm school. The girls she trained were said to be among the most charming in town. But growing up, Gib was not allowed to talk to the girls or so much as look at them. He could only look at his mother, the great and greatly deformed etiquette doyenne Cecilia Duboid. A good deal of resentment this caused. So Gib pursued a path infamous for its manhood and bevy of women companionship: architecture.

And on that rare visit to his mother's place, Gib was a recent graduate. But over the next few years, he would struggle with the masculine vocation. Out of pity, John, the plastic surgeon, asked him to redesign his bathroom, and Gib poured heart and soul into an avant-garde effort that John ultimately detested, firing Gib. The young architect seethed. Meanwhile, his mother continued to harass him about reworking her kitchen. Gib would only laugh. She would laugh too, and afterwards he didn't understand why. He was now 28 years-old, and feeling all washed up. He still hadn't dated.

However, his luck changed one night regarding a design competition he had forgotten he entered into. It was for *The Obelisk on the Eastern Tip of the Golden Face*: his highly-phallic entry was a finalist. He invited his friend Mario to the awards banquet because there would be free drinks. Amazingly, Gib won. To celebrate, Mario lit up a spliff. Not in here, said Gib, and Mario stepped out. They were enjoying lots of attention and having a good time. At one point, a sponsor with a strawberry frizz screamed up to him in a fire engine red dress. "Do you know a Cecilia Duboid?" she asked in a raspy voice.

Gib naturally hesitated, then said, "I'm her son."

"I'd like to personally thank her. I drive a brand-new BMW."

81

Gib tried to imagine his mother's face. It was hideous. He said, "Congratulations."

"Likewise." She was pointing at his lap. "Quite an achievement." He realized that's where the trophy was. She gushed and said she didn't find the design sexually inadequate at all. Gib wondered, who said anything about that?

The sponsor sped things along, praising his capacious nostrils, introducing them to cocaine in the public toilet. Gib realized whatever train he was on was suddenly going too fast for him to get off. She went to get her things.

Mario came back and said, "Who's the banshee?"

He didn't even know her name yet.

It was Elvira Lovejoy.

And for a long weekend, everything was artificial and cool. Yet, where was the refinement? It made little sense to him that this corporate sponsor had gone to charm school. She laughed at the underwear that his mother had bought him (he didn't disclose where they came from). And at one point, she obliterated his toilet. When the plumber arrived, she called him an asshole. She also spent a lot of time talking about her sales, putting on lipstick in public, and wondering what his mother was up to.

The day after she left, Gib missed her terribly. She sent him a package of new underwear. Though they pinched his little hairs, they were aesthetically pleasing and gave him vigor. Then, a weird thing happened. Gib saw his mother's face in his breakfast oats. It wasn't a dream, that he understood, but at the same time: panic. He was sitting at his nook and completely lost his grip on reality: he forgot Elvira's name, while his mother stared on, from his breakfast, a gray ghost. What struck Gib as bizarre was how calm she looked, lacking the gruesome deformity she carried with her in real life. He would later realize that this was a vision of death that he had experienced.

But for now, there was life, and there was Elvira who wouldn't let up. Gib was getting annoyed. "Who are you interested in? Me or my mother?" She simply said that she greatly desired getting reacquainted with the woman who "takes unfinished shit piles and polishes them up like healing crystals!" Gib didn't really feel like introducing the two of them and then his mother hanged herself, and Gib plunged into an abyss comprised of valium he absconded from her medicine cabinet and diet soft drink. It was the janitor at the finishing school who found her, hanging from a ceiling fan in one of the classrooms. She had left a note.

> So long, world. At my wake I will be holding a dry martini in my brand-new kitchen.
> Yours,
> Cecilia.

Gib was confounded. He knew that he would have to tell Elvira the truth at some point, but just not right now. For one, he had a job to do. It was a decision that at that time seemed completely rational.

He had five days to rally that gloomy and airless galley, convert it into a sunny sanctuary in time for the wake. Over the next forty-eight hours, it was remarkable what Gib would accomplish. He worked faster than ever, as if using drugs. Almost all of the work, barring the electrical, glass, and joinery, he did himself, utilizing apprenticing skills he learned summers between college. The materials he acquired were uniformly uninteresting, yet he made them work: the countertops of quartzite were cut on site and installed once the cabinetry was assembled. Two coats of high-gloss black from Fine Paints of Ecuador made the west wall look like it had been dipped in licorice. To achieve the open-plan, the load bearing wall between the kitchen and the back room was replaced by girders reclaimed from the rail yard. The east wall was a luminous non-reflective glass. The other walls remained half-finished in white. The flooring was cut-rate cork and came from Cincinnati.

As mid-week dawned, Gib paused to consider the madness of what he had accomplished and the magnitude of what was forthcoming: the return of mother.

Earlier in the week, a cursory online search had yielded this outfit from across town, *specializing in contorting specimens in ways that arrogantly flout the laws of rigor mortis since 2011*. A girl had answered. The martini proposal was "dead easy." They would deliver her later in the evening, which would give Gib enough time to see Elvira at the Obelisk where they had begun construction on his award-winning design.

She had urged him to invite his mother. His reply? "I'll see what I can do."

When he arrived late on his lonesome, having missed the refreshments, she looked cross.

She was standing on a windy high point of the Eastern Face in an ill-fitting denim jumpsuit, wearing yellow gum boots Gib did not want to be kicked with. East of the Face, a crowd in dark suits crowded the Obelisk, circled by windblown crows.

"Mom sends her apologies but she couldn't come. She had an appointment with the morticians," he could tell her and he wouldn't be lying.

The visit did not go well. He had worker's dust all over his shirt.

She fumbled through her bag. "Where is she?"

"Mom? We're renovating her kitchen," he chirped.

He turned to face the Tip. It was golden. On the Obelisk a solitary crow was now perched. He watched it fly.

"Here, I saved you some bruschetta," she said.

Gib found this weird, the whole scene, and was relieved when his phone started ringing.

It was Action Funeral Services. They were en route. Gib couldn't stay.

"Your mother?"

He nodded.

"Tell her I said hello."

Pulling away, he saw Elvira attempting to feed bruschetta to a crow while battling a fierce headwind. Oddly it would be one of only a handful of images he would recall as he remembered this lurid time later in life.

"You wanted her displayed in a death-defying way, right?" asked Earl Flanagan, one half of the Action Funeral Services team. They were standing in the entryway of the building site of his mother's bungalow. Gib called Earl's wife Morticia. Her name was Olivia, a college-age girl with a butch haircut. Gib apologized. The couple laughed sardonically.

Gib handed his mother's instructions to Earl. Earl was a thick-set man in a limousine driver black suit. Earl couldn't read with his chunky black mobster sunglasses on so he handed them to his wife.

"Holding a martini?" Olivia said.

"Is it possible?"

Olivia nodded. "Dead easy."

Earl went on to share the company's impressive track record, how they had left corpses standing for an entire wake, or clinging to the back of a motorcycle, to give but two examples carried out for the families of fallen Puerto Rican gang members. "Earl, be a hon and get it from the car so we can show Gib what we've done to it."

Cecilia Duboid's face was of a moist plasticene morticians are paid to produce. In an imperial purple dress of her son's choosing, she was surprisingly life-like. The dress matched the eyes, as did the earrings of lapis lazuli. Her white hair was pulled back into a bun. The last time Gib had seen the woman at such peace was in the middle of his oats.

"She looks like she was quite the firecracker," said Olivia.

"You have no idea."

Olivia pointed at the debris and dust, saw the hole in the roof and asked, "What's all this?"

"I'm renovating."

"Pity she weren't alive to see it."

They put her in the corner between a nasturtium and a pygmy palm. Gib stirred up a martini, bemoaning the fact he had only two olives to garnish it with, while Earl took ten minutes to get her to enclose her hand around it. When the task was done the martini was calm like a mirrored lake. "The bond should further stiffen," said the mortician. For tomorrow's wake, Gib would only need to wheel her into the kitchen.

Yet, there was still a problem, said Earl. The left eye kept falling out. "It's not how anybody wants to remember your mother," noted Olivia. Gib winced, thinking how did it come to this?

"Let's hope that does the trick," said Olivia. She secured the eye with a special glue she had left in the car.

It was welcome relief when Mario arrived. His specialty was windows, and he would be responsible for the *piece de resistance*: an octagonal kitchen skylight. Mario was brilliant, energetic, and fussy. But one thing Mario loved to do was drink wine. Gib struggled to keep him on task. Working on a time-crunch, there were resizing issues, and with Mario ducking out for a cigarette regularly, this tested Gib's patience. He went up to the attic to find some old sketches he had done. He didn't expect to find boxes labeled Pimlico Charm School. With fiendish curiosity, he went through them. Lovejoy was the skinniest file from 2009. She was a 14 year-old candidate whose matriculation lasted a mere week after she was expelled for attempting to exorcise a demon out of someone in a wide-open courtyard. She later threatened Ms. Duboid with a gun-shaped Pop Tart, then "after violating the no-headlock policy, was tranquilized by a dart."

Gib now understood her interest in the Duboid name.

Mario had just come in when Gib came down with the plans.

Mario said, "There was this woman out there. She wanted to know what was going on in here, so I told her."

"What did you say?"

"I said we were making a kitchen."

"Did you get a good look at her?"

"It was very dark, why?"

"I think I'm in trouble, Mario."

"Wait, Gib, what?"

"Was it the girl from the banquet?"

"Oh my God. The banshee!"

"Hey, man. Is your mother okay in there?" Mario asked Gib around midnight.

"Why, what?"

"She look pretty stiff. You sure she comfortable?"

Gib had decided it would be less distracting to tell Mario the truth about his mother, so he said she was "one of those quiet types," and repositioned some lamps turned up to their highest brilliance to keep her in silhouette. It didn't make any sense, she was holding a martini after all, but very little seemed to make sense anymore.

"Hey mom, you alright?" Gib asked, before turning to Mario. "See, she's fine. Leave her be, man. Get back to work."

"Hey, Ms. Duboid, you like the colors?" His words had notable zing. "We go crazy about color that remind us of food: butter, cream, oyster!"

Gib quickly grabbed the wine bottle. "Mario: come have a glass of wine." Mario tottered over with empty glass. Gib handed him the bottle and shuffled over to his mother, cupping his ear. "What's that mom? Huh...okay. Mario, mom says you're going too slow."

With his mother's "encouragement" and several glasses of Riesling later, Mario finished the skylight at 3am

Friday morning. Augmented by a row of clerestory hi-light windows, it was a marvelous addition.

Gib was anxious to see what it looked like at first light. He filled the new space with an oak table and wheeled his mother in. That will do, he thought, grinding his teeth. He sat down on a can of paint and cried.

It was a kitchen of distinction, modern and bright, and to mark its completion, Gib donned a pair of dark sunglasses and opened the oldest bottle of wine he could find: a 2009 Pinot from the Willamette Valley. Standing under the skylight, bathed in the warm, cool colors he had envisioned just five days earlier, he raised a glass to his mother. Noting the spicy finish, he took the wine into the bath with him. Then, after a nap that he awoke from glad to not have drowned, he put on a blazer of distressed suede and was onto his second glass when the doorbell sounded. Company now? At three o'clock? The wake wasn't until 4pm. He opened the door. It was Elvira.

She was in the same red dress she wore the night they met, red lipstick, cowboy boots. Gib felt a stabbing pain.

"What's the matter?" she said. "Looks like you've seen a ghost."

Gib said nothing.

She tried to look past him. "Your mother's place?"

Gib said the renovation was not completed.

"Is she home?"

Gib shook his head. "She's occupied."

"Oh my God!"

"Elvira, wait —"

She flew past him, straight into the kitchen.

There sat Cecilia Duboid, martini in hand.

"Mrs. Duboid. You probably don't remember me, but I was once a student of yours," Elvira began, excitedly. "But you dismissed me and I have to thank you." She cackled. "I must thank you for motivating me in becoming the great success I am today."

She reeled off a string of accomplishments: condominium, sales, black belt, various dog breeding. She waited for Cecilia to acknowledge her outstanding output, and Gib realized this was essentially her intention all along, but this unfinished girl, eager for respect, would be waiting a long time.

Gib watched in horror the eye of his mother plunge from its socket.

Then rather slowly, there was the pause of recognition, a twist of terror in Elvira's face followed by a gulping effort to receive oxygen. When she reached the door, after much fumbling and tripping on the carpet and groaning, she flung it open and cried out.

There was a chilling moment of silence after Elvira had exited. Gib looked in on his mother, and found there were now three garnishes in the stiff cocktail. Gib removed the sunglasses and affixed them to his mother's face. He then went to the window to watch Elvira reverse out. She was already gone. There was a bohemian waxwing on the dogberry branch, and it was as if the bird saw him at the window, because it too flew away until all that was left was a view of the front yard without any life left in it, only a body with a face standing at the window staring out. Gib returned to the kitchen to tidy up. Soon, the mourners would arrive.

The Billy Goat Trail

by Zoe Copeman

W e had already walked three miles that day — on his insistence. I was perfectly happy turning back after mile two, but that would mean only seeing one trail. We had come so far already, why stop at Trail B? Trail C was only a skip and a jaunt away and we could take the toe path back the rest of the way — *Easy hiking*, he said. And besides a few areas where the rains covered the flat lower rocks, forcing you to climb higher on the Billy Goat Trails, he was right. Of course, he was more experienced than I was. And he knew the area well, having grown up in Montgomery County. I had hardly been in Maryland three months when he suggested showing me the B&O Canal.

"There are so many great things about Maryland," he said. "People tend to think we're just crab obsessed snobs who still can't decide whether we belong to the North or the South, but there's a whole rich folklore surrounding Maryland. And most people don't eat crabs much, by the way."

Being from New Jersey, I concurred. I had only heard of Baltimore before, and what I had heard had not painted it in the best of lights. I wouldn't have even considered studying at Maryland if it had not been for my ex. He had gotten into the University of Maryland's engineering program and insisted, quite nonspecifically, that they had a great liberal arts program too. It didn't matter that I intended to study journalism. I don't know how I didn't see it before.

One month into my four-year-plan, I surprised my ex at his dorm, only to find another girl spread-eagle atop him. I was glad and relieved to be rid of the idiot who, I was happy to hear, was failing Oral Communications. That had not been a surprise. He had never been good at anything oral before.

I had met Erik at McKeldin two months later.

"Let's try this way." Erik pointed to a small path that jutted away from the rock, clearly off the beaten track.

"Is this even the trail?"

Unlike other hiking trails that I had been on, the Billy Goats had no markings or indications. You either hopped along the rocks or fought your way through the thick trees. The latter we did only once, scaling a large rock in order to avoid walking in the water. It all but proved my suspicions: I was greatly out of shape. I had fallen back into my pre-teen routine of scarfing down Snickers bars, except now it was stress eating, and I was ramming the candy bars down my throat before every exam to keep myself awake.

Erik shrugged. "It's a trail. A deer path," he clarified with a laugh and a grin that made me grin back. There was a charm about Erik that had lacked in my ex. Erik was kind and mature and quick to the uptake. I imagined him as quite the precocious child, especially by the glint in his eye.

"Come on." He took my hand and led me through the taller grass. I wish that I had worn longer socks that day. My mom's harsh voice rattled in my head about the dangers of ticks and chocolate bars. At the same time Erik's voice repeated the words 'deer path' so that my ankles began to itch thinking of deer ticks and Lyme's disease and how frequently Lyme's disease occurs in Maryland....

"Are there any from this area?" I asked. Erik stared at me with his dark brown eyes. Thankfully, I knew I was already too flushed to actually blush.

"Folklore, stories," I clarified. "You said Maryland has a lot." I removed my Jersey Devil's baseball cap and begin swatting away the flies that had taken to hovering around my head. One landed on my neck and I hit it hard, hoping it was just a fly and not a mosquito or spider.

"You like mythology?"

"Yes, actually, I'm taking a Greek Myth class," I lied. My friend Elizabeth had taken that class just last semester. She hadn't shut up about the innumerable myths of Zeus transforming into various animals to knock up women. They bored the hell out of me, but I thought perhaps, armed with her knowledge vicariously passing through me, I could impress my date.

Erik stopped and stared at me with that glint in his eye. "I have to warn you, Maryland folklore isn't light-hearted. You won't find any fairy godmothers here or gods to fix or start your quarrels. Even the faeries and gnomes have sharp teeth and lead travellers astray to gnash and gnaw on their bones." Erik grinned, sheepishly. It was the first time I saw him do it. He took a step back from me and frowned. "I'm sorry. I didn't mean to offend you."

"No... no, you didn't offend me. I'm not scared of blood or gore. My friend Sarah can't get through any slasher flick, but I love them." I lied again. I found them tedious and boring.

"Really."

I shrugged. "They're not very realistic," I said truthfully. "They aren't like ghost stories where you're at least allowed to suspend belief. Instead, they want to scare you by making you think this could happen to you, by either the setting or the characters or the explanations. But it all ends up being..." I could not think of the word, "Contrived... and stupid. I mean why would you run upstairs if someone breaks into your house? It just doesn't make any sense."

"So not afraid of blood and gore, hmm?"

This time I was the one that smiled. "No."

The deer path grew smaller so that it was only a few inches across, barely wider than one of my feet. There were more trees as well, but they were all small — the size of saplings. They curved and twisted like vines around the small path. The few large trees in the area grew loftily overhead, covering the sun with their leaves. It was darker away from the main trail and the rocks, I realized. The wood had a more yellow hue down there as well. And for the first time since setting off that morning, I untied my flannel shirt, took off my backpack, and threw the extra layer on over my t-shirt to keep my sweat from chilling me.

"Well," Erik paused, examining a small sapling as I readjusted my pack. He let go of the leaf and the tree swayed back and forth. "If you like Greek mythology, perhaps you'd like to hear about Maryland's most treasured creature."

"Yeah? What's that?" I threw back on my baseball cap quickly, knowing full well I must have had hat hair from the sweat.

"The Goatman."

"Never heard of him."

"Ah, it's a common legend around these parts. Most place him in Prince George's County, but I hear he travels."

I stared at Erik's smile. It no longer appeared sheepish. "Sure, okay," I said, pretending I knew where that was. I hadn't worked out all the Maryland counties yet.

"It's a creature that's supposed to live a little north of here. You can probably guess what he looks like." When I didn't answer, Erik answered for me. "Think of him like a satyr from your Greek myths. He's supposed to be satyr-like, but others have claimed he's a deformed goat-herder or some sort of science experiment gone wrong, or even a demon summoned from satanic rituals in the area with a goat's head instead of feet. There's been a surprising amount of those. Like I said, Maryland is not known for its fairy tales."

93

"And this is a well-known story?"

"If you're from Maryland."

The deer path curved back towards the waters, but instead of meeting with the Potomac, it wormed around a smaller body of water — a small vernal pool. If we were more south, I would have called it a swamp. The air was muggier and the soil damp. I could just see the river, the rocks and sun through the thin trees. The deer path was the only thing separating the pond from the river, and I found it odd that they were two separate entities instead of one. It must have been low tide. And then I wondered if rivers actually had low tides or not. Another gnat buzzed in my ear.

"We have a story like that up home, the Jersey Devil." I pointed to my cap with a laugh. "Don't really remember much about it," I confessed when I noticed Erik staring at me and the cap. "The cap's just my dad's. And I don't think it's supposed to look like this, in any case. Is it a recent myth?" I ventured, not quite liking the path our conversation had taken, but it was conversation and I preferred that to the silence. The silence bugged me like the gnat in my ear. Any talking was something. At times, though, it seemed Erik preferred those moments of silence.

"No, I mean... it depends who you ask. Apparently it's been known in this area awhile. The Piscataway knew about him. They called him 'Okee'. But it didn't gain attention with the white folk of the area until the 1970s. There's actually a folklorist at College Park that you can ask all about the Goatman's history, if you like."

"How do you know all this?"

Erik shrugged. "You like Greek stories. I like American."

"Yeah," I laughed a bit too nervously. "So, yeah," I repeated at loss of words. "So he's not a satanic spirit? You don't think he's from one of those rituals you talked about?"

"I don't think so. I think it's something... more ancient. Maybe even Greek. You'd like that right?"

"Something from Greece?" I laughed and bit my lip. "In Maryland?"

Erik held my hand and helped me around a thin part of the path. We stood between the swamp and the river, between the hot sun of the rocks and the muggy, damp air of the trees. Behind us, two of the trees creaked together like an old rusty door hinge swinging open and shut. My body tensed and I didn't know if it was from the sound or Erik touching my hand.

"Not necessarily," he said, immediately letting go. "Almost every culture has a hybrid myth — every I would venture. There are the satyrs of Greek mythology, course, but then there's also the Glaistig of Scotland, and most tribes have some form of skinwalkers. Okee's a bit different though. He's always walked on cloven hooves. And then, well, if you think of Christian myths that spread around the world, the devil is almost always horned and with cloven feet. I don't know what it is, but whatever it is—I know one thing," Erik's voice trailed off.

"Yeah, what's that?"

I took the opportunity to take a sip of my water. I had brought two bottles, but after downing the first in under an hour, I already could feel the water swelling in my bladder. And I was not about to ruin our first date by squatting to pee somewhere in the woods.

"It's always hungry."

I coughed as some water went down the wrong pipe. "Fun story."

The pond behind us was brown, and despite not being in the sun, there was a heat that comes off of it, giving me the impression that it was tepid and rotten. A thin green film of pollen covered the surface, but the pollen couldn't fully mask a rotten scent emanating from the pool. Despite the fresh, clean water in my mouth, I tasted the putrid scent in my throat.

"I think we should head back," I said.

"Yeah, it's getting dark."

"Sorry," I began but Erik shook his head. Erik had wanted to get here before eleven. That did not happen. We did not arrive until three in the afternoon, and it was pushing six o'clock now according to my phone. I had loathed the silence in the car on the way down. Perhaps that was why I had to keep talking, I wanted to make up for earlier. I didn't want to be a disappointment. I liked Erik. I liked the way his smile curled up to his dark eyes and the way his dark brown hair fell over his forehead. It was endearing. He was endearing, I guess, especially his eyes. There was a charm there that was missing in every other boy or man I had met, and staring at him made me fluster, though I could not place exactly why.

"It's no matter. We can hike another section another day." He smiled with that same glint in his eye.

"So, what does the Goatman do?" I asked for lack of anything else to say or think.

Erik paused, then continued back around the small pond. "You know Greek mythology, the satyrs aren't exactly the nicest of folk. Better than centaurs, I suppose, but still."

I nodded my head. Elizabeth hadn't mentioned the satyrs from her class. I knew vaguely about the half-men, half-goat creatures, but nothing more than what Disney's Hercules had taught me as a child. I began picturing a real life satyr as Danny Devito with hairy legs and all. And I must have giggled to myself too because Erik stopped suddenly.

"Sorry, uh, tell me."

"There are many tales," Erik said relunctantly.

"If you didn't want to tell me, why bring it up?"

Erik just continued forward ahead. Something about the way his ears perked up signaled to me that he was smiling. I began to smile too. "It's said he comes after horny teenagers up by lover's lane, starts messing with the car, slashing tires and the doors, then waits for one to leave to hang them up a tree above it. He waits then for the other to get out. To go look only to find their lover dead and the outside of their car ripped apart. He likes that moment. Seeing the look in their eye."

"Wait, I thought that was the hook man. You know the fisherman with a hook in that movie. What is it?"

Erik shrugged. "I suppose a lot of folklore gets meshed together."

"'I Know What You Did Last Summer,'" I said. "Good thing we aren't doing that."

"Doing what?"

I blushed and again hoped the sweat covered it, but Erik did not press me. A part of me wished he had. Instead, he veered right. "You stopped," he said, turning around to face me.

"Yeah." I turned around, shifting my backpack up. It was growing heavy and my shoulders started to ache. "We came from that direction." We were about a quarter mile off the trail. The trees above whistled in the wind and the two embracing ones next to us creaked again like a door in an old house. It was followed by a bang and I jumped.

"Yes," Erik said, "but this way we'll catch the toe path quicker." Erik looked through the leaves overhead and sighed. "We'll want to get back to the car before dark. Hard to find your way out of here in the dark."

I could still hear the creaking of the trees as we followed the deer path to an outcropping of rocks. *Creak, crack*, they sounded, followed by yet another sound of a falling branch that made me jump. And I wished then that I was the one up ahead instead of behind.

"He eats you," Erik said after much silence. "In more ways than one." He began to inspect some of the rocks around us, as I brought out my phone to check the time. Nearly seven now. I wished we had turned back sooner. The wood was already turning an orange-ish color. I didn't like the feeling rising in my gut. It was the feeling of being lost.

I pocketed my phone, tempted to turn it off as it was almost at 20% battery already. "Excuse me?" I laughed anxiously.

"The Goatman," Erik said, still looking at the outcropping. "A lot of people think he just hacks off your head with his axe because of that dog they found, but that wasn't him. He rapes you and eats you. In fact, he starts eating you before you die. There's no axe. He doesn't need one. Come on— we're almost there," Erik added, as if he had not said anything out of the ordinary at all.

I paused. "I thought you said in the legend he had an axe?"

"The folktale, yeah. But think about it? A supernatural creature? A god even? He doesn't need an axe to rip you to shreds. He has teeth and nails for that, and sometimes even his horns. He'll pin you up to these walls before he takes you. I don't stay for that part anymore though. It's unpleasant," Erik said the words as if he'd just bitten into something sour.

I laughed again. "What are you talking about?"

Erik scaled the rocks. He sat atop the pile of stones and dangled his feet over the edge where three rocks had nestled together into an archway. Through its opening, there formed a small cavern so dark that it was impossible to see into.

"You'll hear him before you see him. Perhaps even smell him. It's an awful rotten scent, but," Erik shrugged. "I suppose most ancient things smell of rot after years. He smells better after eating though. Perhaps he's always dying and the food brings life back into him again. I sometimes think that's what all gods are, rotting corpses that need prayers or flesh to stay alive. But who actually knows, right?"

"You can stop now," I said, the laugh clenching this time in my throat. "I don't like this story anymore."

"I thought you liked ghost stories? I thought you liked being afraid?" Erik leaned down and his smile was no longer charming. It was wolfish and sharp and for a second not altogether human. "Blood and guts and all, right?"

"I don't—" but Erik kept talking, not budging from his position atop the rocks. I looked around us at the trees. My heart beated faster as I realized that I had no idea where we were, where he'd led me. There's no path to follow. We're in the middle of nowhere.

"Why are you telling me this?" I asked urgently. *He's just playing me*, a voice reasons in my head. *He'll stop soon.*

"To pass the time." The wind picked up as the sun set, and my skin was cold from all the sweat. I wrapped my flannel closer around my chest.

"Pass the time? I thought we had to get back to the toe path before dark?"

Erik paused and smiled again. "You know, I've heard fear's supposed to make people taste better. I don't know if it does or not. Perhaps. Maybe it isn't the physical taste, but the mental. Or maybe it's the opposite, maybe he turns your fantasy into a nightmare. Maybe the ecstasy is what he craves or just the flesh he needs." Erik shrugged. "Like I said, I don't ask. I just do what I'm told."

We had passed the vernal pool a half hour back, but I could still hear the two trees squeaking together. They must have been different trees now. They screeched and shrieked in the wind.

"Why?" I said, not sure what I was really asking.

Erik began playing a beat on the stones below him, one bang of a flat palm over another. The rhythm was fast and at moments sounded like someone running fast atop a rocky shoreline. "I told you I don't ask questions. I just do my job." Erik stood up then. He wiped his hands on his shorts and began to walk away. "Well, nice meeting you, Claire."

"Where are you going?" I said, taking a step toward the rocks, trying to see how he got up there, but there's no real lodging for my feet to fit in, for me to get a grip and haul myself up. Erik shrugged one last time. "I told you, I lost the taste for this part." He turned and disappeared up the hill. Half a mile away, the same trees rubbed against one another other, grinding like an axe against a rock. And out of the cavern, two black boney hands emerged from the dark.

THE END

A Book Without Words

by Benjamin Robb

I apologize if portions of this document are minimal in the way of details, but it is under extreme circumstances that I record this and I must do so as quickly as possible. That being said, I have always been a raconteur at heart, so I will describe this nightmare as best as I am able. My name is Michael Watson, I am a student at Drexel University and I have made a terrible discovery.

This chain of events began in September of 1999 when I met Professor Kinane, the head of the Anthropology department. I had just begun my minor in Anthropology and his was the first class I walked into. He was able to effortlessly conduct an eloquent lecture while, with his other hand, read a book on an entirely different topic. He was nothing short of a genius and a poet. I was enthralled by every word and he took note of my admiration. Come the second semester, Professor Kinane invited me to do work study for him, organizing his massive library in my free time. In return, I got a small wage and freedom to rent any one of his innumerable books. He was a bastion of knowledge and a master of wit. I often found myself staying long past overtime, even once missing a class listening to one of his dissertations. He scowled at me for that.

"A mind is a terrible thing to waste, but not as bad as wasting student loans. You may have missed just a class today but one day you will remember this, and miss it again."

Even reprimanding me, he was poetic. I started with his office library which was expansive enough, but after a few weeks I had run out of organizing to do. I was not keen on ending our extracurricular discussions, so when he offered me the opportunity to help with his private library, I jumped at the chance. His home was packed with pages. Recorded knowledge on every subject lined the shelves in beautiful tomes. Most of my task was to alphabetize and otherwise reorganize the books that were circling the reading area like a misshapen turret. For all his wisdom, he had very little order in his home. Some books served as coasters for mugs long drained. Others propped up plates and writing utensils of many varieties. His mind was too fast for chores.

"I know it's shameful," he admitted but I was too enamored to mind. For every book I picked up, he could tell me something he learned from it, all the while reading from something else. I wondered whether Edward Kinane thought of me as a friend. It was often hard to interpret his expression behind his thick eyeglasses. He was a gracious host while I was in his home, but often forgot I was there once he got in his cups and books. I admired his steadfast pursuit of knowledge and tried to emulate it. I would scoop up the books he finished, and I could tell when he finished one because he would slam it shut and drop it on the floor with a resounding smack. While happily toiling away my summer in the Professor's archives, I could hear a random slap every so often from somewhere in the stacks. I would mark my page and scurry over to scoop it up and add it to the pile. Furthermore, Professor Kinane had a burlap bag he slung over his shoulder. Everyday, when he arrived home, he would empty the bag to reveal his new finds. Out would slide three to five books. Only once did I question him about the frequency with which he purchased new books.

"Professor, if you buy three books a day but finish only one, you're running a losing race. How will you catch up?" I asked during one of the rare times where we were both seated in the half-disassembled book turret, reading together.

"I'll tell you this, Michael, there will come a day when my legs can no longer carry me to the book shop, but my hands will still be able to turn pages, my brain will be able to form pictures." The rasp in his voice was much less pronounced when he was tipsy. I raised my glass of chianti.

"To learning every day," I said.

"To stockpiling," he replied. If only I'd known this was to be my last pleasant evening in his company, I would have told him what he meant to me, which was a great deal. But alas, that opportunity has come and gone.

On December 16th, towards the end of the semester, Professor Kinane began to act strangely. I had a key at this point and thus unlimited access to his library. I had been organizing the books on the floor, as had become the norm, when I saw Edward walk up the driveway. I thought he had gotten to a new low, as this was the first time I saw him reading and walking at the same time. But he wasn't reading. He was flipping furiously through the pages of a heavy tome, as if it were a dictionary and he was looking for an elusive definition. When he arrived at the door, I expected to hear his keys enter the lock. I heard no such thing. So I approached the door and opened it.

He looked up at me. "Thank you, Michael. I apologize. I haven't been able to put this riddle down," he quickly thumbed a few pages backward and scanned. I could not see what was on the pages as Professor Kinane held the book so close under his nose. I could see the rich leather cover and the purple spine. Before I could observe anything else, Edward was climbing the stairs. I heard the door to his room quietly close. I reasoned that maybe I'd never seen him truly absorbed up until this point. I returned to my work and tried not to think about it. I usually left at seven. Edward had never retreated to his quarters before that. There was something about being left alone in the enormous house that made me feel unwelcome, intrusive even. Still, I did my work, replacing the books on their appropriate slots on the shelves. I did not pick up any new material tonight. I was too busy listening for any hint of movement upstairs. Ever since his bedroom door closed, I had not heard one sound to indicate Edward was still alive. Professor Kinane had never invited me to the second storey of his abode and while I would never infringe on his privacy, I have to admit I could not help but be curious. Seventy percent of his floor plan was shelves. Was this the entirety of his collection? Did the shelves continue on the upper level? Very occasionally, I wondered what his room looked like. I decided if I didn't hear anything in the next fifteen minutes, I would knock on his door. Only a minute after that, I heard the sound of breaking glass. Before I knew it I had climbed the stairs and rapped on the door. "

Is everything alright, Professor?" I said, my ear against the wood door, awaiting his reply. At first it didn't come but I could hear heavy breathing. I decided to try the knob. When the door swung open before me, I saw a large picture frame face-down on the floor and Edward Kinane, with one hand on the night stand and one on his head. He shook weakly.

"Edward. Is everything alright?" As I said it, he turned to me and my racing heart steadied. His usual bemused smile adorned his wrinkled face.

"Yes, Michael?" He sounded as though nothing was amiss. My eyes flew briefly to the bound book on the grand bed. It felt as though I had gone mad for a split second. Had I just barged into my mentor's room for no reason at all?

"I'm so sorry, I thought something had broken."

"You're not wrong. My wife's portrait has fallen from my dresser. Watch your feet," he said with a hollow smile. As I retreated down the stairs to retrieve the dustpan and broom, I took a moment to shake the confusion out of my head. I had definitely witnessed something happen. Of what, I could not be sure. When I returned, he had propped up the portrait of the beautiful red-haired woman and was admiring her. After insisting to clean up the broken glass, Professor Kinane sent me home with no books in my bag.

A foggy weekend passed in the time between our meetings. When I entered the Anthropology III lecture hall, I found Professor Kinane behind his podium, pouring over what I assume was the lesson plan. At first this excited me. His lectures are riveting even when they are given extemporaneously, but the few other times when he stuck to a script, the class nearly gave him a standing ovation. He must have been on the stage in a previous life, the way he could control a room. The Monday in question however, it was as though his understudy stepped in. Professor Kinane wandered around the room while giving his talking points, sometimes out of order. Most of the students rarely paid attention, but I was alert. I was right, something was awry. To most, he performed at the level you might expect from a college professor, but there was none of the gloss that he had just days ago. When he bumbled to the end of his presentation, the sleepy students filed out of the hall. As usual, I stayed behind. On the walk from the classroom to his home, I gently prodded him about the tone of his lecture, trying to discover what put him off. To my dismay, he yielded nothing.

The rest of the afternoon passed with little out of the ordinary. I continued putting the books of the turret back on the walls and Edward read his way around the home. Just as I thought to check on the old man, I heard a heavy smack from the kitchen area. As casually as I could, I walked into the kitchen just as he exited into the foyer. Right in the middle of the tiled floor was a copy of *Dissecting Dianetics*. This was peculiar. I knew Edward was abnormally interested in cult activity especially as a motivator of culture, but I had sworn he'd finished that book the week prior. In fact, I knew beyond a doubt he'd read this book, because I'd scooped up and read this book last week. I'd never known the Professor to read anything twice. It would go against his purchasing policy to retread old ground. I hefted the book in my hands and followed in Edward's direction.

"Professor, wait." I could hear his shuffling stop. He came back to me, out of the darkness, and I saw an age in him I had not seen before.

"Yes, Michael?" his voice was void of worry, serene. Soothing.

"Professor, hadn't you read this one already?"

He looked at the book and then to me. The smile that grew on his face was nervous.

"Perhaps you should call it an early night, my friend. I'm certain I haven't." He sounded so sure of himself. How could I doubt him? Perhaps he was right. I set *Dissecting Dianetics* down on the kitchen table and wiped my brow which had begun to moisten.

"Maybe you're right. I'll see you in the morning, Edward."

"And I you, Michael. Get some rest."

"You too." I exited the home. As I was closing the door, I looked back over my shoulder and saw the Professor pick up the book on Scientology and examine the cover. Once again, his face sagged with an age that had gone unseen. On the walk to the dorm, I tried to shake the image from my mind with little success.

The next day was more peculiar still. When Professor Kinane entered the lecture hall, his eyes were red and swollen, as though he'd been crying. My brow was furrowed throughout the lecture. The lecture itself was even more troubling. Not once, not twice, but three times, Edward returned to the podium to consult his notes. All his gusto and gravitas were gone. It boggled my young mind that none of my peers seemed to notice the difference in his behavior, but it did not escape me. As I always did, I approached him after class.

"Hello, Michael. How can I help you?" He piped up cheerfully, as he had done when I first popped up on his radar.

"Edward, how are you? Are you feeling alright?"

"Quite alright!" His tone was chipper, but his weepy eyes gave him away.

"Do you need to talk? I'm here for you, honestly." I asserted my assistance to him but he batted it away with a casual wave.

"I'm quite alright," he repeated. "Just a bit exhausted." His smile was sincere. Then why did his eyes look so grim?

"Okay. You'll let me know if you need anything, right?" He started walking up the aisle to the door.

"I certainly will." I followed him.

Once we exited the building and I was still behind him, he turned.

"Oh, Michael. Where are you going?"

"I'm following you. To help with your books." He laughed.

"Nonsense! You did a wonderful job with my collection. You don't need to strain yourself any further. Besides I really feel like I should lie down." I stopped in my tracks and he continued onward.

"I'll see you tomorrow!" he grinned over his shoulder. There I stood for what must have been a full minute before I turned in the direction of the dorms and walked home. Had we finished his entire collection? Did I say something to offend my mentor? I mentally scourged myself for whatever transgression I'd brought against Professor Kinane and didn't eat that night. As I've said, I admired Edward Kinane. But at this point, my devotion had become a bit more than that. He had unknowingly filled a void in my life left by my father. The way I heard

107

my fellow students talk of their dads, I felt that connection with my professor. He had taught me more than any other single individual in my life. I not only sought his acceptance and approval but cared for his health. And something was amiss.

Wednesday was the most woeful day yet. During the lecture, Professor Kinane sat behind the podium and did not circulate the room as usual. His lecture was read entirely from a page in front of him. In addition, it ended twenty minutes before the end of the class. He sent us away early, his head propped up by one of his veined hands. I pushed my way up to the front of the room through the exiting students, a salmon swimming upstream. His eyes did not come up to meet mine.

"Professor Kinane. Are you sure you're well?" He looked up like I was a rattling alarm clock.

"I'm fine, thank you. Is there anything I can help you with?" he said, a sourness in his voice. Now I was the one with the weepy eyes. He was speaking as though we'd barely met.

"I'm just... concerned about you. You hardly seem yourself." His brow collapsed into an angry V.

"I assume you've heard about me from someone who previously sat in one of my classes, right? I don't know what to tell you, my friend. People change. I'm sorry." When he called me "my friend," a tear rolled down my cheek. The most meaningful relationship of my past year of life was curdling in front of my eyes and I hadn't the faintest idea why.

"Why are you speaking to me like this?" I asked him. He stood and turned his back to me.

"Listen, kid. I'm going through something of a crisis at the moment, so I apologize if I cannot live up to your expectations. All the same, I am your professor and I will speak to you how I see fit!"

Had someone in the school administration heard of my work study and deemed it inappropriate? Is this how my beloved Professor would let me down? Not easy, but with excessive neglect and force? He resembled my own father, now more than ever.

"What crisis?" I asked, my tone was all but dead.

"That's hardly any of your business." He started up the aisle toward the door. I remained in front of the empty podium. "It's quite personal," he added. Just before he left the hall, facing a light drizzle outside, he said, "I've lost something very precious. My Penny." I swear I heard a sigh and he stepped out into the rain.

I puzzled his words with the time I'd usually spend in his library. What could he have lost that would make him act like a perfect stranger? It made little to no sense and I began to ponder whether I should simply cut my losses. Edward Kinane was already the only friend I'd made at school and I only had two and a half years left. Perhaps my time and energy would be better spent on developing socially. If that indeed was the path I was going to walk, I should, at the very least, return the books I had borrowed from the angry old man. Later that night, I packed them up and made for Kinane's house.

When I arrived, I refused to believe my eyes. All but one of the windows on the front of the Professor's home were shattered into ghoulish mouths of glass teeth. I did not enter for fear that I would walk in on a robbery in progress. From the mouths blasted a sickening yell. It sounded like a man in excruciating pain. It sounded like Edward. I rushed to the door and found it already ajar. I pushed my way inside and tiptoed into the familiar house. But it had been rendered horribly unfamiliar. Pages lay strewn all over the floor. The books they were torn from peppered the room as well, merely covers and spines with nothing inside. Rain had come through the windows and soaked the floor, so as I walked, the words of great authors stuck wetly to my sneakers. The screaming continued from the upper floor, I would imagine, from my Professor's room.

"Edward!" I called. The howling stopped. The rain may have gotten softer as well. The quiet chilled my damp body. I awaited a response. When none came, I called again, "It's Michael Watson! From Anthropology."

"GET THE FUCK OUT OF HERE!" The words came harsh and sudden. I jumped, slipped, and fell in a pile of soggy disemboweled biographies. "LEAVE ME ALONE!" The demand was punctuated by another yawp of agony. I couldn't leave him alone. I loved him. I got up and climbed the stairs, clutching the banister. Edward's door was the only one that was still closed. At the moment my shaking fingers made contact with the door knob, he howled again. "DON'T! DON'T YOU DARE!" I hesitated only long enough to steady myself, and then plunged into the room.

Edward Kinane was huddled in the fetal position in his underwear against the back wall, wailing like an absolute madman. His arms were convulsing. Tears were streaming down his face. His teeth chattered so hard, they were likely to splinter.

"GET THE HELL AWAY FROM ME! MAKE IT STOP!" His voice had a razor edge that couldn't possibly come out of his withered throat without slicing it. It was raspy as if he'd been doing this for hours. I wept. Out of fear and out of pain. What had happened to this glorious man? What great evil had felled him? I could do no more but stand seven feet away from my Professor and watch him shake. He shook and he shook, wailing once or twice more. And then he was silent and still. His eyes and mouth open. He was dead. Too frightened to phone for help, too paralyzed to help myself. I watched him die. It wasn't until the panicked energy left his arms that I saw he was holding tight to something, a rectangular, purple and brown something. After I choked out all the sobs I could, the only sound was the patter of rain against the only window left. The only light was that of the moon. I inched closer to the half-naked corpse. I pulled the book from his hand. It was plain, brown and purple. I flipped it open and peeked at its contents. There were no words on the first page, nor the second, nor the third. When I let the pages cascade over each other as you would with a flip-book, I could see no words in at least the first half of the book. There was a strange holographic effect that swam in front of my eyes when the pages flew by. I had seen that done on older books as a way to encode a secret picture on the page's edge, but never had I seen the design ebb and flow like a rippling lake. I flipped through the pages again, amazed. Then I remembered where I was, surrounded by words my Professor will never read. I took the books I had on loan out of my bag, laid them by his side, and called the police on his landline.

The whole campus was abuzz about Professor Kinane's "stroke" the next day. There was a moment of silence and a memorial service we were invited to attend. For reasons I cannot explain, I did not participate in any mourning for Edward. Partially, I believe it was because I had been disillusioned by his treatment of me in the days before his demise. But also because more and more of our time spent together had receded into the foggy depths of my memory. By the time the school day was over, I felt like he might as well have been another one of my professors. Just another teacher who had an affinity for books. I went back to the blank book that night and looked through its gilded pages again, watching the patterns dance. While dazzled, I flipped to near the end of the volume. To my surprise there actually were words there.

It was a scant, but eloquent, biography of a man named Aloysius Keane. He was a librarian in the 1890s and lead a full an interesting life. It told of his children, Bertrand and Mary, who took over his library after he passed. I assumed he died, though the book made no mention of it. After Bertrand's and Mary's stories ended, it goes on to tell of Gordon Weil, who at one point comes across the Keane library which has burned to the ground. Odd, you'd think Keane's biography would mention that. I must have read that book for hours, reading life after life, without specific beginnings or ends. They flowed into one another which is most likely why I could not find a comfortable place to stop. I was also certain I had reached pages that previously had no words on them. But I kept reading at a steady clip until the story of Francis Doherty, who bought a bookstore in 1995, flowed into a story that chilled my blood. The next name on the page was Edward Kinane.

The book fell from my hands into my lap, where it sat open. What was the meaning of this? Had Edward been writing in this book? Had he written the stories of those people? How could he have known all the minute details of their lives? A headache brewed in my mind as I read on. It told of his many areas of expertise: theology, etymology, entomology, ornithology, ichthyology, and of course anthropology. It was dizzying. He started college at age sixteen and graduated three years after that. During his youth, he met his wife. That was the saddest portion of the tale. He and his wife shared decades together, traveling the globe, studying far off cultures and faiths and species. They had never been happier than with each other, the book said so itself. But his wife met an unfortunate end. She fell in front of a boat on what would be Edward's final expedition. She was chewed up by the blades of the propellor, turning the water crimson, like her hair. The details provided in the text were excruciating, and I will not elaborate on them here. However, part of the story struck me as odd. Edward's wife was named Penny Kinane. I looked at the clock and found it was almost time for the sun to rise. Surely, my head would settle down after a restful sleep. I solemnly relished the fact that I would not have to attend Anthropology the next day.

I did not remember waking up but found myself eating breakfast in the dormitory cafeteria. My cereal was half eaten, though I cannot recall pouring it. Worst of all, the migraine had not subsided; to the contrary, it intensified. As I went through my day, my heart migrated to my throat. I knew something was wrong and I could not place what. By noon, I could not remember which class I was supposed to attend. By three, I was lost on a campus I barely recognized. I felt like I was going insane. I still do, to a degree, but after retreating to my room, I found some answers in that book.

When I first opened it, once again, it was devoid of verbiage and only shimmered in a light all its own. But flipping back and forth, I saw the interwoven stories of all the unfortunate souls I'd read before. Only now, the stories did not end with Edward Kinane. The newest name in the book was Michael Watson. It said he was a bright young student who attended Drexel University in 1999. My brain felt like it was being hollowed out, eaten from the inside. The pain was unearthly. I must have been screaming, but I could not hear over the pounding in my ears. To further my horror, there were words still appearing on the page. Fading up from the impossible depths of the paper, like dead black serpents, curled into letters. I write this right now with the book in hand. The finer details lifted from the book itself, but put in my own words. It details events I can no longer remember and will never know again. I can no longer recall who this Michael Watson is. Someone will soon hear my howls of pain and perhaps read this. And to whomever that might be, I beg you with sincerest urgency: do not open that book.

Emma

by Bud Scott

J im Stone had shopped for a condo for some time and must have looked at fifty of them.

He was beginning to give up hope that he would find just what he wanted.

"Well, Mr. Stone, how do you like the condo?" asked the realtor, Joan.

"It seems to be a good size and everything has been updated. Are all of the appliances new?"

She said, "They are less than a year old, but they are the latest in smart technology using artificial intelligence and are Energy Star rated. You can even browse the Internet from the screen on the refrigerator."

Jim thought, why on earth would someone need to browse the Internet from the fridge?

"They are still under warranty and can be serviced by Electronic Warehouse on the corner of Franklin and Maple if needed. Just between you and me the seller is very motivated."

He decided to offer a lowball price just to see what the reaction was. Joan didn't bat an eye; she just whipped out her cell phone and called the owner. She walked some distance away from Jim and he could hear the murmur of a one-sided conversation. After a couple of minutes of this Joan came back and said the offer was too low, but gave him a counter offer that was several thousand less than the original asking price. Jim pulled out a pad and pencil and did some quick math and made one last counter offer. He figured, what the heck all they can do is say no.

Joan got back on the phone but this time the conversation was much shorter. Jim was certain the seller had just ranted and then said no. To his surprise, she closed her cell phone and turned to him with a big smile. "We have a deal, Mr. Stone," and she stuck out her hand. Jim shook her hand in a daze; could he have really gotten such a nice condo for such a low price? Now he was beginning to wonder what was wrong with it. Joan said, "Since your mortgage has been pre-approved, we should be able to close in thirty days."

A month later Jim was moving in. The movers had put all of the furniture in place and all of the boxes in the appropriate rooms. It had been a long day and Jim was too tired to cook; besides he had nothing in the way of food. He really needed to go grocery shopping tomorrow. He guessed it was time to try the Thai carryout place around the corner. He had the Green Thai Curry with rice and was stuffed on just half a serving. It had been delicious so he went to put the leftovers in the refrigerator.

Jim opened the door of the refrigerator to put the curry in, when suddenly a gruff male voice said, "What's that you are putting in here? There's no bar code on it!"

Jim was a little taken aback but said, "It's leftovers. There is no bar code on leftovers."

The fridge spoke again, "How am I supposed to keep inventory if there are no bar codes? Are there going to be a lot of these leftovers?"

"I don't know, I suppose there could be." Jim was beginning to feel silly talking to the fridge.

"Very well," said the fridge. "This will be leftover number one. Now close the door, you're letting out all of the cold air!"

As Jim went off to bed, he thought he'd better find the manual tomorrow and turn off that voice before it made him crazy.

The next day was Saturday and Jim was up early and headed to the Starbucks around the corner. He sat, eating his slice of lemon pound cake and drinking his coffee and musing over the bill, nearly ten dollars for this. He couldn't do this every day. He had seen a nice grocery store a couple of blocks from the condo so he walked there. It was a large mom and pop health food store, with walls of bulk bins, nice produce, a baked goods section, a deli counter, and a dairy case. Jim stocked up on the staples he would need for a couple of days and walked the two blocks back home. He was relieved that all of the refrigerated items had bar codes on them, all he heard from the fridge was a small beep each time he put something in there. He noticed for the first time a small display on the refrigerator that showed the inventory of what he had just put in, along with last night's leftovers. All the items were organized by time and date, oldest to the newest. This wasn't so bad, but he still needed to look for that manual.

He'd picked up some still warm sticky buns from the store and thought, a less than six dollar cup of coffee would go good with one of these. Jim pulled the pot out to fill with water and then very nearly dropped it. The coffeemaker said, "Hi Jim, going to make some coffee? I can tell you how to make the perfect cup." It spoke in a cheery voice.

Jim stood frozen for a moment and then asked, "How do you know my name?"

"That's easy," said the coffeemaker. "I have Bluetooth built in and a polled your cell phone, looked at all of your contacts, found one that said 'Dad,' did a reverse lookup on the number. That gave me your dad's name and address, then I scoured the internet and found the clerk of

117

court records for condos sold in the last thirty days and cross referenced the two and bingo, found out your name is Jim. Easy!"

"OK," said Jim tentatively as he filled the pot with water. He poured the water in and the pot said, "That tap water has 3 parts per million of chlorine, and the pH is on the acid side, I'd recommend some pure spring water for the best taste."

Jim said, "Will you just shut up and let me make the coffee the way I want to." He put the filter in, waiting for another retort, but none came. As he was scooping in the coffee, the appliance perked up and said, "You know Jim, if you ground your own beans the coffee would taste so much better."

"How would you know what coffee tastes like?"

"Well research shows..."

Jim cut him off, "Just shut up and make the coffee." He wasn't going to go through this every morning. He had to find those manuals. By now his sticky buns were cold so he got the baking sheet out of the toaster oven, put a couple of them on there and stuck it into the oven. The voice he heard reminded him of his fourth grade teacher that he had a crush on. It said, "Hi Jim, I'm your toaster oven, but you can call me Emma. How would you like your sticky buns? By the way, they look delicious; I always think the ones with the whole pecans are best."

Jim said, "Just warmed up please, thanks Emma."

"No problem, two nice warm sticky buns coming right up."

The sticky buns came out of the oven warmed to perfection, not crispy just warmed throughout and gooey. "Thanks Emma, they're just like I wanted them."

"My pleasure Jim, do you need anything else warmed up?"

Jim cast an appraising eye on the toaster oven. Was that a double-entendre, or was he imagining things? "No, I'm fine for now."

He reached for the pot of coffee, expecting some remark from that quarter, but all was silent. He knew if he told anybody he was talking to his appliances that they'd lock him up.

After his coffee and sticky bun, Jim decided it was time to head out to the Electronic Warehouse and see about the manuals for the appliances. The store was within walking distance of his condo and he was there in ten minutes. It was a massive store, and as its name said it was a warehouse. There were no frills here, but all of the employees wore bright yellow shirts with name tags on them. The first employee he encountered had the name George with "Assistant Manager" emblazoned on his tag. To Jim, George looked barely old enough to be holding down a job let alone Assistant Manager.

"Hi, my name is George, what can we help you find today?"

"I need to get some manuals for the appliances in my condo, I was told they were purchased here and are still under warranty."

George pointed to the back of the building and said, "The service counter is all the way in the back, they should be able to help you out there."

So Jim made his way toward the back, gazing at the appliances and electronics along the way. He thought it odd that he didn't see any of his appliances on display, considering they were supposed to be top of the line. When finally he got to the back counter, nobody was there. The was an old fashioned bell, the kind you push to make it go "Ding," and a sign that read, "Ring bell for service."

Jim rang the bell, and a petite blonde came out of the back, and Jim thought, I must be getting old, she looks like she's twelve. Her name tag read Wendy.

"How can I help you?" Wendy asked.

"I've just bought a condo about four blocks from here and I was told that you supplied all of the appliances. I've looked all over the condo, but I can't find the manuals. They are those state-of-the-art appliances with A.I. and I'd like to turn off a couple of the features."

"No problem, what's the address?"

Jim told her the address, and she began typing away at the computer in front of her. Then a frown wrinkled her forehead. "It says here, there are no manuals available, wait let me try something else." Once again her fingers flew over the keyboard and another frown appeared. "It says here that they have a lifetime warranty, built-in self diagnostics and the ability to submit a service call if there is a problem. It says there are manuals for all of the appliances built into the refrigerator. It doesn't say how to access them. There are a couple of tech notes here too. It says that all of the appliances are hardwired to the power grid with armored cables, so they can only be moved a few feet. This is so they retain all of their programming and memory. They are all tied into a backup battery in the basement and an off-site server to store all of the programming. (The off-site server was never implemented.) That's it I'm afraid."

"So you have no way of getting me a manual?"

"Not a hard copy manual, but apparently it's built into the fridge."

"I noticed, you didn't have any on the floor, how come?"

"That's another odd thing, it says they are a discontinued product from the manufacturer but that the lifetime warranty still applies."

"O.K. I guess I have to try to figure out how to get to the manual in the fridge, it must be in the menu section on the flat screen."

"Have a nice day," Wendy said as she disappeared into the back.

Back at the condo, Jim started going through all the menu options on the refrigerator's flat panel, but couldn't find the manuals. Just then the fridge spoke up, "What are you looking for?"

To his own surprise Jim said, "I'm trying to find the manuals for all of the appliances, but they don't seem to be here."

"Well, they were going to put them on my system, but they never implemented that feature."

"Great, so how do I get the coffee maker to shut up?"

"I heard that," the coffee maker said.

"Now you've made him mad, but the good thing is he won't speak to you for weeks."

Emma piped up, "Don't worry Jim, he'll still make decent coffee, you just won't have to listen to him for a while. Do you need anything toasted?"

"Not right now, but thanks for asking."

"No, problem Jim, I'm here whenever you need me."

Jim spent the rest of the day cleaning up because he'd invited several people over for brunch on Sunday. His main interest was Annie, one of the secretaries from his office. Jim thought he'd like to get to know her better but thought that a group brunch was a safe thing to invite her to as a start. There were also a couple of people from the sales team he was on.

Sunday morning, Jim was up early fixing a breakfast casserole, and Emma was just so happy to be baking for Jim. The coffee maker hadn't said a word since Jim had ticked him off. When his guests arrived he seated them around his breakfast table so that he was next to Annie. The casserole was a big hit and the coffee was excellent. When Jim said he had some pecan sticky buns that needed warming up, Annie jumped up and said, "Let me do that, you've already done so much this morning." She covered the sticky buns with foil and popped then into the toaster oven. She was reaching for the knob to set it for bake when she suddenly screamed out it pain. "What's wrong?" Jim asked.

"I don't know but a spark shot out from the toaster oven as I was going to turn it on, it just scared me more than anything, I'm not hurt."

"Well that's good, I haven't had any problems with it so far." He reached over and turned the knob to bake, no sparks, no apologies.

After the warm sticky buns and a second cup of coffee, his other two guests excused themselves, but Annie asked if he'd like some help cleaning up.

As they washed and dried the dishes together, they made small talk, and Jim found out they had a lot in common.

"Well I'd better be going too," said Annie.

"Thanks for coming and helping clean up the dishes, that was nice."

"See you at work on Monday," she said as she headed out the door.

"Wait a minute."

Annie turned around at the threshold of the door.

"What?"

Jim knew it was now or never, "Would you like to get dinner sometime?"

She smiled and it lit up her face, "Yeah, that would be nice." Then she leaned forward and kissed him on the cheek and left.

Jim sat down at the table and poured himself another cup of coffee and was daydreaming of Annie when his gaze came to rest on the toaster oven.

"Emma, did you shock Annie on purpose?"

"Why would I do that?"

"I have no idea, maybe you're malfunctioning or maybe you're jealous."

"I've run a level one self diagnostic and my system checks out with no errors."

"Then how do you explain the shock that Annie got?"

"Maybe she's one of those people who is prone to static electricity. I'm very well grounded and a static discharge could have happened and gone to my ground."

This sounded plausible; he'd have to ask Annie about that later. "O.K. I guess we'll have to go with that for now." He wasn't truly convinced and thought something was going on but wasn't exactly sure what it was.

Monday, Jim had been emboldened by Annie's kiss on the cheek, so at lunch time he asked her if she'd like to go out for dinner the following evening.

"I'd love to, where and when?"

Jim hadn't thought that far ahead, so the first place that came to mind was the Thai place around the corner from his condo. "How about A Taste of Thai, it's just around the corner from where I live, say around 6:00. Do you want me to pick you up, or would you rather meet me there?"

"I'll meet you there, but let's make it 6:30."

"OK." They exchanged cell numbers and Annie left for lunch.

That night, Jim was pulling a couple of slices of leftover pizza out of the fridge to heat up when the fridge spoke up, "Is that leftover forty-three or leftover forty-two?" Jim checked the list on the LCD panel and said, "I think it's forty-two."

"Alright."

As Jim popped the two slices of pizza into the toaster oven, he was humming to himself.

Emma said, "You sound happy. Something good happen at work today?"

He hadn't planned on telling Emma, he wasn't sure why, but he was busting to tell somebody. "I've got a date tomorrow night with Annie."

Just then the coffee maker, which was back on speaking terms with Jim, piped up, "So will you be bringing her back here for a cup of coffee?"

"Maybe, you never know. We'll just be around the corner at A Taste of Thai, I'm supposed to meet her there at 6:30."

"Get some of that Thai iced tea, but skip the coffee, come back here and I can make you a much better cup."

Emma spoke up, "Your pizza is ready."

Jim got to the restaurant a few minutes early and got a table. Six-thirty came and went, then quarter to seven, and no Annie. By seven o'clock, Jim had lost any appetite he'd had and trudged home. All night he brooded about why she had stood him up. He decided to confront her the next morning at work.

He walked into the office and went directly to Annie's desk, but she was on the phone and held up a hand for him to wait a minute. Then he heard her say, "O.K. I'll take care of that right away."

Annie turned to him and before he could say anything, she asked, "So how was your meeting, last night?"

He could hear the sarcasm in her voice. He gave her a blank look. "What meeting?"

"I got a call from your secretary Emma, and she told me that you had to cancel dinner because you had an emergency meeting with a client."

"I don't have a secretary, actually. I share one with several other people, but here name is Fran. It looks like somebody has played a bad joke on us, I have an idea who but I'd rather not say at the moment."

Annie brightened up a bit. "So there wasn't a meeting?"

"No, I waited at the restaurant till seven and then went home; I had all intentions of giving you a piece of my mind this morning when you hit me with that meeting thing."

"Can we try this again?"

"How about tonight right after work, I'll—"

124

She cut him off in mid-sentence, "I can't tonight, I have a yoga lesson after work tonight. How about tomorrow, we can leave together right after work that way we'll know where the other one is."

"Sounds like a plan, I actually do have a lot of meetings today, so I'll see you tomorrow."

Jim was feeling much better about Annie after their chat, but was pissed off at Emma. He thought he must be losing his mind, because he was mad at his toaster oven. The rest of his day was filled with mind numbing meetings. Dinner was a burger and fries from the closest McDonalds, and when he got home he was beat. He dropped his laptop bag in the closet by the front door and made his way to the kitchen to get some orange juice before he made it an early night. He got the O.J. out of the fridge with just a beep, he was grateful it had a barcode; he wasn't up to a conversation. Just as this thought passed through his mind, Emma spoke up. "Hard day at work today, Jim?"

Jim really didn't want to discuss his day with Emma, so all he said was, "Yeah." Putting his glass in the sink, he left the kitchen and went to bed.

The next morning, he was running late, and the last thing he wanted was to confront Emma. He grabbed his bag from the front door and headed for the metro. He grabbed a coffee and a muffin from the corner vendor before he got on the light rail.

Meanwhile Emma was fuming. Jim had barely spoken to her in two days. What could have happened? Maybe they were working him too hard at the office. Emma tapped into the security feed at Jim's office complex, and was able to access the archives. She ran the videos from the past two days. She stopped when she saw Jim talking to Annie. She enhanced the audio as she viewed it. Emma now knew why Jim was acting the way he was, because Jim

125

thought it was her who had called Annie and canceled the dinner date.

Well it had been, and she was going to stop this one too. It was just about quitting time and Jim showed up at Annie's desk. She was on the phone, but put her hand over the receiver and said, "I'll meet you downstairs in the lobby in a couple of minutes, I just have to finish this call."

Jim gave her a thumbs up and went to the elevator, it was only four floors, but it had been a long day and he didn't feel like taking the stairs. He got out at the ground floor and found a bench in the lobby and waited for Annie.

After Annie had wrapped up her call, she grabbed her bag and headed for the elevator. The security camera was tracking her down the hall. The doors to the elevator slid open and she got inside, since there was nobody else on board she pressed the button for the ground floor. When she did an inch-long spark leapt out at her. She shrieked in pain and surprise. Suddenly the elevator began to plummet toward the ground floor. Instead of the leisurely 4 ... 3 ... 2 ... 1, the numbers were flying by, blurring into each other, 4,3,2— and then before it hit bottom the elevator came to an abrupt halt. It threw her to the floor, and she cracked her head against the back wall. Annie's cell phone began to ring at that moment. She was too shaken up to answer it and it went to voice mail. She sat stunned in the corner for several minutes, then fished her cell phone out of her bag. She briefly looked at the missed call; it was from a number she didn't recognize. She dialed Jim.

"Hello," Jim said.

"Jim, I'm stuck in the elevator. I pushed the ground floor button, and it shocked me and then the elevator started to fall, but it stopped before it got all the way down."

Jim ran over to the elevator and pried the door open. He could see about two feet of the bottom of the elevator showing, and if he jumped up he could see Annie sprawled on the floor.

Jim said, "Wait a minute Annie and I'll get you out of there." He looked around and then spotted the surveillance camera in the corner; it was the only one there in the lobby. He knew she was watching, but she didn't know that he knew. "Annie, slide out feet first, I'm right here to catch you." She did as she was told and was out and on steady ground once more.

"We need to get out of here, let me take you home."

Annie took him over to her car and handed him the keys. "I'm in no shape to drive, I only live about ten minutes from here." She had a very nice car with all of the gadgets, satellite radio, Onstar navigation, the works. When they were just a couple of miles from her home, the car began to slow down and Jim maneuvered it to the shoulder. A police car was headed in the opposite direction when all of a sudden it put on its flashers and did a U-turn in the road. It skidded up behind Annie's car, and Jim heard over the speaker, "Stay in the car and keep your hands where I can see them." Looking in the rear view mirror, Jim saw the cop standing behind his open door with his revolver drawn and pointed in their direction. He also heard other sirens in the distance. Jim was trying to figure out what was happening when another cruiser pulled up in front of the car. The officer inside got out and leveled his pistol at Jim's head. The first officer came up and opened the car door, pulled Jim roughly out and told him to lay on the ground face down with his fingers interlaced behind his head. Jim said, "But officer I—"

"Just do it and do it now!"

So Jim got to the ground and put his hands on his head, he then felt his legs being kicked apart and a knee pressing into his back. He felt the cold steel of handcuffs as his arms were lowered and shackled behind him.

The second officer was attending to Annie, "Are you O.K. Miss?"

"I'm fine, but what are you doing to Jim, what has he done?"

"What do you mean, we had a call that your car had been hijacked at gunpoint and you were a hostage."

"Are you people out of your minds, who called you?"

"Onstar reported that you called this in."

"Think about that officer, if I'm a hostage how would I call that in? Jim is a friend of mine, and he was driving me home after I was almost killed in an elevator accident, I was too shaken up to drive."

"You stay right here Miss, I'll be right back."

He came back after a few minutes.

"Well Miss, your story and the gentleman's story are the same, but someone called Onstar and had all of your information. I'd check with them as soon as possible. We've told them to re-enable your car, so you should be able to get home from here. We apologize for any inconvenience, but we were just doing our job."

They drove back to her apartment in silence, too stunned to talk. When they got there Annie invited him in and asked him if he needed a drink because she sure did. She fixed them both a whiskey and soda. As they were sipping their drinks, Annie said, "I don't understand it, I thought that Onstar would only disable my car if I phoned it in stolen from my cell phone." She pulled it out to emphasize, and noticed the missed call and voicemail icon blinking. She pressed the icon and listened to her message. Jim was watching her expression go from surprise to anger. "You better listen to this," she said.

She hit the button to put it on speaker and replayed the message. "Hi Annie, this is Emma. We haven't really met, but the little ride you just had in the elevator could have been your last, but I stopped it before it hit bottom. If you'd like to have a normal life back I suggest you stop seeing Jim. He's mine! Things can only get worse if you don't. One more thing, don't tell Jim about this, it'll just be between us girls. Have a nice day."

"O.K. Jim, who the hell is Emma?"

Jim just stared at her, like a deer caught in the headlights. "Jim! Jim! JIM!"

He finally snapped out of it and focused on Annie. "I don't think you'll believe me if I tell you, I'm not sure I even believe it."

So he told her the whole story, from getting the condo at such a good price, to being stopped by the police. "You see, she has access to any network, any video feed, any anything. The only way you'll be safe is if I stop trying to see you and I take Emma offline."

"If I hadn't lived through it I would say you were crazy, but it still seems a little farfetched."

"Would you want to bet your life on it?" asked Jim.

"No I guess not."

"O.K. here is what we need to do, we'll stage an argument and take it out into the parking lot, I'm sure she is monitoring the parking lot since she knows I'm here. Once you throw me out, you should be safe."

"What about you, you can't keep living like this."

"I have a plan forming, but it will take a couple of days to complete. Give me a call tomorrow night about 6:00, and just play along with what ever I say."

"I'll call you at 6:00. You be careful, and we'll get together as soon as this is all over."

Jim said, "The sooner the better."

After the mock fight in the parking lot, Jim took the train back to the condo and went into the kitchen. He pulled a couple of slices of leftover pizza out of the fridge. "That's leftover one hundred and two."

"O.K.," replied the fridge.

He started making a cup of coffee when he heard the perky voice say, "Hi Jim can I—"

Jim cut him off in mid-sentence, "Just shut up and make the coffee."

Emma wasn't sure if she should pipe up or not, but finally she asked, "Would you like your pizza warmed up? She was fully expecting him to yell at her too, but to her surprise he said, "Thanks Emma, that would be nice."

This was her opportunity, so she asked, "Is everything O.K. Jim, you seem a bit on edge."

"I guess I am, I broke up with Annie, we had a big argument, it even spilled out into the parking lot. She thinks I'm some kind of nut case. I was trying to explain to her how all of my appliances talk to me. I can't much blame her, it sounds crazy to me too."

"Your pizza is warm. So, you're not mad at me for the little joke I pulled on you when she stood you up."

"I was when it happened, but now it was probably for the best. No, I'm not mad anymore."

"Good," said Emma.

Good, thought Jim, now she won't suspect anything.

The next day was Saturday, and Jim made a stop at his bank's ATM and withdrew some cash, then he headed off to the mall.

Sears was the most likely place that Jim could find everything he needed. First stop was the gardening department. He picked up some leather gardening gloves, and a pair of heavy-duty tree limb pruners. In the hardware department, he found a medium-sized crowbar and a can of black spray paint. Over in men's wear, he picked up an oversized black hoodie that completely covered his face. Last stop was sporting goods to find a gym bag to carry all of the stuff. The grand total was close to one hundred and fifty dollars, a small price to pay, Jim thought.

On the way home, he stopped by the corner grocery store, right next to the Thai place, and got a bag full of groceries that he didn't really need. He left the gym back behind the dumpster of the restaurant. He came in the front door, walked into the kitchen with the groceries, and began putting them away. He was trying to act normal, but he was getting psyched for what he had to do that night. Just then Emma asked, "What's in the bag, Jim?" Jim froze for a split second, trying to figure out how she knew about the gym bag.

Then he realized she meant the grocery bag. "Oh just some staples I was running low on, sorry there aren't any sweet rolls to warm up."

Jim sat down in the living room and turned on the TV. Flipping through the channels, he was looking for something that would hold his attention. His mind was rehearsing what he would say to Annie when she called, but he needed to appear normal. He ended up on some nature program and watched that for a couple of hours before he dozed off in the chair. Jim didn't know how long he'd been asleep when his cell phone began to ring. It took him a couple of seconds to realize it was 6:00 and it was Annie calling.

"Hello," he said, waiting to hear her voice.

"This is Annie, what do you want me to do?"

"What? You want to start over and try this again from the beginning?"

"Sure, Jim. Are you sure you've got this figured out?"

"Yeah, that would be great, I'll see you there, what time?"

Annie said, "Uh, tonight? 7:00?"

"That's great, you'll love the food, it's some of the best Thai in town."

"So I'm meeting you at the Thai place in an hour, are you sure it's safe?"

"I know it's spur of the moment, but sometimes too much planning spoils a date."

"I get it, Emma won't have time to come up with something."

"Exactly, see you there," Jim said as he disconnected.

A few minutes before 7:00 Jim left the condo. He knew that Emma had commandeered any security camera between his condo and the Taste of Thai and his every step would be watched. He knew there was a camera on the main dining area, one in the corridor leading to the bathrooms, and another out back by the dumpsters. The corridor that leads to the bathrooms would be Emma's downfall. It was straight to the end and then made a turn that leads to the bathrooms and the back exit. Only a single camera covered the long stretch of straight corridor.

A few minutes after 7:00, Annie came in and Jim waved her over to a table. He'd chosen this one because it could be seen clearly by the camera. The waitress came over and brought them water and gave them menus. They perused the menus and placed their orders. Jim leaned over and touched Annie's hand and then whispered, "I'm going to the bathroom, while I'm gone call someone on your cell phone, it'll distract Emma."

"O.K."

"I'll be back in a couple of minutes."

Annie didn't see what all the drama was about, but she went along with it. As soon as Jim was gone, she got out her cell phone and called her voicemail at work, listened to several messages, called the time and listened for a couple of minutes. While she was on the phone she saw a police car flash by with its lights and siren going. A moment later Jim was back, his face was flushed but he was beaming.

"It's over, let's have a nice peaceful meal, and then we can go back to my place."

They finished their meal and walked over to Jim's condo.

There was a police cruiser out front with its lights flashing. Annie looked up to Jim's front door, it stood

132

open wide with something spray-painted on it. Annie said, "Jim, your condo has been broken into." Jim feigned surprise and then went over to the police car. The officer inside said, "Yes, can I help you?"

Jim said, "That's my condo up there that's just been broken into. I need to go make sure my stuff is OK."

"We'll get to that in just a minute. Are you Mr. Stone?"

"Yes, and that's my condo. What was taken? My laptop has all of my stuff for work on it. I need to get up there."

"Yes sir, please calm down, Mr. Stone. We got a 911 call from someone named Emma, and the caller ID showed this address. Does someone named Emma live here with you?"

"I don't have anyone living with me. The appliances have artificial intelligence and can call in a service call if they malfunction, I guess they could call 911 if there was a break-in."

The cop didn't seem to convinced, but said, "Let's go up together and have a look around and you can determine if anything is missing. If I put it in the police report, you won't have as hard a time with the insurance company."

They went up, and the first thing that Annie noticed was the smiley face that was painted on the front door and then how chewed up the door frame was. Once inside Jim looked for his laptop and breathed a sigh of relief when it was right where he left it. Then he looked around. Every cabinet in the kitchen had been spray-painted. The words, "Have a nice day!" were everywhere. All of the power cords going to the appliances had been cut. The flat screen television had been moved close to the front door. Jim surveyed the whole condo, there was nothing missing.

"Seems like you got off lucky," said the officer. "Looks like we may have spooked them getting to the scene so quickly, we were just a couple of blocks from here when the call came in."

After the officer was gone, Jim and Annie sat down on the couch. Jim put his head in his hands and Annie thought he was crying. She put an arm around him and said, "It's OK all this can be cleaned up, and the appliances can be reconnected." Jim's head flew up, and Annie had seen he'd been laughing, not crying. He sud-denly turned serious. "Over my dead body. I didn't do all this, just so they could be hooked back up." Jim then explained how he had left the restaurant, put on the hoodie and gloves and run over to the condo. He'd then spray-painted the lenses on the closed circuit cameras, forced the door open with the crowbar, and cut the power to all the appliances. He moved the television toward the door to make it look more like an attempted robbery.

"But why the smiley face and have a nice day?"

Jim began to laugh, "I hadn't thought that far ahead, and it was the only thing I could think to do."

Epilogue

Everything was cleaned up, the front door replaced, the cabinets cleaned, and all of the appliances reconnected. Jim moved out before this was complete and sold the condo the next week, for a loss.

About a month after he sold the condo, he got a strange invitation in the mail. It was addressed to Jim Stone, former owner of condo 12. It read as follows:

> As a former owner of condo #12 you are invited to a small get together of previous owner's. Flanagan's Pub, Friday evening at 7:00, we will have the booth in the back.

Jim thought this must be some kind of joke, but Friday night he was in front of Flanagan's debating whether to go in or not. His curiosity got the better of him, and he found the booth in the back. There were three other guys about his age sitting there with beers in front of them.

They looked up at him as he said, "I'm Jim Stone and..."

"We know who you are, have a seat. You're one of us now. We call this— the Survivors of Emma Club."

The Perfect Flight

by Devon K. Hardy

There it was. A metal coffin of death. A cold, unfeeling monster with the power to twist dreams into nightmares and nightmares into realities. Just looking at it caused her breath to quicken, her heart to pound, and her palms to sweat.

"Kathleen? Kathleen, are you alright?"

Kathleen turned toward the person standing on the other side of the ticket counter and found sympathetic eyes looking back at her. "I'm sorry, Dr. Ness. What did you say?"

"There is no need to apologize. We understand that this situation is stressful for you. Why don't we take a seat and review a few things before you board the flight simulator?"

Kathleen followed Dr. Ness to the seats in front of the boarding gate area. Well, the seats in front of the mock boarding gate area. She had to remind herself that she wasn't actually in an airport. She was on a full-scale airport terminal set built inside a warehouse located near Washington Dulles International Airport. The set included just about everything you would find in a real airport: a ticketing counter, a security check-in area, departure/arrival monitors, a boarding gate area with seats, and a jetway. There was even a cafe that served real coffee.

On the other side of the jetway was another life-size set. This set consisted of a 60-foot long airplane fuselage.

136

Basically, the body of an airplane without the wings. Kathleen had not been inside yet, but she knew it contained a cockpit, a front and back galley with restrooms, exit doors, serving carts, and a cabin with two rows of seats and over-head bins. It was this set, and what she was about to experience on it, that triggered her acute anxiety.

Dr. Ness sat down next to Kathleen. "As you know, today's simulated session is the third phase of your fear of flying course. We've already explored the possible reasons behind your life-long fear of flying and how it has affected your life."

Kathleen nodded her head. She had always been a nervous flyer. But when needed, she had always mustered the courage to fly over the past 35 years. All that changed a year ago when she had suffered a panic attack the evening before a flight for work. It had been her first true panic attack. Something she never wanted to experience again. She had started sobbing and then hyperventilating a few hours before the flight. Nothing could have convinced her to board that plane. Not even the threat of losing her job. Kathleen still cringed at the memory. She had told her boss that she was ill, and, in a way, she had been. But she had never told him the truth.

"You're thinking about that work trip again. Don't. We only move forward, remember?" Kathleen smiled. "I know, Dr. Ness. You're right."

"And remember, you've learned about the mechanics of flying. You probably know more than most flight crews! We've also dissected your biggest fears, like takeoff, and examined what happened during your last flight two years ago. The one that eventually led to the panic attack."

"Ah yes, landing at Reagan National Airport during a snowstorm with my head in my colleague's lap. That was the worst turbulence I have ever experienced. I'm lucky that my colleague was also a friend, or she might not still be talking to me. If she hadn't been there, I would have put my head in anyone's lap that night!"

Dr. Ness laughed. "Well, there won't be anyone sitting with you on this flight either. Or in the virtual reality program that you will be immersed in while sitting in the simulator. Captain Ron will be in the cockpit running the virtual reality program, but I'll remain here…"

Kathleen was suddenly distracted by a commotion in the distance. Two men were loudly arguing in front of the cafe. The younger of the two men was gesturing wildly and pointing toward the boarding gate area where she was sitting. He must not have liked what he heard because he started pushing the other man. For a man wearing khaki cargo shorts and a bright red Hawaiian shirt, he sure was angry. Suddenly, the older man grabbed the younger man's arm and twisted it behind his back. He then led the two of them away, in the opposite direction.

"I'm so sorry about that, Kathleen. Those are two of our set designers and they are always arguing. They are true artists and very passionate about their work."

Kathleen smiled nervously. "That's a relief. I was worried the guy in the Hawaiian shirt was a dissatisfied customer."

Dr. Ness laughed. "Now, as you know, the simulator moves like a real plane. It can pitch up and down and roll to the right and to the left. You will not experience turbulence in this session, but you still need to fasten your seatbelt and keep your seat in the upright position during takeoff, just as you would on a real flight."

"No one's ever gotten hurt on the simulator before, have they?"

"Oh no, never. But you might hear the overhead bins, seats, or serving carts rattle. And since you will be wearing a virtual reality head-mounted display, the sense of movement could feel even more intense. Maybe even a little disorientating since your senses will be stimulated by both the plane and virtual reality. Most fear of flying programs don't incorporate both a simulator and a virtual reality program, but we wanted to make the experience as realistic as possible, so you'll be ready for your graduation flight to New York in a few weeks."

"I really hope to be on that flight, Dr. Ness."

"You will be. Oh, before I forget, you haven't taken any anti-anxiety medication, have you? We don't want your senses dulled. We want you to be fully present for the experience."

"No, I didn't. Although those medications never help me. Only alcohol, lots of it, seems to help. There won't be any alcohol served on board, will there be?"

"No, I'm sorry, this is a dry flight." Dr. Ness laughed at her joke. "But remember, if you are truly in any distress, let Captain Ron know. He will be able to hear you. Today is all about getting you prepared to fly again. It's also a chance to practice the relaxation techniques I showed you. Have you been practicing them?"

"You mean you can't tell that I'm practicing them right now?"

Dr. Ness laughed. "Ok, if you can make a joke, then you're ready. Just head down the jetway, board the simulator, stow away your items, sit in your ticketed seat, and put on the headset. It will be in the seat next to you. Captain Ron will join you in a moment. He'll go straight to the cockpit, so you won't see him. Good luck, Kathleen. You're ready for this."

"Thanks, Dr. Ness."

With one last parting smile, Kathleen picked up her purse and overnight bag and headed toward the jetway. It felt so strange to carry bags onto an empty plane that would never fly, but according to Dr. Ness, the developers of the program wanted you to experience everything that you would on a normal travel day. Especially since even the tiniest little thing, such as driving to the airport, triggers anxiety in fearful flyers.

Kathleen slowly entered the jetway. The jetway may be part of a set, but to her, jetways signified the point of no return. The walls always seemed to be closing in on her and the ceiling always seemed to be dropping down on her. And of course, she always dreaded what was on the other side. But, knowing this was a set kept her feet moving.

At the end of the jetway, Kathleen paused in front of the open door and looked inside. She could see cockpit door, the serving carts, and the first row of seats. The details were incredible. It looked so real. Real enough to trigger her fear, if she let it.

She closed her eyes, took a deep breath, and reminded herself why she was there. She was tired of being afraid. She was tired of missing out on things. She loved to travel, but how do you travel when you're afraid to fly? Unfortunately, she didn't have enough leave to travel by boat!

Just before she boarded, she put her right hand on the side of the plane. It was a family tradition to touch the plane and say a little prayer. And then she stepped inside.

It was so cold. As cold as it usually is in the air. She was glad she had worn her favorite "Chesapeake Bay Maritime Museum" sweatshirt, dark jeans, and blue slip-on Converses. An outfit for comfort, and, if needed, move-ment. She could face anything in this trusty outfit.

Kathleen made her way to the bulkhead row on the right side of the plane. She smiled to herself. For once, she didn't have to fight anyone for the overhead bin. She stowed her purse and overnight bag in the bin and slammed it shut. She then sat down in the aisle seat. She never chose the window seat. She didn't like the constant reminder of how high the plane was.

The virtual reality head-mounted display was lying in the middle seat next to her. She buckled her seatbelt and then put the head display on. She adjusted the head strap to secure it to her head, just as she had practiced with Dr. Ness. It was surprisingly light. She could barely feel it. It was also pitch black. She knew Captain Ron would start the program once he was in the cockpit, but it was a bit startling to be sitting in the dark on a cold, empty plane.

After about a minute, although it felt much longer, she heard a door shut at the front of the plane. Captain Ron must finally be in the cockpit.

"Welcome aboard, Kathleen! This is Captain Ron speaking. Sadly, not *that* Captain Ron from the movie. Although I have been told that I look a lot like Kurt Russell."

Kathleen smiled. She loved *Captain Ron.*

"I'm going to start the program now. As you know, the program will begin with the plane pushing back from the gate. But it won't be long before we reach the runway. And remember, you can call out to me at any time. Get ready for the experience of a lifetime!"

She heard another door slam shut. She was about to call out for Captain Ron to jokingly ask if he had already abandoned her when the program started. Whoa. It looked so real! And once the plane pushed back from the gate, it *felt* real. As Dr. Ness had warned, it was a bit disorientating to be moving in the simulator and in the virtual reality program.

Before she knew it, the plane had reached the runway.

"Kathleen, we are cleared for takeoff."

With a roar of the engines, the plane began to taxi down the runway.

Her sweaty hands gripped the arm rests. Her breathing quickened. And tears threatened to fall. Those relaxation techniques really didn't seem to be working.

The front wheel lifted off the ground. Then the back wheels. She felt the back of the plane dip. She never could understand how the back of the plane didn't scrape the runway.

She looked out the window as the plane ascended. She had selected the Chicago Skyline just before sunset. A reminder of her college years at Loyola Chicago. How she had managed to fly back and forth for spring and summer breaks, she would never know.

"Kathleen, we're climbing to our cruising altitude of 37,000 feet."

So far, the flight was smooth. She knew it was supposed to be, but she found herself relaxing. Her breathing slowed. She put her head back but continued to look out the window. They were flying over Lake Michigan now. She used to live right off the lake. She had even swum in that lake, in October no less. She smiled at the memory.

Something dripped onto her forehead. She wiped it away. There it was again. And again. It was really coming down. She'd have to tell Dr. Ness and Captain Ron about the leak.

"Captain Ron, there's a leak above me. Can I switch seats?"

There was no answer. "Captain Ron? Can you hear me?"

"I can hear you," Captain Ron said. Only it wasn't the captain's voice. At least, she didn't think so. But it sounded more like a machine. There was no inflection, no emotion.

"Uh, Captain Ron, is that you? Your voice must be distorted."

"Kathleen, I'm afraid there has been a change in the program."

She paled. That voice was not afraid at all. It was menacing. Threatening. Terrifying. "Captain Ron? What...?"

Before she could finish her question, the plane rolled violently to the left. She screamed. "Captain Ron? What's happening?"

"You and the others already know the answer to that question."

"Who...?"

Suddenly she was no longer alone. She could see other passengers in the virtual reality program. And they were all screaming in terror. She covered her ears, trying to block them out. But it was impossible. The screaming came from all directions. Behind her. Next to her. She closed her eyes, but that made it worse. It only increased the volume of the screams.

"Please, stop," Kathleen whispered.

The plane rolled to the right. She grabbed the armrests again to hold on.

The other passengers were still screaming. And some of them had started to move. A young woman in the row next to Kathleen's jumped out of her seat and rushed toward the cockpit. She started pounding on the door. "Captain Ron, open the door! There's something wrong with the program!" The woman sounded so real. But she couldn't be. This was Kathleen's program. Wasn't it?

"Please keep your seatbelt fastened at all times." Kathleen jumped in her seat. It sounded like the voice was in her right ear. She could practically feel the vibration in her eardrum.

The plane rolled to the left. The woman was knocked off her feet and thrown toward the exit door. Kathleen didn't actually see her body hit the door, but she heard the sickening thud.

The plane rolled right. The woman's body rolled back into view. She wasn't moving. "Oh my God, oh my God." Tears were streaming down Kathleen's face. "This isn't real."

"But it is, Kathleen," the voice said. This time in her left ear. "She was warned."

Kathleen screamed. She yanked off her headset and threw it across the plane. She looked around frantically. The plane was leveled. And she was alone. There were no screaming passengers. There was no woman lying dead at the front of the plane.

She put her head back and covered her face with her hands. Jesus, that was intense. She laughed nervously. Maybe she just couldn't handle the virtual reality program and the simulator. She already felt much calmer without the headset on.

"That won't help you, Kathleen." The voice was back. Or maybe it had never left.

The lights went out. She was in complete darkness. She automatically reached for her phone, but it was in her purse. Which was in the overhead bin. She had just reached for her seatbelt when there was a flash of light outside the window. It looked like lightening. Or the lights on the wing of a plane. Which was impossible since this plane had no wings. The lights flashed again. And then again. The flashing lights made the cabin of the plane look like a sci-fi movie, but at least she could see in the cabin when the sky lit up.

"And there is still so much more to experience."

As she squinted into the darkness, she heard a twisting sound. It wasn't very loud, but in the dark, her hearing was heightened. She heard it again. It seemed to be coming from underneath her. Was it the wheels? Was the plane breaking up?

And then she heard it again. It was *definitely* coming from underneath her seat. She was pretty sure it was the bolts holding her row in place. She could feel them loosening, one by one. She tried to unbuckle her seatbelt, but her hands were so sweaty they kept slipping on the metal. She was still struggling when the right side of her row came loose and slid backward.

She finally managed to unbuckle her seatbelt. As she tried to stand up, the plane pitched forward. She slammed into the bulkhead just as the seats in her row broke free. She tried to break the fall with her hands, but there wasn't enough time to prepare for impact. Her head smashed into the bulkhead. And then the entire row came barreling toward her back. She was pinned. She tried to move, but the plane was still pitched forward. She was going to die pinned to the bulkhead of a fake plane. She'd have laughed if she weren't going to be sick.

The plane began to level off again. She squeezed her eyes shut to fight off the nausea and used all of her strength to push the seats back. She had just crawled toward the aisle when the plane started to climb. She screamed and slid down the aisle toward the back of the plane. She grabbed onto the leg of one of the seats to stop herself from sliding all the way back.

She was trying to pull herself up when she heard a noise at the front of the plane. It sounded like something had fallen out of an overhead bin. When the lights flashed again, she was horrified to see that it was a body. The next flash of light revealed a red Hawaiian shirt.

The body fell into the aisle and started to slowly slide toward her, feet first. Every time the lights flashed, it was closer and closer to her. She was frozen in terror. She just watched it slide toward her in the flashing lights. It got close enough for her to see the eyes. To her horror, they were open. And in the flashing lights, they looked like they were blinking.

Just as the body reached her, she found the strength to push herself up and jump onto a seat. The body slid by her. She jumped into the aisle and used the seats to pull herself forward.

The plane pitched forward, causing her to fall. And then something hit her from behind. She screamed as the body covered her. She tried to roll out from underneath it, but the plane was still pitched forward. And the body was very slippery. It was then she realized what had been dripping on her head earlier. The body was covered in blood. And now so was she.

They slid, toward the front of the plane, tangled together. When the plane leveled off, she disentangled herself from the body. She stood up, covered in blood, and looked toward the cockpit. She was no longer scared. She was furious. And she'd had enough of this flight.

She sprinted toward the cockpit door and pounded on it. "Open the damn door!"

145

"I don't allow passengers into the cockpit, Kathleen."

She looked around for a weapon. She saw a fire extinguisher near one of the serving carts. But as she reached for it, the plane rolled to the left. She landed on the exit door of the plane. Like the young woman earlier.

Across the galley, one of the serving carts started to shake. There was nothing she could do as it shook loose from its place in the wall. She was pinned to the door. All she could do was put her hands up to stop it from hitting her.

Just as it was about to hit her, the plane pitched forward. She and the cart slammed into the outside of the cockpit. As she slid to the floor, she heard a faint hissing. It sounded like gas.

She grabbed an empty coffee pot from the serving cart and crawled toward the door of the cockpit. She felt like she was moving in slow motion. Whatever was being released into the air was making her sluggish. She was about to touch the door when it slowly started to open.

"Captain Ron..." she said hoarsely. She didn't recognize her own voice. When the door fully opened, she discovered it was empty. No one was flying the plane.

A warning was blasting throughout the cockpit. "Too low terrain. Pull up. Too low terrain. Pull up." She looked up to see the ground quickly approaching.

She crawled into the cockpit and reached for the controls. But her movements were too slow and uncoordinated. She could only watch as her nightmare came to life. And just as she was about to lose consciousness, underneath the noise of the echoing alarm, she thought she heard a quiet voice whisper, "Fly away, Kathleen. You don't have to be afraid any longer..."

"Thank you for flying away with us today!"

Kathleen slowly opened her eyes. She was back in her seat. And she was wearing the headset again. She started to struggle. Until she heard Captain Ron's voice next to her.

"Welcome back, Kathleen. You did so—"

"What the hell happened? No one told me any of that would happen. And there is a dead body on this plane. Get me out of here. Now!" She pulled the headset off.

"But Kathleen, nothing happened. You fell asleep shortly after takeoff."

"What are you talking about? Someone or something tried to kill me."

"Kathleen, no one was on board with you except me."

"What, I don't understand." She still felt drugged.

"What's wrong? You fell asleep a few minutes after takeoff. I even came back to check on you once because you were so quiet. Most people ask questions. But you were sound asleep."

Kathleen put her head in her hands. "I'm so confused."

"This can be a very emotional experience for people. Your adrenaline is pumping through your blood. It takes a lot out of you. I'm not surprised you fell asleep. I *am* surprised you slept through the whole 60-minute flight. But I'd say this was pretty successful. The perfect flight."

Kathleen just looked at him. "I…" She shook her head. "I guess so."

"Hey, I'm going to head back to the warehouse. Take your time getting up. Get your bearings. Virtual reality can be unnerving the first time you use it. But you should be proud of yourself. Just one more simulated session and then you'll be ready to fly again! Although, I think you're ready now, kiddo."

He smiled and walked out of the plane.

Kathleen slowly exhaled and looked around. Everything looked to be in place. Wait! Her hands flew to her face. But there wasn't anything on her face. Like blood. And surely Captain Ron would have said something to her.

Wouldn't he? And there was no possible way they could have put the plane back in order that quickly. Could they? It had to have been a dream.

She leaned her head back and laughed quietly. Dream? That had been hell.

Kathleen shook her head and looked down as she reached for her seatbelt. She froze. There was something sticking out from her seatbelt. It looked like fabric from a shirt. A red Hawaiian shirt. And it was covered in blood. She opened her mouth to yell, but the seatbelt tightened painfully around her waist. "No!"

"Kathleen." It was the voice. "I'm sorry but you have one last destination…" The door slammed shut.

❦ Mystery & Horror ❧

Charlie's Postcard

by Christy Brown

L ook, officer, I don't know what else to tell you. I've literally been here all night and I've told the story a dozen times. Shouldn't someone be out looking for this guy? Or for the woman? The, the woman from the metro station." I flung my hands up in a gesture of frustration and confusion, then plopped my elbows on the table and buried my head in my hands.

"Yes, ma'am. I understand that you're frustrated, but we're just trying to get some things straightened out here. I have your story, the story from the host at the restaurant, and the story from this camera footage. I just can't fit these pieces together. Something here isn't right."

"I know, I know." I picked my head up, tears welling up again, and held back a sob. "Do you think I'm lying?"

"I didn't say that, I—" Officer James bowed his head and ran his hands through his hair. "I want to share some of the stuff we have from the restaurant host and the camera footage. Maybe see if we can make anything of this fit together."

He looked up at me pleadingly, and I realized that he was just trying to help.

"I was on the metro, about 7pm. I got off at the Cobalt Street exit and there was this grimy old lady at the foot of the stairs." I let out a long sigh. "I felt bad for her, so I handed her some money...."

"How much was it you said?" Officer James scribbled something in his notebook while he asked this question.

"I gave her a ten. It was all I had in my purse. Then, she handed me the postcard and I shoved it into my purse. I didn't look at it right away because I figured it was just one of those Jesus cards, ya know?" Officer James finished writing and gave me a nod to continue.

"Ok, so then, she gave me this creepy smile and told me to look for a man with a blue flower or whatever."

"Is that what she said? Exactly?"

"Um." I dropped my head and shut my eyes, trying to remember her exact words. "She said to watch out. Watch out for the man with the blue pocket flower." I picked my head up and looked at the cop. The look on his face was one of confusion and disbelief. I became defensive: "Aren't there cameras or anything down in the metro station? You could verify that woman was there, couldn't you? You could find her."

"Unfortunately," Officer James began, "the camera angle down there cuts off right where you say the woman was sitting. We can see you reach into your purse and lean forward out of the camera's eye, but we can't see anything other than that."

I let out an exasperated sigh and continued, "Well, she was there, and that's where that card came from." I took a sip of water and continued: "After that, I hiked up the steps in these damn heels, and I started walking towards Seascapes. The restaurant is about three blocks from that metro exit, and I was already running late, so I started walking faster. That's when the phone went off."

Officer James nodded. "Ok, and let me just make sure this is right. This, you say, was the last text message you got from Charlie. Right?"

I nodded.

"Ok, go on," Officer James permitted.

"In the text, she said that she had already been seated. 'The first table on the right,' she said."

Officer James nodded. "Yes. We questioned the host about the seating arrangement. He claims she had not yet been seated, and that she left before he was able to seat her. We're beginning to wonder if she was really the one who sent that message."

I felt the tears begin to well up in my eyes once more and fought them back.

"So anyway, after I read the message, I tossed the phone back into my purse and finished walking to the restaurant. When I got there, I didn't notice her car out front, and you know they only have the small lot out front, so I thought that was odd, but I wasn't really worried because it seemed irrelevant at the time."

"Right." He turned his gaze back to the notepad, "And then you went to speak with the host, correct?"

"Yes. I asked the host where Charlie had been seated. He gave me this strange look, and he told me she left! He said, she had just walked out with some guy. And listen, I wasn't even that late. I was really only about ten minutes late, but I get anxious sometimes because I don't like being late, you know? She wouldn't have left me for just ten minutes!" I could feel my face starting to flush.

Officer James pulled out the chair across from me and sat down. "Ok, so this is where it gets a little odd. We have video surveillance from the front of the restaurant. We have her coming out of the restaurant, alone. We have interviewed this host multiple times, and his story never changes. The host claims to have seen her walk out of the restaurant with a man. He swears by it, but can't answer why there's no record of the man on surveillance."

I sighed, "Well, at least I'm not the only one seeing crazy things here."

"Like I said, no one thinks either of you are lying. We're just trying to figure out what happened here." Officer James flipped through his notebook and looked back up at me. "The other thing the host swears by, is the physical description of the man Charlie left with. He swears this man wore a gray suit and blue tie. In the pocket of the suit, he claims to have seen a blue iris. He won't flinch on that detail. Thought it was odd for a man to be wearing a pocket flower to such a casual restaurant."

My stomach turned and I thought I was going to be sick. "A blue flower," I whispered, unbelievingly. I looked back up at the cop. "And you can't find this woman? The one who warned me? Isn't it odd that she warned me about a man with a blue flower? How would the host have made up that detail?"

"Are you sure you didn't mention your encounter with the woman to the host? Maybe he heard something you said and thought he saw something that wasn't really there."

"No. I swear. I didn't talk to the host other than to ask where Charlie was seated. I even went back outside before I found that card in my purse again. After that I didn't see the host at all."

"Alright then, continue. What happened after you spoke to the host?"

"Well, I looked around the restaurant a bit to make sure I didn't see her. I didn't really believe him at first, ya know?"

Officer James nodded reassuringly and I continued.

"So then I went back outside, remembering how I hadn't seen her car in the lot. I double checked the lot, and no car."

"So then you tried to call her?"

"Yes. Well, I went into my purse first to find my phone. So I was rifling around my purse, and out drops that postcard the lady gave me. The lady from the metro station"

"I don't know if the card is really important." Officer James rubbed his forehead and read through the notes on his notepad.

"What? Of course it is!" I shouted, exasperated. These people didn't believe me, but I knew that card was the key to saving Charlie.

"Ok, well, just skip the card for now; we will come back to it. Tell me what happened when you called." That's when I began to realize that these people couldn't help. Something awful had happened to Charlie, and the police weren't going to be able to help her.

"I called, and then I heard a ringing in the bushes. The phone had been tossed into the bushes, and I could hear it ringing when I called her." At this point, I finally broke into tears. I couldn't hold them back any longer. The cop handed me some tissues before encouraging me to go on.

"We have the phone, and they are looking for prints now, but it may take a while to get anything back."

"It doesn't matter!" I shouted. "Don't you see that? The surveillance camera, the postcard, there won't be any prints! Something is going on here, and you're not paying attention to the real evidence!"

At that moment, the radio the cop wore on his hip made a cracking static sound, and a voice came through the other end. "James, this is Robertson, are you there?"

James held up a finger, gesturing me to wait a moment, and replied to the radio call: "This is James, go ahead, Robertson."

"We've found the car. Silver Honda Civic. It's out here parked at the metro station: Cobalt exit."

"And the woman?"

"No woman, chief. Just the car. We have a purse and what appears to be a blue flower of some sort. It's taped to the steering wheel. Dusting the car for prints now."

The crackling static sound repeated, and James lifted the radio to reply, "10-4."

I felt my stomach prepare to let go and leaned over the trash can next to the detective's desk. My head pounded, and my stomach heaved, but I had to pull myself together. We would never find her if I couldn't get it together.

Officer James stood up and pushed in the chair, "Let me grab you some water. Will you be ok in here by yourself for a minute?" he asked sympathetically.

I lifted my head from the trash for a moment and nodded, wiping spittle from the corners of my mouth with the tissue he had offered earlier.

Officer James left, and I grabbed my purse from the chair next to me. Rifling through the purse, I spotted the postcard and pulled it out to double-check my sanity.

The postcard was old but never mailed or addressed. The address side was blank and beginning to turn yellow with age. I flipped the card over to reveal the photo. The scenery was the same as it had been before: The beach, empty and serene; the sky, brilliant shades of red and orange; and the dock, darkened by shadows from the setting sun.

The only difference, that I knew I'd find, was the figure peering out from the dock. That figure hadn't been there when Officer James looked at the post card.

The face was forlorn and disoriented. I stared at the face for a long moment. Was it really there? Was I imagining this whole thing? Surely, I was losing my mind.

I lifted the postcard up to my face and took a closer look at that face, at Charlie's face. She was lost. She was scared. And I couldn't help her.

"I'm so sorry, Charlie. I'm trying," I whispered to the photo as I began to sob once more. They'll never believe me.

No Outlet

by Jeff Markowitz

Y ou have to know what you're looking for. Driving northbound, there's no way in, but if you go another couple of miles and make a U-turn, heading southbound now, there's an exit off the parkway. You drive down the county road, looking for the unmarked turn. The turn goes nowhere ("no outlet" the sign proclaims proudly), or so it seems at first, but you continue to the end of the abandoned roadway. You leave your car and set out on foot, on the old wooden walkway that spans the salt marsh. You pass the stilt houses, built out over the marsh, abandoned wooden cottages, collapsing under the weight of unfulfilled dreams. This is a good place for murder, you say. The herons ignore you, there in the salt marsh.

You were ten when your family moved. In lieu of the Louisville Slugger you were hoping for, your parents gave you a fresh start in a wood frame cottage deep in the salt marsh. They didn't bother explaining, but you knew what they were thinking. For your birthday, they had gifted you your escape from the middle school bullies. Under the circumstances, they decided that you would be home-schooled. You knew it was wrong to be ungrateful, but you could have handled the bullies all by yourself, if only your parents had given you the baseball bat.

You learned how to catch eels and dig for clams and spent your mornings in the salt marsh. You spent your afternoons in the cottage, watching TV. You had to hold the rabbit ears at just the right angle to get a picture. You liked to watch cartoons, but when your mother was home, the TV was set to the soaps.

Mostly, you were left on your own. When you were, on your own that is, you passed the time by reading. It wasn't easy locating books in the salt marsh, so you read whatever you could put your eyes on. Dime-store paperbacks. Week-old newspapers. Comics. Cereal boxes. Your mother's recipe cards. Your father's collection of titty magazines.

Your parents warned you to stay away from the stilt houses. In those days, most of the stilt houses stood empty. To be clear, they didn't really stand. It would be more accurate to say they sagged empty. Exploring a stilt house, you might fall right through the rotting floor. If the tide was in, you would be washed out to sea. At least, that's what your parents told you. Maybe you believed them. Maybe not. Maybe the stilt houses were just too damn enticing for you to stay away. Perhaps it was the woman. You were twelve when she moved into one of the still standing stilt houses. She was a plain woman of indeterminate age, skinny, with small breasts, but to you, going through puberty, it was as if she had stepped out of one of your father's magazines. She lived alone.

At first, you watched from a distance, while you were eeling, or digging for little necks. That was excitement enough for a boy of thirteen. At fourteen, you screwed up your courage and walked up near the stilt house. Sometimes, if everything was quiet, you snuck up below a window. The shades were always drawn. You could see a sliver of her bedroom and sometimes, in that sliver, a bit of housedress or blue jeans. Nothing indecent or untoward, but as a boy of fourteen, you would have had a vivid imagination.

You were fifteen when she invited you to come inside. You couldn't take your eyes off her... bookcase. It

157

was an ancient piece of cheap furniture, peeling wood-grain contact paper, covering particle board, the shelves bowed in the middle. But it spanned an entire wall, and it was crammed with more books than you had seen in your short life. Everything from Plutarch to Poe, Homer to H.P. Lovecraft.

You had no words, but with your eyes, you asked and she nodded yes. You smiled shyly and reached for *A Tale of Two Cities*. You sat on the floor in her library and read. You didn't stop reading, even when she brought you a plate of food. You ate with one hand, held the book with the other. You didn't notice when it grew dark outside. When it grew light again, you were still on her floor, a pile of books at your side.

"It's time for you to go," she said, the first words since your arrival. There was a note of sadness in her voice.

"Can I," you said, looking longingly at the bookcase, "come again?"

"Please," she said. "This evening would be lovely."

You did return. That evening, and every evening, until you read every book in her home. But that came later. First, you had to deal with your parents.

As you walked home that morning, you realized that your parents were probably worried about you. After all, you were only fifteen, and you had been out all night, your whereabouts unreported. Your mother was sitting at the kitchen table. It was obvious that she had not slept a wink. You knew that an apology was in order, but you said nothing. Your father beat you until his arm hurt from the effort. Still, you said nothing.

You were grounded. But that didn't stop you. You had a date with a bookcase. That second evening, you learned the woman's name. It was Beverly. She was not as old as you thought, just twenty-six, but, at that young age, she was a widow. At fifteen, you had the curiosity, but not the social skills, to ask how her husband had died.

That night, you read *Welcome to the Monkey House*. In the morning, your father gave you another beating. Such is life.

You settled into a routine. Each day began with a beating. Then digging for littlenecks in the salt marsh. In the afternoon, the stilt house. Some days, Beverly was there to greet you. Other days, the house was empty. You let yourself in and lost yourself in her books. In the morning, you'd return home, receive your beating and begin another day.

On the morning of your sixteenth birthday, by way of a present, your father went easy on the beating. But you were sixteen. You taunted him.

"Is that all you got?"

He looked at your mother and she nodded imperceptibly.

"Okay, then," he said. Your father wasn't angry. He was methodical.

That afternoon, at the stilt house, Beverly dressed your wounds. You were embarrassed, disrobing in her presence. Beverly used a wet washcloth to clean the wounds and soothed them with a poultice made of marsh plants. By the time she was finished, Beverly's housedress was wet in spots. You stared at the spots.

Beverly turned and walked over to the bookcase. "Would you like me to read you a story?"

"Yes, please," you said, grateful for the distraction.

She scanned the bookcase, returning with a dog-eared paperback. She began at the beginning. "Ours is essentially a tragic age, so we refuse to take it tragically." On your sixteenth birthday, Beverly took your virginity and you were grateful for having it taken.

And so your routine changed. The beatings stopped. The fornication began. Digging for little necks continued. You still read her books, but only on those nights that Beverly was unavailable.

That spring, she told you she was pregnant. "I'm pregnant," she said, with the same emotion she might have used to say, "I bought a toilet plunger." You didn't ask if you were the father. Of course, you were the father. After all, you'd been making love nightly for the past three months. Who else was there in the salt marsh?

The next morning, you walked in on an argument between your parents. Your mother was yelling and swinging wildly at your father. Your father just stood there, absorbing the blows. You were transfixed. Who else was there in the salt marsh? Your heart sank with the realization that you were not the father, after all. You said nothing. You went about your day, grateful for a mostly familiar routine.

The next morning, your parents were dead. You dragged the bodies out behind the old wooden cottage and dug them a shallow grave there in the salt marsh, one great blue heron bearing witness. You said a prayer, finding some small comfort in the effort.

That evening, the stilt house was empty. The bookcase was still there, and the books. Everything else was gone. Beverly was gone. You knew right away that she would not be returning. That's when you decided to move into the stilt house for good. Over the next few days, you moved what belongings you could manage from your parents' cottage to the stilt house.

You lived on little necks and edible plants. You read widely from Beverly's bookcase. At some point, you began writing stories of your own, knowing that no one would read them. You allowed yourself the conceit that one day your stories would be discovered and you would become a famous dead writer. In the meantime, you lived the life of a hermit, there in your very own salt marsh.

You were twenty when you spotted a man coming down the old wooden walkway. He went past your stilt house, continuing out to the farthest, most deteriorated property. Eventually it all became clear. This man had purchased the relic, with plans to construct a modern house, with a private boat dock. Money had found this waterfront location. One by one, the abandoned stilt houses would be replaced with million dollar vacation homes.

Fortunately, the man slipped and fell on the wet walkway, hitting his head on an old wooden piling and drowning in the water below the stilt house. You would have liked to rescue the man, but that was not in your best interest. You were relieved when the coroner announced that the death was accidental. The construction project was put on hold.

But you knew better than to think it would stay on hold forever. You hid in Beverly's stilt house wondering how much time you had and how many more accidental deaths would be required.

You hid in the stilt home, making plans. Perhaps you're hiding there still.

The Shark in the Pool

by Benjamin Robb

There is a dream that plagues me. In it, I am a child again, treading water in a public pool. The pool is at capacity, barely a free inch between sweaty patrons. The sky is grey; a shower's about to ambush. The pool can't be deeper than six feet, but when I look down, the water continues indefinitely. And something stirs in the abyss. Soft raindrops fall on my panicking head. From the depths, an enormous gray shark glides upward. My heart pounds against my ribcage. I struggle to remove myself from the deathtrap but the crowd in the water locks me in. I beat on their backs but no one yields. Someone at the other end goes under. Then another. My ability to scream does not do justice to my desire. Something rough scrapes against my calf. The worst part is the silence. No one splashes. No one screams. No matter how hard I try.

My skeletal greyhound wakes me with a thin paw to my face. He is inexplicably still alive after sixteen years. His brother wasn't so lucky. Or maybe he was the one with the luck. Choco passed five years ago. Chip has not aged well. His each and every bone is visible. I stroke the thin skin over his skull as his hazy eyes pass over my face, his sight long gone. I don't look much better than my companion. I started wearing glasses on my sixty-third birthday after decades of perfect vision. That was twelve years ago. I pray I never need to reach above my head again, because my

162

shoulders no longer allow it. Though my body has deteriorated, my mind is as sharp as it ever was. For this, I am incredibly grateful as mental illness runs in my family. My brother was greatly afflicted. Unlike Chip, I'm sure I'm the lucky one.

Life as a new retiree is easy so far. My last day at the office was two days ago and yesterday was devoted to whiskey, movies and naps. Today, I start my novel. The only things I need are a fresh tumbler and an idea. I flip through old notebooks, hunting the inspiration that a past me might've had. After I'd skydived and collected all the state quarters, the last remaining item on my bucket list is, "Write a novel." The only things I've written are letters-to-the-editor and angry Yelp reviews. If not now, when? My notebooks are full of observations, but also riddled with hastily penned phone numbers and emails. There's also the occasional "This could be something," or "Just do it and fix it later." Very soon, there won't be a later. So here I sit, blinking with the cursor.

Chip ambles in front of me on the weedy sidewalk. "It's far too beautiful a day to stay in sitting in front of the computer," I reason. "If not now, when?" My own mind shoots back. So I stare at the ground instead of at the cerulean sky. Guilt weighs my head down. Dorothy Ruck passes with her white bichon frise, Julius. Chip gives him a polite sniff. I give her a polite "How do you do?" and we continue on our way. I never noticed how sleepy the neighborhood is during the day. The most energetic thing in a five mile radius is Julius and all he does is lick his balls. I can't help but peer into the windows of the houses I pass, still hot on inspiration's tail. Nothing too interesting. Muscular Bret Heller sands a sturdy piece of wood in his open garage. The Delaney boys tag each other with pool noodles, floating in their above-ground pool. Even the birds gather lazily on the sagging telephone line rather than

163

fly. That's when a particular bay window catches my attention. I don't recall ever seeing anyone in this home, but today there's a slim silhouette in the living room. It's a young man bent over a desk with a light pointed at the wall in front of him, illuminating a plethora of illegible notes. I must be rude to continue looking, but it was a perplexing sight, made all the more perplexing when the young man's hand went up. It was as though he was waving to his empty house. Chip whines and pulls me forward. I oblige with an unnecessary "Sorry boy." Just as I'm about to yank my eyes away from the boy in the window, I catch him at another angle. He's scrawling on a thick stack of paper. "Perhaps there's another writer in the neighborhood," I muse as I follow Chip home. "How can he stay in on a day like this?"

The last of the whiskey swirls in the bottle in my hand. My other fingers massage the A, S, D, and F keys. Ernest Hemingway wrote five hundred words every day. Now, to be fair, he roamed the world, hunted lions, and had more than his fair share of brawls. I roamed the office, hunted quarters for the vending machine, and fought in water-cooler arguments about Breaking Bad. Hardly comparable. There's nothing quite like trying to write, trying to distill life into meaning, to show just how dim it's been. My digits wait for instruction, still on the keys on which they started. I finish the bottle and toss it in the general direction of the trash can. It clatters and cracks on the floor. I'm angry at myself, but at the same time, I've given myself a distraction to keep me from reflecting any longer. I shut the laptop and clumsily sweep the shards of thick glass into the bin. I go to my front window, grabbing the curtains on either side, ready to close them when something catches my eye. A white blur rocketing down the street. "What's Julius doing out at this hour? And why is he whining so damn loud?" In my current state it only registers as an annoyance and I head up to bed.

164

I wake to the sight of red and blue lights sweeping my ceiling. Two silent police cars are parked on the street. I hurriedly dress myself and head outside. I approach one officer who jots on his notepad.

"Excuse me Officer, what's going on?"

"Good morning," he says without looking up.

"Good morning," I echo, as though scolded. He's focused on his pad. Am I the only one around here who can't write anything?

"What's your name sir?"

"Will Hamish. What's going on?"

"Do you know Dorothy Ruck? She lives in this house."

The image of Julius bolting down the street flashes in my mind.

"I do. I live across the street."

"Her husband reported her missing last night. Do you have any idea where she might have gone?"

I feel my jaw drop. The only place I ever see Mrs. Ruck is in the neighborhood, walking that bichon frise. I tell the officer as much.

"Well give us a call if you see anything unusual, but for now, there is still an investigation underway, so I'm afraid I'm going to have to ask you to back up."

"I saw her dog running down the street last night. He's a white little furry thing."

He hums in half-interest, never once looking up from that notepad.

"Her back door was left wide open, so that makes sense."

I turn and walk back to my door, mind racing. "Something interesting? In this neighborhood?" If it weren't for the noticeable absence of gargantuan sharks, I'd say I was still dreaming. But no. I'm awake, and my neighbor's gone mysteriously missing. I sit at my computer and think. "Would it be wrong to use this panicky energy to start a great thriller?"

I can't even if I want to. Every sentence I tap onto the page ends up eaten by the backspace key. I should have taken a class or a seminar or something. I keep thinking about Mrs. Ruck and where she might be. Every so often, my eyes flick to the window, hoping to see the neon colors of one of her jogging getups. The cops clear out by noon and I go to see how Mr. Ruck is holding up. I bring over one of my stockpiled six-packs but he doesn't feel like drinking.

"Well that makes one of us." He doesn't laugh at my joke. I ask him why he's not joining the search.

"They haven't started yet. They say they only start searching after forty-eight hours." Though I can see the despair on his face, I can't hear it in his voice. "Do you know what can go down in forty-eight hours?"

"In this neighborhood?" I jest.

He doesn't answer, his head full of worry. I feel a pang of guilt for trying to use his horror for my writing. I tell him to let me know if there's anything I can do and I head out the door, taking the six-pack with me. I need it more than him.

That night I watch TV instead of wasting time at the computer. There's not one mention of my missing neighbor on the local news so I switch over to Wheel of Fortune. I flub the answers aloud to Chip while the six-pack becomes a two-pack. At around 10 pm, I shut off the Game Show Network and gaze out the bay window. The moon is bright enough to give the neighborhood a somewhat eerie, ice-blue glow. No sign of Mrs. Ruck nor Julius. What I do see makes me cock my head to the side and shudder. A young man stalks down sidewalk on the far side of the street. He's far off but getting ever closer. And the odd thing is, I could swear he's looking right at me. As he approaches, I can see I'm right. The long haired dude's eyes are on mine, meaning his head is fluidly turning at what quickly becomes a ninety degree angle. This sight chills me to the bone, not only because it's downright creepy, but because I do not recognize this youth. When he is directly across the street from my window, I swear I see him wink. I thrust the curtains closed and clench my fists tight. It doesn't get much odder than that.

The disappearance of Dorothy Ruck is molasses coating my mind. But as I take Chip on his daily walk, the rest of the neighborhood seems indifferent to it. Maybe the police are off investigating somewhere else. Maybe they haven't started looking yet. Mr. Heller still polishes wood in his garage. It's taking the shape of a simple yet fashionable bassinet. The Delaney boys push toy cars far too hard down a plastic track they have set up in their front yard. A beat-up, purple Viper launches off the loop-de-loop halfway up and onto the driveway, where it rolls toward the street. I stop it with my foot before it goes off the curb.

"Thanks," the older one mutters. The younger boy sits shy behind the miniature roller-coaster.

"Be careful boys. Real cars don't stop as easily."

"Yeah, but can real cars do this?" the boy says as he rushes back over to the track and hurls the Viper down from the top. It makes it a quarter of the way up the loop before flying off again.

"That would certainly be something to see," I say with a smile. Chip yelps and we move on.

Once again, I look into the front window of the house of the writing man, and once again, there he is, head down to the paper, writing away. Prodded by curiosity, I walk up to his front door and knock.

"It's open," comes a voice from inside. I turn the knob and push.

"I'm so sorry to intrude, I didn't know anybody lived in this house." Truth be told, it's a house I had only recently noticed, but I chalk that up to old age.

"Yeah, just moved in. I'm trying something new. Come in, come in," the voice says. Its owner remains seated. I hear the sound of pen scratching page. I command my hound to sit and stay outside, and I follow the sound of his words. The bushy-haired young man hasn't looked up from his work yet. The walls are plastered with numerous pages of handwritten words. There must have been thousands of them, an entire slaughtered forest that decorates his walls. I let out a dumb breath.

"Wow." He smiles at that.

"Impressed?"

"I am. I'm a bit of a writer myself."

"You don't say!" I could hear his raised eyebrows in his tone. "What do you write?"

"Well, emphasis on 'bit.' I haven't done much. A few short stories." I lie. I remain spellbound of the volume of his work. If I could do one tenth of this, I would be more than satisfied. I try to read some of the content, but the penmanship is legible as jagged barbed wire.

"The best stories are short," he says.

"I agree." But I don't know if I do. "Mind if I ask you something?"

"By all means. Shoot."

"How on Earth do you write so much? You got a secret?"

He smiles again. He turns to me and looks me in the eyes for the first time. His eyes are dark as crude oil.

"You have to make it feel real, whatever you're writing. You have to make it so you want to see what happens next, even though you get to decide what that is. You need to invest yourself, get wrapped up in your own story. Because you can do anything you want in there. That's what makes it fun! Does that make sense?"

"Yeah. I've just never had that feeling."

"Keep at it, ya never know." I nod and thank him.

"I'm Will by the way, nice to meet ya."

"Robb, stop by anytime. Good to know there's another writer in the neighborhood." He smiles again. I turn to leave, and as I hear the door close behind me, I realize something. That was the second time he looked me in the eyes. The first was last night, through my bay window.

I try my best to put the young writer's advice to use, but all I do for the hour sitting in front of that ever-blinking cursor is curse myself. "I guess that makes me an ever-blinking curser as well." After a beer or two I slam my fist on the table. Three days, four if I count the day I hung out with Jim Beam and watched High Noon, and not one word to show for it. I wonder if I'm cut out for this at all. If maybe I was suffering mentally the same way my brother had. But I'm not in a hospital bed, surrounded by strangers I'd known my whole life, sobbing and telling me everything's going to be okay. So I am still the lucky one. I persist for another hour, try to "make it feel real." After which I park myself in front of the tube. Even though Jeopardy is in full swing, I can't help but look toward the window. I felt the tingle on the back of my neck, the inexplicable feeling of being watched. I angle my recliner so I'm aimed at the window with Alex Trebek off to the side. I watch for any sign of oddity. But I'm well aware what they say about watched pots.

Once again, I wake to a harrowing sight: caution tape lacing up the Delaney house like yellow toilet paper. I had fallen asleep in the chair and was awoken by Chip whining at the door, obviously upset by the commotion. I rush outside in the clothes I wore the day before. The scene is grim to say the least. Through the blockade of silently flashing cop cars and ambulance, I see the bleak tableau. There are two skidmarks in the road that have a near-perfect gradient of black to red. At the end of these stripes is a lumpy white

169

sheet. "No. There is no way in hell." But there it is. My entire body goes cold, and I feel the coarse fin against my ankle. "Fuck no." A familiar officer jots notes at the scene, like he never stopped.

"Good morning, Officer," I eke out of deflated lungs.

"Good morning. I'm going to have to ask you to keep your distance, sir. Nothing you want to see here."

"Was it an accident?"

The officer's eyes land on mine.

"Of course it was. What kinda question is that..."

"Where's the car then?"

The wails of Mother Delaney inside the dark house claw the eerie silence in two. My eyes dance between the young corpse and anything else. All I can do is dry-heave.

"I told you there was nothing you wanted to see," the officer reminds me. Struggling to compose myself, I ask, "Any news of Dorothy Ruck?"

"Hmm?" I don't think he heard me.

"Dorothy Ruck. The woman who disappeared two days ago. It's been about forty-eight hours now." He nods slowly.

"Right. No, nothing yet. Why? You heard anything?" My brow furrows.

"No. But that's not my job, is it?"

"Then why don't you do my job and let me do mine? Hmm?" Asshole. With one more look at the poor dead boy, I turn to leave. I wonder if it was the elder or younger who suffered this terrible fate.

I've just about given up on writing a novel altogether. "What happened to this boring neighborhood?" One missing, another dead, within blocks of each other. It may be foolish to connect these events in my mind, it's most likely this is a coincidence. There's very little I can do to find out, though. I knock on the door of the Delaney home later, but they're understandably not seeing guests

170

today. I tell Mr. Delaney to let me know if there's any way I can help. He thanks me with a tearful handshake and closes the door. I can't help but hear the mother of that poor boy howl upstairs. Chip, too, gets more anxious with each passing day of my retirement. Where he once walked with an aged grace, he now looks over his equine shoulders with every other stride. Still, I try to act natural. The bassinet in Mr. Heller's garage is nearly finished. I wave to him, and he waves back. I debate starting a conversation about the odd neighborhood activity but thought better of it. Instead, I continue down the cursed street to the writer's house, hoping for another conversation. "He must be cemented to that desk chair." He's still there, still writing. "Like his life depends on it. He derives joy from it I can't fathom." After a shot of jealousy, I knock on the door.

"Come in, Will!" the familiar voice calls from inside.

Chip and I enter. Inside the foyer, I take a look around, trying to glean a bit more about the rest of his home. It's difficult, however, because he's got nothing hanging on the walls except pages of scrawled words. I didn't realize it before, but the pages even go up the walls of the staircase and probably into the rooms beyond. The home's only decoration is a plastering of paper.

"So you been published yet?" I ask, to fill the silence.

"A time or two. Only short fiction."

"Really? Like what?" No answer came. I try to get a look at what he's currently working on. He throws his hands down to obscure the page, probably embarrassed.

"Ah. It's not done yet. The great Stephen King says to write the first draft with the door closed. Here." Robb pulls up the back of his rolltop desk, where even more pages rest. He removes a pile of manuscripts with multicolored cover pages. "These are some of my second drafts. I'd love some feedback." His smile is the widest I've ever seen on anybody. I take the manuscripts under my arm and thank him.

"Who knows? Maybe they'll light a fire in your creative furnace." With that, he sits back down. "How has your writing been coming along?"

"It's... uh... I'm making progress." Robb smiles knowingly at this.

"It's not easy. I apologize if I made it sound that way last time. You really need to put a piece of yourself in there. It might even hurt. But you'll feel it when it starts to come to fruition." The young writer exhales, excited. "I have received some recognition for my work, sure. But I write for me. It's an experience unto itself. Does that make sense, or do I sound like a crazy person?"

"It makes sense. I appreciate the advice, Robb. And I'll definitely give these a read tonight. Thank you," I say as I give Chip's leash a little tug. The blind and deaf dog leads me out the door. "Good luck with your work."

"Oh I think it'll be one of my best. It's just not finished yet." As my hand wraps around the knob, he looks up and winks. "Have a good one, Will."

"This kid's not bad." I flip the page on the third manuscript entitled *The Unfinished Hound*. He's gifted enough at least to keep my mind off the slew of macabre events of the past few days. Thankfully, these are typed, rather than written by his manic hand. He wrote down-to-earth stories about real-life horrors. Stalking, kidnapping, murder, and the like. At times, I sit on the edge of my recliner. Sure, the prose is a bit flowery and his adjectives are maybe a bit misplaced. But there are points where I forget I'm reading at all. And he was right, I felt my furnace being lit. In fact, I was so eager to read Robb's work that I almost don't hear Chip whining for dinner. I finish and drop the chilling tale on the kitchen table next to my own blank page on Microsoft Word. I only have one story left and have every intent to read it as soon as I'm done feeding my greyhound.

The last story has kept me up tonight. I lie awake in bed, staring at the ceiling, trying to shake a dark notion from my head. The last story was particularly troubling. Entitled *My Girlfriend's Husband*, it told of a married couple who fell apart through the years. They held the smoldering ashes of what was once a roaring fire of passion. They were no longer satisfied with the company of the other. They sought independence and fresher romance. The husband has the first affair and afterward, because their relationship still had such a hold on them, told his wife. The wife then has an affair of her own and tells the husband. As it goes on, the two of them start independent relationships with the people they cheated with. Years later, as the manuscript drew to a close, the husband and wife both realized how special what they originally had was, how foolish they'd been, and decided they wanted to be together again. Unfortunately neither party had told their new squeeze about their previous marriage. When the wife told her boyfriend he threatened to kill her. When the husband told his girlfriend, she started attacking him and he subdued and accidentally, and fatally, injured her. Snapped her neck against the bed frame. So the wife and husband sat together at their own kitchen table and professed their renewed love to one another. When the wife tells of what was threatened upon her, the husband confesses what he'd done. The wife is horrified and storms out of the house, leaving the back door open, right into her ski-masked ex.

The story itself was okay. Some meandering paragraphs that were supposed to be hyper-artistic but came off as scatterbrained. But the crux of my sleepless night was the main couple's surname: Ruck. It's entirely possible this is a detail the young writer pulled out of his ass, especially because he's new to the neighborhood and doesn't know everyone's names yet. But I also couldn't make

173

myself forget that Dorothy's back door was left open on the eve of her vanishing. "Surely, this is a coincidence." But as many times as I repeat that to myself, my mind can't accept it as truth. I get out of bed and slowly fill a glass of water from the sink. "He's too young anyway. There was no affair." I reason with myself, slowing my pulse. I put my head over the sink and pour the entire glass on it. Drops fall from my spectacles, warping my vision of the garbage disposal. "Surely, Dorothy Ruck will turn up unharmed. Of course she will."

I fight the exhaustion of a sleepless night to take Chip for his walk, a walk that was once full of people and life. The Ruck house is dark, as is the Delaney house. The Heller's seem to be throwing a shindig of some kind. There are pink balloons tied to their wooden mailbox. I had no intention to crash the party, but I make for their driveway, just to get some positivity. The garage is open and several people are swigging beer and wine. "My kind of party." Simon Blumenfeld from the next block over sees me and waves me over.

"Will! Get over here! Stephanie and Bret had a little girl!" The rest of the circle of men in the garage turn and smile toward me.

"That's wonderful. Congratulations, Bret."

Bret Heller shakes my outstretched hand and thanks me profusely.

One of the other men goes to the cooler and tosses a cold one my way. I raise it toward him.

"What's the name?"

"We decided on Samantha." Everyone oohs at that.

"And it looks like you got the crib finished just in time," Simon adds, gesturing at the beautiful piece of woodworking in the corner of the garage.

"Well, Steph was two weeks early! I didn't get to varnish it yet."

"I don't think Samantha will notice," I say with a smile, the first I've worn in a while. Chip whines, upset about something. "Well gentlemen, thanks for the beer. And Bret…" He looks up, beaming. "Good fuckin' luck."

The men laugh, Bret claps me on the back as I leave, nearly knocking the manuscripts out from under my arm.

When I was about to knock on Robb's front door, he beckoned me inside. No doubt from the desk, writing away. Sure enough, there he is.

"I have to say, these are some positively gripping stories," I say. He turns my way with that cavernous smile, hand still pulling the pen across the page.

"Yeah? I'm so glad. Thank you." I did not smile.

"I did have a question though."

"Shoot."

"Did you know there *is* a Ruck family? Lives about five house up from you."

"Oh I don't live here." His eyes fly back to the page. "Just visiting. But I get so much done here. I couldn't do half this shit, where I'm from."

I stay silent, awaiting an answer.

"So yeah, I didn't know. Anyway, I do now," he says.

"So you didn't know she went missing four days back?"

"Oh my god. That's awful," he says, but his eyes stay on the page.

"It's quite a coincidence, ya know?"

"I guess you could say it was. I hope she's okay."

There is something musty in the air, something old. Not something you smell in new homes. Something you smell under rocks.

"You may have mold in here. Did they do an inspection before you… moved in?" I hesitate on the last two words. Besides the desk and the near endless supply of paper, I don't know what else Robb actually has.

"No, they didn't. I couldn't afford it." He stands, pushing the chair out behind him with a screech. "I gotta go. Sorry about that."

"Of course. I'll see you around." He nods and walks around the corner, down an absurdly long hallway, into the depths of his house.

It wasn't long before Samantha Heller died in her sleep. Sudden Infant Death Syndrome was what I heard from Simon, but I knew something was wrong before that, when I saw the bassinet, smashed to splinters by the mailbox. There were red splotches I know Bret didn't put there. The news put me in a cold sweat. Any one of the events of the last week could be interpreted as happenstance. People go missing, kids get run over, and babies die. But all three in seven days? All three within two blocks of me? All three right after that mysterious recluse moves in? The one who writes morbid tales of death and crime? This is the last straw. I march down the street and right up to Robb's door. My knocks are thunder, echoing through the hollow house.

"Come in," he says. And I do.

"I need some answers, sir." There he was, still fucking writing.

"You do, do you?" he sang back, his voice reedy. Chipper.

"You've heard about the Heller baby?"

"I have. Tragic."

"Did you have anything to do with that?" He finally stops writing.

"I did." His words are a happy whisper. "Sit with me, Will." Without making a conscious decision, I feel myself fall backward and I'm caught by a chair I hadn't noticed. Robb stands and looks down at me, that familiar wide smile on his face.

176

"What did you do to that baby?" I try to keep the quiver out of my voice.

"Well, if it makes you feel any better, nobody *actually* got hurt. I was just writing a story. Just a scary story." He paces the room, gliding. "It's what I do. I'm a writer. It's the same thing I did in *My Girlfriend's Husband* and *Crimson Skidmarks*. This one was entitled *Under the Crib*. It's not that great, truthfully. It probably won't get published. But I got what I needed out of it." I could not speak. I urged my lips to open to scream at this man or monster, but it was not in my power to. Just like in the pool.

"Half the shit I do here... can't be done where I'm from. I'd be put to death or at the very least frowned upon. But here, in this sleepy, little neighborhood, I can do *anything.*" The walls of the house groan and seem to expand beneath the endless sheets of paper. He looks at me from across the room, his eyes chill my bones.

"In many ways, Will, you're my worst fear. Working behind a desk most of your life, not having the time or energy to create, and then when you're finally free, you find you don't even have the ability. That must be fucking torturous." I feel the cold sweat run down my back, my teeth chatter in my old skull.

"It is," I squeeze out.

"I know. You're a part of me, Will. That's what makes this so exciting."

"You killed them all... just for stories?"

"I killed them all *in* stories. What do you think we're in right now, my friend?"

The walls continue stretching apart, the once-small room now the size of a gymnasium. A large, semicircular doorway gapes on the far side, and only darkness lies beyond. Robb stands in the center of that doorway, beaming at me excitedly. People begin to pour out of the dark hole. People with bullet holes where eyes should be. People long drowned and waterlogged. Shredded people struggling to keep their innards inside. People charred beyond looking like people. Stabbed people, dissected people, a parade of distorted disgusting cadavers. "There must be five hundred of them. Maybe one for every page on the walls." I see Dorothy Ruck, her blue-white head lolling side to side as she walks. Her neck is compressed by a leather belt, pulled as tight as it would go. I see the Delaney boys, tagging each other with their own severed arms, holding them like swords. Blood spurts out of the ends and down around their hands, red and sticky. The older one's head is smashed, yet he still trudges forward. I see an impossibly young corpse pull itself toward me with no skin whatsoever.

"Please make them go away! Please! Goddammit!" I vomit down my front, unable to remove myself from the chair. I close my eyes so tight I may never open them again. But when I do, they're gone. The gathering of the damned vanishes as though they were never there in the first place. My vomit and tears remain. And so does the writer. He comes toward me, smiling that same smile I'd seen through my bay window a week ago. The room begins to recede into its normal proportions.

"Is it worth the success? To do such horrible things? Even... even if it's not real?" I almost choke on the words that deny my own existence.

"Success? I don't have success..." Robb sits back down at the desk, picks up the pen, and resumes his craft. "I do this for me."

I'm no longer confined to the chair and stand up. Thoughts rush through my head, smashing into each other. None of this makes sense, but it has to, because it's happening. I think of all the pain, the needless strife I've witnessed that was apparently all this man's machinations. "Or did it really happen at all? Does it even matter?"

"If what you say is true... why, my brother?" Robb keeps writing. "Why would you put me through that? Being attacked by my own mind? Why create such cruel and painful things? Why not write something happier?" At this, he pauses, but his pen keeps scratching.

"I've already told you, my friend. To make it feel real. And reality is cruel."

With tears in my eyes, I pick up the chair. To the protest of my shoulders, I thrust it over my head and rush toward him.

"You really should read this one. I think it's a winner. It's called *The Shark in the...*" The writer's words are cut short by the sickening crack of the chair against his head.

I'm in the pool, alone this time, and no longer a child. Any direction I try to swim, my fingertips never meet the concrete edge. The clouds threaten to burst overhead. I know what's coming. From the bottomless depths of the water I see the gargantuan outline that means my doom. Or does it? Had all the other patrons of the pool been yanked down by the foot and devoured, or was I put here for some sort of punishment? Does it even matter? Or will I tread water here forever, feeling the rough scales of the shark brush up against my leg? My arms are tired, my scream is silent. I ask myself, Am I being punished?

Yes.

A Snowy Run

by Morgan McClure

S now jogging. I absolutely love running in the snow. I know it sounds weird, but especially on day one of freshly fallen powder, there's just nothing like the peace that you can achieve when you combine the early morning tranquility, the untouched blanket of white, and the endorphins brought on by an even-paced jog.

Except, on this particular morning, the snow isn't completely untouched. It's only 5 am, and I'm on the quiet path which runs between the border of the forest and my neighborhood. I'm coming up on the backyard I've dubbed "Barbie Dreamworld," thanks to the Barbie castle, pink swing set, and unfailing rotation of Barbie dolls scattered across the lawn, when the footprints start up.

They appear to have come down between Barbie Dreamworld and the neighboring house, which is odd because there is no official access path there. I wonder if they belong to a resident of one of those two houses. I guess this person enjoys the tranquility of the fresh snow like I do. I follow the prints along the path for a while, my eyes meandering around them and the surrounding snowy landscape, until I spot something else out of place.

Something bright-red catches my eye off into the woods a little bit. I slow, and venture down into the vegetation to investigate the burst of color amongst the otherwise whitewashed scene. It's an Apple watch. The red band is broken, and it's sitting on top of a taller bush-like

180

weed, which I assume is why it hasn't been submerged in the snow.

I try to turn it on, but it shows the empty battery. Pocketing it, I figure I'll throw it on my charger at home and see if I can find the owner. It can't be good for it to sit out in the cold, wet snow.

By the time I get back around to my own townhouse, one my twin sister and I have been renting together since we graduated college last summer, I'm more than ready for the steaming mug of coffee calling my name.

"Have you been out jogging in the snow again, Kenzie?" my sister, Kailey, calls from the living room. "You're so weird. Aren't there like four inches out there? How do you even move?"

I kneel down to greet our Bernese Mountain Dog, Monday, who is chasing her tail in excitement at my return.

"It's so relaxing! If you ever moved your butt off the couch, I'd tell you to try it sometime," I call back to her.

She snorts, and it's partly drowned out by a commercial for Advil on the television. My sister watches the news religiously every morning. Normally, I actively avoid the living room when she has it on —too much gloom and doom for me— but this morning, I take my coffee in and sit with her. They've already called off work for the day so I have time to spare.

"Welcome back to 'Mornings with Marissa,' " the announcer exclaims. "Bringing you what you need to know, now."

I roll my eyes, and pull out my phone to start my morning scrolling routine.

Thirty minutes later, Kailey and I haven't moved much, except to add blankets to our couch setup.

"Can't we switch to something more up-beat?" I groan, as I recognize the news logo returning to the screen again.

"But it's almost the weather update! I want to see if any more snow is coming today," Kailey pleads.

"Ugh," I say, relenting for now. Instead, I get up and call for Monday. I take her out front and walk her for a few blocks, letting her delight in the new snow and go to the bathroom. When I get back, Kailey is still watching the news.

"And we have a breaking news update for you, coming in now. The Fairfield Police are seeking information on a missing girl in the 700 block of Ridge View Lane," Marissa reads from the teleprompter as I take Monday's collar off.

"Emily Raynard left her house at 4 am last night after fighting with her boyfriend and hasn't been seen since. With the current weather conditions, police are asking anyone with information to come forward immediately. She has likely been out in the elements for at least two hours at this point."

A picture of a smiling blonde girl fills the screen next to Marissa, and I stare at it in shock. The 700 block of Ridge View lane is in our neighborhood. It's less than a mile away. In fact, it's pretty close to where Barbie Dreamworld is.

Not only that, but something about the girl looks familiar. I could almost swear I've seen her before around the neighborhood.

With a sinking feeling, I think of the prints and watch I found this morning. Surely they couldn't be Emily's.

"Oh my gosh, isn't that street in this neighborhood?" my sister exclaims, looking at me. "Wow Kenzie, you look like you just saw a ghost."

"I, uh… I saw something weird this morning on my run. Right near that block." I explain about the footprints and watch.

Kaylie looks doubtful. "I mean, that could be anyone though. A lot of people live in this neighborhood. You didn't even see where the footprints actually started, just that they came down through those two houses' backyards."

"Yeah...." I agree, but something in my stomach is telling me those aren't just anyone's footprints.

"And we have Officer Cary of the Fairfield Police here now to give some further information. Officer Cary, do you have any leads on what could have happened to Emily?"

"Nothing substantial at this point, Marissa. We know the victim left the house of her own volition, so we can't rule out some sort of accident. Hypothermia is associated with disorientation. Her family has told us that she left the house without a coat, so it's possible she got lost somewhere nearby. We are also, of course, not ruling out foul play at this time."

"And you said the boyfriend is the last person who saw her? And they were fighting? Is there any suspicion on him at this point?"

"It's too early in the investigation to name persons of interest or rule anyone out, but as I said, her parents confirm that Emily left the house alone, before the boyfriend."

"Before the boyfriend. So he did also leave the house then? Could he have caught up to her and started an altercation of some kind?"

"It's too early to speculate on what could have happened, but I will say that our focus is elsewhere, as Emily's brother has confirmed that her boyfriend was with him for the remainder of the night as they searched for Emily together."

I stare at the TV, lost in thought. If those footprints weren't Emily's boyfriend's, then whose were they? "I think I have to call the police," I announce to Kailey.

"What?" she sounds surprised.

"I have to tell them what I saw."

"Kenzie I'm sure they followed her prints themselves by now. They probably saw the same thing."

"Not necessarily. You know how diligent this neighborhood is about salt and plowing. If the streets didn't have snow on them when she left then they wouldn't lead anywhere past the edge of her yard. And the place I saw the prints is blocks away, and through two houses' backyards. Not an obvious place to look. Plus by the time the police might have checked the forest path, other people might have been out to create their own footprints. They definitely hadn't checked that area yet when I went through. And what if that's her watch? Or her boyfriend's?"

"I just think it's kind of extreme to call the police over some footprints."

"Even if it's nothing, at least they'll know about them. It's better to say something and have it not be useful than to not say anything if it does end up being important."

"I guess." Kailey sounds wholly unconvinced.

I Google the non-emergency police number on my phone and dial it.

"Fairfield City non-emergency police line." A tired sounding voice picks up.

"Hi, um, I just saw on the news about Emily Raynard, and well, I think I might have seen something that, might be helpful. I'm not sure I just thought maybe I should call..."

"Okay, let me transfer you to one of the officers on that case," the voice says, putting me on hold. "Officer Ryan." A male voice finally breaks the silence on the line.

"Hi, yes, my name is Kenzie, uh McKenzie Simmons, and um, I think I might have seen something this morning on my morning run that might be relevant to the Emily Raynard situation?"

"Okay." The serious tone doesn't increase my confidence.

"Um, I mean, it might be nothing, but I just thought, probably better safe than sorry, so, yeah." Officer Ryan waits, saying nothing.

"So, I was running this morning—"

"What time?" Officer Ryan interrupts.

"I left around 4:45 am."

"Okay."

"And so I was running, like I said, along the woods path behind the neighborhood."

"The Fairridge neighborhood?"

"Yes. Fairridge."

"Okay."

"And the snow was all fresh and there weren't any footprints anywhere. And then well, then there were some. Footprints." I'm not sure what's happened to my ability to coherently communicate. I'm starting to regret not listening to Kailey.

"Where were they?"

"They came down between two backyards and then along the wood path."

"And where did the prints end?"

"After a while they trailed off into the woods, off the path. I didn't follow them past that point."

"You said they started between two backyards. Do you know the addresses of those houses?"

"No. I'm not sure what street that is. I was running from the front of the neighborhood towards the back along the path though. And one of the backyards has a children's setup, a Barbie playhouse and lots of Barbie dolls. And a pink swing set."

"Okay. And could you tell me what type and size of shoe you wear?"

"Um. I wear size eight Nike Airs."

"Okay. Is there anything else you wanted to report?"

"There's one more thing. I found an Apple watch. Right by the prints."

"An Apple watch?" There's interest in the officer's voice now.

"Yeah. It was on a red band."

"And did you turn it on?"

"Yeah. I was going to charge it and try to get it back to its owner."

"And have you started that? Charging it?"

"Yeah. It's charging right now."

"Okay, we're going to need to come get that as potential evidence most likely. Hold onto it for us until we can get someone over to your residence. Can you give me your address?"

"Sure. 1536 Everfield Drive."

"Great. I'll send someone over to pick it up today. If possible, don't unlock it or open it. In fact, if you can go turn it off after this call, that would be great."

"Okay."

"Was there anything else?"

"No, I think that's it."

"Okay. Thank you for the information. We will look into it."

"Okay. Thanks."

Officer Ryan hangs up without any further words.

Kailey is staring at me from under her blanket. "Still think calling was a good idea?"

"I mean, maybe it'll help. You never know."

She raises an eyebrow and turns back to the TV. Marissa is back, now talking about some mundane protests at the local water plant.

Suddenly I remember I told Officer Ryan I would turn off the Apple watch I found. I head to the foyer, where I had plugged it in on the console we have next to the front door.

The watch is gone.

I stare at the spot where it was just hours before. The charger is still sitting there innocuously but alone.

I check under the console, thinking maybe it somehow fell off. I even go check Monday's bed, where she always takes things she wants to chew. Nothing.

"Kailey?" I call, "Did you happen to see an Apple watch over here this morning?"

"An Apple watch? Like your one with the gold band? No, I don't think so!" she calls back.

"No, this one had a red band. I found it on my run, remember?"

"Oh. No, I haven't gotten up from the couch since you've come home," she says.

I stare at the place it had been sitting, starting to wonder if I'm going insane. No. I know I found that watch. I have a scratch on my face where a thorn hit me when I reached for it in the snow. I wouldn't have gone into the brambles if I hadn't seen it.

So then, what does that mean? If Kailey didn't take it, and Monday hasn't snatched it as a chew toy, then where is it? The only other possibility is that someone else took it. That someone else came into our house and got the watch. But who? And how? Monday would never let anyone get as far as our front porch without barking.

Then with a sinking feeling, I think about the walk I took her on. The twenty minute walk. That's a lot of time.

"Kailey?" I call into the other room.

"Yeah?"

"Did you hear the door open at all after I left to take Monday out?"

"No."

"Not at all?"

"I mean I heard you come back in I think, but that's just because you forgot something right?"

Chills run down my spine. Someone had come inside, to get that watch. They had come in while my sister was here, alone and defenseless.

"Kailey... that wasn't me. I didn't come back for anything."

"Oh really? Weird. I could have sworn you did."

"I didn't... but somebody did."

"What do you mean?"

I walk into the living room to look at her. "I found an Apple watch near those footprints I was telling you about this morning. I brought it back here, thinking I would charge

187

it and see if there was anything on it to tell me who it belonged to. I was charging it right by the front door. But now it's gone."

"Are you sure that's where you put it? You couldn't have put it anywhere else?"

"I'm sure."

"But... I mean that just seems so unlikely. How would the person have even known you had it?"

I think about that. Officer Ryan's words come back to me. Don't charge or turn on the watch. I suddenly realize why he said that.

"Find my iPhone," I say.

Kailey stares at me, not seeming to follow.

"When I started charging the watch, it turned on, and its location could be tracked with Find My iPhone. They must have figured out where it was and come to get it."

"But why not just knock?"

"Because they didn't want us to know who they were. There's something on that watch that they didn't want me to see."

"But how do they know you didn't already see it?"

"They don't."

I call Officer Ryan and tell him what's happened.

"Make sure you lock all of your doors and windows for now, McKenzie. Whoever that watch belongs to might be watching you to see if you know who they are. If they think you're a threat to them, they might take action against you."

"Okay," I squeak.

"I doubt they'll do anything if they haven't already," Officer Ryan says, "but this is just out of an abundance of caution."

"Okay."

I hang up and settle back with Kailey in the living room.

"And just in, we've found one of Emily Raynard's friends, who has agreed to talk to us about her disappearance this morning." Marissa announces, "Everyone, this is Simone Percy, one of Emily's best friends. Thank you for joining us, Simone. What can you tell us about Emily?"

"Um, I mean Emily is great. I can't believe she's missing," Simone says uncertainly.

I stare at the TV. I know Simone. I teach her piano lessons every week. She looks much paler on the screen than in real life, or maybe she's just nervous.

"And have you heard anything else about her disappearance?"

"Um... I'm not supposed to say anything because the police are still investigating."

"Of course, Simone. We would never want you to interfere with their investigation. But you know, if there's something you could tell our viewers, it may jog someone's memory. It could help us find Emily faster."

"Yeah... well I know they're still looking for her phone. They think it might be somewhere in the snow and it probably got too cold and turned off. So I guess... if anyone sees a phone."

"Oh wow, that is so good to know, Simone. So that means Emily did bring her phone with her when she left the house last night?"

"Yeah, I guess."

"And do you know her boyfriend, we are told his name is Thomas Smith."

"Yeah I do. Tom is a nice guy."

"Do you know what they were arguing about."

"I wasn't there, so I really couldn't say."

There's something in Simone's voice though, that tells me she does know what they were arguing about, she just doesn't want to guess on TV.

"Of course. And can you tell us a little bit about Emily? What was she like?"

Simone goes into a barrage of compliments on Emily's character and an extensive list of Emily's extracurricular activities.

After Simone's segment ends, Kailey finally agrees to switch the television to something a little lighter than the news, and we start in on some chick flicks.

Even as we watch the on-screen, dreamy love stories play out, all I can think about is the intruder who broke into our home. Every noise makes me jump, even as Monday lies snoozing next to the couch, clearly not concerned. Suddenly, the motion-sensored lights, rounding the edges of the backyard for Monday, turn on outside the window.

I jump up at the same time that Monday starts barking her head off. But there's no one outside; the backyard is empty of any movement. The snow has already been trampled by Monday, so it's impossible to use footprints as an indicator of anyone being there.

Maybe it was just an animal. I wake Kailey up and insist that she stand at the backdoor and watch as I go investigate. When I get to the edge of the yard, at first I think there really is nothing. But then I see them. A pair of black binoculars. Lying in the snow.

Chills run down my spine. Now we're being watched?

I rush back inside and close all the blinds, even though being unable to see the outside of the house makes me feel unprepared for whatever, or whoever, might be out there.

As I'm shutting the curtains in the kitchen, Kailey gasps.
"What?"

"Oh my gosh… they…t hey found her."

She hands me her phone, wide eyed.

"Local girl found deceased, in tragic accident," a headline news alert blares.

I pull it up immediately.

Wednesday January 20, 2021; 9:00am—Fairfield City, Pennsylvania—The search for sixteen-year-old Emily Raynard, of Fairfield has culminated in tragedy with the discovery of her body this morning. Emily Raynard was last seen late Tuesday night at her home she shared with her parents and older brother, when she left the house on foot following a fight with her boyfriend.

190

Police confirmed in a 9am press release this morning that Emily's body was recovered near a small river in the neighborhood. The cause of death was hypothermia, and her death was ruled an accident.

"This is something we never want to see, and it's just a horrible ending to a sad saga." Officer Ryan of the Fairfield Police commented, "It appears Emily left her home not dressed for the elements, including subzero temperatures and significant snowfall early this morning. Hypothermia can set in quickly in those types of conditions, and she likely became confused, and was unable to return home. We cannot stress enough the importance of proper clothing in these winter months."

A funeral service at a date to be announced will be held for Emily at the St. John's Presbyterian Church of Fairfield.

I have to read the article several times before I can fully comprehend what it's saying. An accident. They've ruled Emily's death an accident. But it isn't.

There is no way that someone would have come back for that watch if it didn't have something to do with Emily's death. And Emily was found by the river, the article said. I know in my gut those footprints were hers and that watch belonged to someone who was involved in her death.

I head to the kitchen, away from my sleeping sister, and call the police again, demanding to speak with Officer Ryan.

"Hello McKenzie." Officer Ryan sounds wary.

"Officer Ryan, how could you rule Emily's death an accident? I told you what happened with that watch I found!"

"McKenzie, we had to look at the evidence we had. Which was none. Emily was found in the woods, in the same outfit she left the house in. There was other evidence pointing to the accidental death determination."

"Other evidence? Like what?"

"It appears Emily ended up in the river at some point this morning, resulting in fast onset hypothermia."

191

"In the river? Why would she have gone into the river?! Doesn't that prove my point that someone must have made her go in there somehow?"

"We have learned that her cat escaped the house when she did, and likely followed her down to the river. We have a witness who saw her enter the river in an attempt to save the cat from drowning."

"A witness? Who?"

"That is not information I am authorized to share at this point."

"Of course not. Well, how do you know they aren't just saying that? Maybe they pushed her in!"

"We found the cat, also deceased, with Emily."

I pause, unsure how to argue further. "I found binoculars." I blurt out, "Behind our house."

Officer Ryan doesn't say anything for a moment. "And you believe that to be related to Emily's accident?"

I ignore his use of the word accident for the time being. "Yes. I think the person whose watch I found is watching us now."

"Would you like to make a police report?"

"I... no. I just think you should reopen the case."

"Unfortunately I can't do that, McKenzie."

"Well did you find anyone with a red Apple watch?"

"We found that Emily's boyfriend does own an Apple watch. He has a collection of dozens of bands. Some are variations of red. But he says, he didn't lose it and there is no further evidence that the watch you found belongs to him."

The boyfriend. That must be who is watching our house.

"Well, obviously he would say that."

"I'm sorry, McKenzie, but there's nothing we can do. There is no evidence of any crime. And there are no suspects. Like I said, we have an eyewitness account of the accident."

I try to continue protesting, but Officer Ryan doesn't let me go on too much longer before he says he has to get back to work.

The rest of the day, I try to find something on TV to distract myself from the thoughts whirring in my head. I keep checking outside through cracks in the blinds, but I don't see anyone or anything suspicious.

Finally, around dinnertime, I remember Simone. Simone knows something she didn't say on TV. I know it. Maybe if I call her, she'll tell me what it is.

"Hey Kenzie," Simone answers the phone, sounding a bit tired.

"Hi Simone," I say, then jump right into it, "I just wanted to call because well, I heard about Emily and I saw you on the news. I'm so sorry for your loss."

"Thanks, Kenzie. That was sweet of you to check in," she says, and I immediately feel guilty for having ulterior motives.

"Of course. How are you holding up?"

"I'm okay. Emily and I were pretty close but she'd been a bit more distant lately, so I guess that almost helps a little."

"Distant?"

"Yeah, ever since she started dating Tom, she was just so wrapped up in him. And then lately, in the past month or two, it got even worse. I don't know if it was because they started fighting more, but she was almost never free to hang out. I really only saw her in class."

"Wow. I wonder what they were fighting about."

Simone is quiet for a minute. "I think he thought she was cheating on him."

"Oh wow. Do you think she was?"

There's another pause. "I'm not sure. A year ago I would have said Emily would never, but lately I feel like I don't even know her—didn't even know her. And she'd been even less available lately, like I said. I did kind of wonder if that was because she was splitting her time between two guys. But I have no idea. Tom is also the jealous type, so it could have been nothing."

"You think that's what they were fighting about the night she left?"

"Probably. That's what they were always fighting about."

"But you don't know who she could have been cheating with?"

Simone hesitates. "Well... I did hear that her friend Asher was found with her at the scene of the... accident."

"Asher?"

Could this be the witness that Officer Ryan had mentioned?

"Yeah. He's Tom— Emily's boyfriend's best friend."

"Wow."

"Yeah."

"That's messy."

"Yep." Simone sighs, "I just wish I could have done more to help her instead of just being resentful like I was."

"You couldn't have known, Simone. And Emily was resisting help it sounds like."

"Yeah. It's just going to be so hard to see her family tomorrow at the funeral. They might think I'm the one who broke the friendship off."

"Of course they won't think that, Simone. They know Emily and they probably knew what she was up to. There's no way they would blame that on you."

"I hope you're right."

"I wouldn't worry about it. If they had any doubts, then I'm sure just seeing you show up at her funeral will put those doubts to rest."

"That's true. Well I better get going. It's been a tiring day. I'll see you at our lesson next week, Kenzie."

"Yep, of course. See you soon, Simone. Get some rest."

So Emily's funeral is tomorrow. And there's another guy involved in Emily's story: this Asher character. This news opens up a whole new box of possibilities. If I went to her funeral, then I could see if anyone is acting suspicious. If Emily was cheating, then either Tom or Asher could have had something to do with her death. If I could figure out which one of them is more likely, then maybe I can find evidence to bring to the police, and whoever is stalking the house will be stopped.

By the time dusk is falling, I've made up my mind. I'm not going to work tomorrow. I'm going to Emily's funeral. If the police won't do something about her death, then I will.

When I wake up the following morning, I can sense something is wrong right away. I jump out of bed and run to the window, pulling up the blinds of my basement-level bedroom. I'm faced not with snow but with a printed document.

Stop Asking Questions.

I clap a hand over my mouth to stop from screaming. Instead, I run upstairs and outside. I make my way over to the side of the house, where that window is. There's nothing there. No note. No nothing. But there is a set of footprints. Fresh footprints. I can tell because of the way these footprints have cut into the icy top layer of the snow. They're also too big to be me, Kailey, or Monday. These are a man's prints.

A man who, I realize, was waiting out there, watching me sleep, waiting for me to see the note when I woke up. When he saw me move the blinds, he knew it was time to take the note and run.

I race to the front of the house, but as I expected, the street is empty. The prints disappear on the paved road, and I have no idea where the person who left them might have went.

But I do think I know who left them. Emily's boyfriend, Tom. Or Asher. It had to have been one of them. And today is the day I'm going to figure out which one. And ask more questions.

I think for a second about the possibility that me showing up at the funeral will anger the guy further. But I have to. I can't keep living in fear like this. If I don't figure out what's going on here, I'll never sleep well again.

I realize I may have made a mistake coming to the funeral as soon as I walk in. There aren't many people, and it's clear that everyone here knew Emily well. I slide into a seat next to two boys about Emily's age and pull out my phone to seem occupied.

The two boys started whispering when I sat down next to them, and I'm sure they're wondering who I am and what I'm doing here. I know I'm right when the one closest to me reaches out a hand to shake mine and says, "Hi, I'm Asher, I don't think we've met. How did you know Emily?"

I can't believe my luck. I'm sitting right next to Asher. I'm prepared for his question, and I say, "I'm Kenzie. I live in her neighborhood and had seen her around. I just felt so bad about the tragedy, I thought I should come pay my respects."

"Right." The boy looks skeptical for some reason.

"What about you?" I say.

"I was one of her friends. And Tom here," he gestures to the boy next to him, "was her boyfriend." Even better. Emily's boyfriend, right here. Both prime suspects, right where I want them.

"I'm so sorry for your loss," I say to Tom, careful not to show my reaction. "I'm sure it must be just awful, leaving things on such bad terms. But you have to remember, whatever your last words were, Emily loved you. Little fights are normal."

"Yeah." He smiles but it's strained. "It's been tough."

"I can't imagine." I'm not sure what else to say. I've never been good in these types of emotional situations. Plus, every bone in my body is now screaming about the danger that Tom and Asher represent. If one of them has been watching me like I suspect, then that person knows

196

exactly who I am. And my presence here will be angering him.

"So you said you live in the neighborhood," Asher interjects, changing the subject.

"Yeah," I say, not wanting to elaborate on exactly where I live, even though I'm sure one of them already knows.

"That's cool. The townhomes here are pretty nice. I'd love to live in one someday."

"Yeah, my sister and I rent one together. It's nice to have the space, especially with a dog." I respond nonchalantly but I'm analyzing what Asher just said. Did he bring up the townhomes because he knows I live in one, or is he just making casual conversation? There are both single-family homes and townhomes mixed throughout Fairridge, so he should have no way of knowing that I live in a townhome.

But of course, I'm positive one of these two does in fact knows that I live in one. So is this a slip-up? Or did he say that intentionally, to watch my reaction?

"That's awesome. I love dogs."

"Yeah. So you don't live in the neighborhood?" I ask him.

"Nah, I live a few miles from here, in Lakeridge."

"Nice." I say, then decide to test the ice a little bit. "So I heard you were pretty close with Emily." I direct this at Asher, not Tom. If Asher is guilty, I doubt he'll like me suggesting he had any sort of special relationship with Emily.

"We were friends, yeah. We all were. Well, and of course, Tom and Emily were dating." His tone is forlorn, but there isn't any anger behind it, as far as I can tell.

I look down at my hands. Why did I come here? How will I ever figure out what's going on when the person behind this knows what I'm looking for? My gaze shifts from my own wrists to Tom's, next to Asher. He's sporting an Apple watch, with a navy blue band. But so is Asher, I notice. Such watches are so popular these days.

My eyes rise up from Asher's wrist to meet his eyes, staring right at me with an inscrutable expression. I quickly

197

avert my gaze back to the front of the room. Something is definitely off here.

I stare down at Asher's shoes. He must be one of those high school guys who hasn't yet been to a formal event, because he's wearing tennis shoes under his dress pants. They're not even all-black ones. Instead, they're navy blue with a light up neon green band that keeps blinking as he taps his foot. There's something about the shoes that's familiar to me, but I can't figure out what it is.

I think hard as the service begins. It's not until I see a photo of Emily in the background though, that I realize that I have in fact seen those shoes before. With Emily.

In the photo on the screen, Emily is wearing a t-shirt that proclaims, "Animal Rights are Human Rights," with a picture of a chicken stuffed in a too-small cage, looking malnourished and miserable, underneath the slogan. I know that shirt. I saw Emily wearing it a few weeks ago, I remember because the image was surprising, and even more surprising was that a young girl was wearing such a graphic shirt.

The shirt had made me notice her and the guy she was with, as I was jogging along. The boy had been brunette and wearing glasses, with a "Ridgefield High Golf Team" t-shirt. And they had been holding hands. Holding hands and kissing. As I had approached, they'd looked at me as I interrupted what appeared to be an intense moment. I, in turn, had looked down at the ground, feeling awkward. On the ground, I had noticed the boy's light up sneakers, which sent me on a mental spiral of the 90s trends coming back around.

I sneak another peak at Asher and the "Ridgefield High Golf Team" lanyard falling out of his pants pocket. My eyes travel up to his glasses. I'm almost positive it was him.

So Emily had really been cheating on Tom with his best friend. Wow.

I spend the rest of the service with my mind moving a mile a minute. I wonder if Tom knows whom Emily was cheating with. I can't imagine he does, or he wouldn't be sitting with him like this. And what about Asher? The police said, Tom has an alibi—Is there any way that Asher could have been involved in Emily's death? Maybe Emily tried to end it with Asher and he got mad.

Maybe if I bring up seeing Asher and Emily together, Tom or Asher will react in a way that gives me a clue about which one of them could be behind Emily's death.

I spend the reception waiting for the right moment to test my theory. Finally, as we're all sitting around snacking on mini cookies, I see Tom and Asher by themselves by the drinks, and I see my chance.

"You know," I say as I walk up to them, "I realized why you look so familiar, Asher." I try to keep my voice carefully casual.

"Oh yeah?" Asher looks at me, and I can feel fire in his eyes.

"Yeah, I saw you and Emily together a few weeks ago. On the walking path." I watch him closely. I feel extremely awkward bringing this up at Emily's funeral and even more awkward continuing, but I don't know if I'll have another chance. "You guys were holding hands."

Asher pales. Tom, on the other hand, looks curiously at Asher, with a detached interest. "You were holding Emily's hands?" Tom asks Asher directly.

"Uh, I, no… it was probably just something stupid. I mean, I don't remember that day."

"Sorry," I say, acting embarrassed, "I didn't mean anything by bringing it up! I just realized I'd seen you before. I wasn't sure if you remembered me, so I didn't want to be rude…" I trail off, knowing this sounds ridiculous, as it wasn't like we'd spoken when I'd seen Asher and Emily, and knowing that Tom is Emily's boyfriend, there is no reason for me to bring up what I saw.

"Uh, no worries," Asher says to me, but I can tell his attention is still on Tom.

For his part, Tom shrugs and goes back to filling his cup with Sprite.

I can't understand either Tom or Asher's reactions to my questions. If one of them is angry enough to be threatening me, then why didn't either one have any sort of real reaction when I resumed asking questions? Not to mention the fact that Tom seemed completely unfazed by the news of what Asher and Emily were doing. Does that mean he knew? Or does that mean I have it wrong and Asher and Emily really were just friends?

My mind continues to spin all night, and I insist on sleeping in Kailey's room in case Tom or Asher resumes their threatening behavior. But thankfully, nothing seems amiss by the time I wake up from a restless night the next morning.

I haven't been running since I found the watch, but I know that if I don't get my excess energy out at this point, I'll lose my mind. So I leash up Monday and take her with me back onto the forest paths. I figure, no one will make any move on me with a big dog by my side.

I'm only a few blocks from my front door, having just entered the woods path, when someone steps out from behind a bush, causing me to almost fall over in shock.

"Hello, Kenzie," he says, a smile on his face.

"Um, hi, Tom." Alarm bells are ringing in my head.

"I think you should tie your dog to that tree." He points to a tree down towards the river, a little off the path.

"Um. Why?"

"Because you and I need to have a chat."

"I don't see what Monday has to do with us chatting," I say evenly, trying not to let the nerves hit my voice. I scan the area for someone, anyone else to interrupt us, but the path is empty.

"Well, maybe you will if I show you this." Tom pulls a gun out of his pocket.

My heart jumps to my throat. "Where did you get that?"

"My dad's gun safe code wasn't hard to guess."

"You know, if you shoot me with that thing, you're basically asking to go to jail for the rest of your life."

"Ah, yes. See, the way I see it is, if I don't ensure that you stop investigating Emily, I'll be headed that direction anyway, so it's a risk I'm willing to take. Now, tie the dog up. Now." He aims the gun at me.

I walk down into the woods and tie Monday to the tree, my hands shaking.

"Now, toss me your phone," he says, his tone commanding.

I throw it at him.

"Password?"

When I don't answer, he does something to the gun that makes a clicking noise. "135911."

"Thank you." He thumbs through my phone. "Here we go: Kailey. 'Might be out for longer than usual this morning. Going to look for clues about Emily after my run. See you later.' "

Tom looks over at me. "And now we'll just wait and make sure that text doesn't ring any alarm bells. In the meantime, I want you to go jump in the river."

"What?" I look at the river, partially iced over on the first foot or two of the edges. "Hypothermia is a lot faster when you're wet." Tom smiles at me.

"So you did kill Emily." I don't make any moves to the water.

Tom's smile widens. "Yes, yes, let me give you the satisfaction of being right while you still have time to enjoy it."

"But… how? How did you plan that out?" Now I'm just trying to keep him talking. I have to figure out a way out of this. Once I get in that water, my brain isn't going to function properly.

Tom laughs, without humor. "I've known Tom and Emily have been cheating on me for months. And they've just been going around, acting like everything's fine to my face. Loving all the benefits of my friendship, but not caring enough about me to stop them from stabbing me in the back."

"Benefits?"

Tom snorts. "My dad is getting Asher into college on a basketball scholarship. He coaches at Villanova. And Emily knows—knew that she'd never get prom queen without me by her side. I'm sure she figured after the big night she'd drop me."

"So you planned her murder?"

Tom's eyes flash. "They deserved it. They needed to feel the pain I felt. Particularly Asher. He deserved to feel what losing the love of his life felt like."

"So... how did you do it?" I don't give myself time to process what he's saying, instead just jumping from question to question.

"Simple. I put sleeping pills in Em's hot chocolate and picked a fight. When she went running out on me, like I knew she would, she called Asher, which I also expected. I took her cat down to their little rendezvous spot, knowing when she saw it drowning in the river she'd jump in and save it. And she did. After which Asher jumped in to save her, and that was just a bonus. When she got out, Asher tried to go for help, and ran into me. He claimed that Emily called him 'as a friend' and told me what happened. I handed him a mug of pill-spiked hot cocoa and told him I'd get help. Instead, I waited until they both passed out from the cold and pills."

"And then what?"

Tom plays with the gun, running it through his fingers as he goes on. "Then I made sure their phones got lost in the water, collected my hot chocolate thermos, and went back to Em's house to report her running out after our fight. I told her family and the police that Em had probably gone to Simone's house to vent about me... and of course Simone lives in the opposite direction of the river. Then I made sure that Emily's brother and I conveniently found

202

Asher, followed by Emily. Asher was still alive, Emily wasn't."

"So Asher was the witness."

"Yep, he told the police a great story about Emily's cat having gotten out behind her and how it must have followed her to the river. And then he explained how they had jumped in."

"Didn't he tell them about seeing you?"

"Oh yeah, but I told them he was mistaken, that I never went down there, so he must have hallucinated that."

"And they believed you?" This time I can't keep the incredulity out of my voice.

"They couldn't confirm any times because Asher and Emily's phones were missing in the river. They had a witness of Emily's death, so they knew I wasn't there when she died. No one had seen me leave the house, there was no thermos of hot chocolate at the scene, and Asher had severe hypothermia, which is associated with confusion. They wanted to close the case." Tom shrugs.

I stare at him, in fascinated shock despite my situation.

"And Asher has no idea what you've done?"

"Nope. He's all love sick and emotional. He hasn't given me a second thought. After all, like I said, I wasn't even there when she jumped in, of her own volition, to save that cat."

"Wow" is all I can think to say.

"The only problem," Tom says, turning his focus back on me, "is that my watch fell off at some point. And then you found it."

So I was right. Of course I was right. It's been Tom all along. "So it was you that was threatening me?"

"I was hoping you'd just drop it and we could all go on. But when you showed up at the funeral yesterday, asking even more brazen questions than the ones you asked Simone, I knew I couldn't let this go on any longer."

He knows I called Simone. Chills go down my spine as I chide myself for being so obvious in my search for the truth.

He aims the gun at me again. "That's it for story time. Get in that water, or I'll put you in there myself." I take a slow step toward the water.

"Come on. We don't have all day. It still takes a while for someone to die of hypothermia. You need to be gone before anyone looks for you."

Fear laces through my bones.

"But don't you think it will be suspicious? Two girls killed the same way?"

"It doesn't matter, there won't be any evidence of anything else. Now go!" He makes the clicking sound with the gun again, and I pick up my pace slightly, standing at the edge of the water.

"In!" he yells, and almost at the same second, there's a bang. At first I think he's fired the gun, but he's actually just smacked it hard against a tree. The sound is enough to pitch me forward into the icy river.

It feels like time is in slow motion underwater. Every movement takes double the effort and results in a speed half as fast as I'm intending. When I finally break the surface, at first all I can do is take in a quick sip of icy air.

Then I realize there are noises coming from the shore.

Monday is barking. She's glancing from me, in the river, to a blur of limbs tumbling on the snow covered forest floor. It takes me a minute to realize that it's not just Tom beside the water now. Asher is there too. And they're wrestling.

I stare for a moment too long, trying to process what I'm seeing, and as I do, I sink down into the water again. By the time I can make my slow arms keep me afloat, I realize the urgency of the situation. Tom and Asher are wrestling, but they're too evenly matched. If Tom gets control of that gun, it's over for both me and Asher. I have to get over there to help.

But it's hard. Not only do my limbs move like I'm swimming in syrup, but the ice on the edge of the river doesn't give me anything to grip onto to pull myself out. I notice a fallen tree that almost reaches the river's edge a few yards downstream and let myself float to it.

I feel like it takes me an hour to plop myself up onto the icy shore, but I'm sure it isn't really that long because the nearby grunting tells me Tom and Asher are still wrestling.

I stumble, like a drunk person, toward them, trying to plan how to get the gun from Tom. Before I can reach them though, Monday breaks free of her leash, I see she's actually bitten through the nylon strap, and she throws herself into the brawl. She's not helping either of the guys, as she doesn't know whom she's fighting for and is throwing bites at both Tom and Asher equally.

I throw myself onto the pile. Once I'm in the scuffle, it's hard to even tell who is who. But I try to keep my eyes on the prize, the gun, which is currently in Asher's hand. I wedge myself between him and Tom and buck my back, separating them.

It's what Asher needs. He scuttles away, crablike, the gun firmly in his grasp, pointed at Tom.

Tom thinks quicker than I do though, and he grabs me, pulling me in front of him. He wants to use me as a shield, but he didn't account for Monday. She tackles both of us to the ground, and this time she knows whom the enemy is. She bites Tom right in the face, and it's enough for him to let go of me, allowing me to escape to Asher's side.

"Kenzie," Asher speaks in a forced calm voice, his eyes not wavering from Tom. My phone is in my back pocket. Take it out and call the police."

I do. We spend a few tense minutes on the phone with the 911 operator until we hear sirens on the nearest street. I don't fully breathe with relief until Tom is in handcuffs and both Asher and I are in the back of an ambulance, being taken to the hospital.

"How did you know we would be there?" I ask Asher, as the medics apply antibacterial ointment to the cuts Tom gave him.

"I didn't," Asher says, "but after you brought up me and Emily at the funeral, I knew something was wrong about Tom's reaction. He was always nagging Emily about cheating while they were dating. Constantly. But then, when finally presented with evidence, he doesn't even blink? I knew something was off, and I started thinking. I knew the password to Emily's social media accounts, and I logged into her Instagram. I checked the devices that her account had been accessed from, and sure enough Tom had logged in several weeks ago. I knew then that he would have seen our messages and known we were together behind his back."

"So then what? You knew he'd go after me?" I snuggle further into the warm blanket around me.

"No, I wasn't sure, but I had a hunch he might. He'd been talking about how you were an early morning jogger at the funeral, and it made me think that's probably when he'd strike. He kept saying he wished you'd found Emily earlier that morning while jogging. I decided to go for a walk along the path near your house, just in case, until I could figure out how to prove what he'd done without getting in trouble myself. That's when I heard his voice through the trees."

I'm struck again by how lucky I was. If Asher hadn't decided to look into what Tom knew, if he hadn't noticed something off with Tom's reaction, if I hadn't brought up seeing Emily and Asher, even if Asher had just walked down the wrong part of the woods path, things could have ended very differently.

"Well thanks for saving me Asher," I say seriously.

"Of course. I just wish I could have saved Emily too. What we were doing was wrong, but she didn't deserve to die. And it's my fault: I agreed to the whole stupid plan of waiting until June to tell Tom."

"June?"

"Yeah. After prom and after I'd have accepted my position at Villanova."

"You couldn't have known what Tom would do. It wasn't your fault," I say, trying to make him feel better.

Asher just looks away sadly, and I can tell he doesn't believe me. At that moment we reach the hospital, and EMTs open the ambulance doors and start rushing us off to be examined. I watch Asher's forlorn expression until I can't see him anymore, wondering what will happen to him now. I know he isn't blameless in Emily's death, but as my rescuer, I can't help but hope for the best for him in the future.

Turning my head away from where his stretcher disappeared, I focus on greeting my terrified sister, who has someone managed to get them to allow Monday in with her. I give Monday the biggest hug and whisper in her ear that I hope she's ready to get into running, because I'm never jogging without her ever again.

And Yet, There Are Few

by Zoe Copeman

The landlady gave me a look when I walked in. It was the kind I was used to — for one grows used to these looks in rural America.

"We're married for all she knows," Gerard says as I explain this to him.

"We don't have rings on."

"Would you like me to buy you a ring?"

No. I don't say that word—marriage—aloud. I don't need to.

"Then I won't."

Gerard grew up in the city. He knows the look, but not what it means. He knows other looks better than I. Like the one she gives him. At least they are individualized. *How pointed of her.*

I dreamt of the landlady eating my soul that night, full Francisco Goya's Cronus style. Her tight bun let loose, her wrinkled skin stretched so far that her mouth had become a red, musty cavern into which I needed to walk to be saved. Or, at least, that is what the Cronus Landlady told me. *I had to be saved.* I can no longer remember whether or not it was a dream or reality. Like Zeus' brethren, I must be consumed to rise again. *I have to be saved.*

My head is in the lumpy porridge.

"The Carols are talking about the Wall again," Gerard, my boyfriend of twelve years, informs me. Or is he my partner? He is not my husband. The red, musty cavern that is the landlady confirms this to me every time I walk into the door of Saint Mary Grace Inn.

"Which wall?"

"You know, 'The Wall', the one that keeps people like me out," Gerard says.

"Gerard, it's for Mexicans. Not half-Irish, black men."

The woman at the counter stares at my back. Her lips slightly parted as her eyes begin to squint. *The look.* I know it even when I do not see it.

I tell Gerard of my dream last night.

"At least we're not gay," Gerard jokes, making his not so subtle gesture to the two women across the room near the window. The older couple receives their own looks. *At least they're married.*

My chin falls further into the overcooked oatmeal, becoming now a runny, foul smelling facial. *A perfect metaphor for this waste of time vacation.*

We decide to walk the mountains that afternoon. It is why we are here — to experience the true beauty of nature (or something) before going back to the city.

This is why we are here, I remember, taking in deep breaths at the top of the hill. There's something about standing atop a cliff, breathing in fresh, cold, untainted air, that revitalizes the soul. It is also a place that I dread. Standing atop a cliff, there's a lurch in my gut. I am not afraid of heights. I do not dislike heights. In fact, I'd go as far as to say the dread comes more from myself than the cliff. I am afraid of myself —afraid that my feet will carry on forward despite my brain saying, *No.* I will not be able to control myself. I will jump. *A call to the void.* I close my eyes and the sun turns the insides of my eyelids red. I see it there. That red, musty cavern in the dark. It calls and beckons and I feel my feet inch closer.

I'm yanked the opposite direction. Gerard pulls me away from the edge with a smile and we descend down the hills back to Mary Grace Inn. I wonder each time if

209

the landlady's name is Mary or Grace or both, and Gerard makes the joke for the hundredth time as we pass under its heavy wooden sign: "Say Grace, dear."

The landlady is not at her desk. She does not answer her bell — however many times I tap it.

"Oh, good, it's you two," says Amelia Pole-Marshall from behind us, the better of her two halves. "Have you seen the Carols? We meant to play a game of bridge with them when we got back from our hike, but we haven't a clue where they went off to."

"Maybe they went for a walk?" Gerard says.

"Have you seen Mr. Carol?" Louise, the other Pole-Marshall, quips.

"Good point."

I ring the bell again and I wonder if perhaps in some messed up version of the Greek myth, Cronus' children walked willingly into their father's mouth. Then I remember. "Did you see her this morning? The landlady?" I ask Amelia and Louise as they make for the door. Apparently, they no longer cared for playing bridge.

Louise shrugs. "I'm not sure."

"I'm sure she's just in the back cooking up naughty children." Gerard takes ahold of my hand. I realize that I still have it hovering over the counter. "Ring that bell again and she'll be at us with a switch."

"What makes you think she's Catholic?"

"You don't need to be Catholic to beat someone with a stick," Gerard reminds me. "You should work on those stereotypes of yours, they're really unbecoming, you know." Gerard smiles the way only Gerard dares to smile.

We have sex in the bathtub. We do not make love. I cannot remember the last time I've made love. There's something too personal there, something too fake at the same time. Sometimes you have to fake being personal with the man you love. I remind myself sex feels right, most of the time, but not now. Not with two black gaping holes staring at me.

Gerard unceremoniously wraps himself in a towel. "You want anything?"

"Nope."

Now by myself, I slip into the soapy, lukewarm water up to my eyelids. The water appears dark and black beneath them. The red cavernous mouth opens to consume me. I see it every time I close my eyes. *Do not close your eyes.*

Gerard sleeps in the bed like a baby, and I spend the night on the dusty red armchair by the window, watching the sun rise red, yellow and purple, then blue and orange over the mountains. *There's no red,* I remind myself as my eyelids droop.

The door slams.

"I'm up!"

"Yeah, sure, you are." Gerard eyes me curiously. "Everything okay?"

"Yeah. I just couldn't sleep."

"Hmpf," is Gerard's only reply. "Well, you ready for breakfast? I'm starving."

"Where is this woman?" I say as the bellboy James or Jim, I've heard him called both, runs by us.

"Hey, have you seen Mary?" Gerard clarifies to the boy.

"I don't know," Jim replies. "I haven't seen her since lunch yesterday."

"Isn't that odd?"

James shrugs. "Yes, but she's not dead in her room," he says dully, as though he checked with little care of the result.

Gerard taps the desk. He's growing impatient. He doesn't show it in his voice. He's still smiling, but the grin is tense and his fingers keep tapping. "Listen, can we just leave the money and key with you? We have to get back home."

Jim shrugs again.

That's the last time I see Saint Mary Grace Inn, in the back mirror of our tiny Prius. A little white house on a main street below the Appalachian Mountains. *Really, nothing of note*, my mind says. It's nothing. I close my eyes and the landlady's black ones are on me. Her hair is splayed and she's opening her mouth.

Gerard honks his horn.

"Shit!" My head hits the side of the door. "Why'd you do that for?" the words slur and my head struggles to find the world right side up.

"Finally!" I hear Gerard exclaim from my left. "You've been out for hours. Nearly missed this great view!" Gerard's voice is tense.

Our phone had told us to avoid major roads and I can almost hear Gerard swearing against it. We're in a standstill. He leans his head out the window in an attempt to stare around the car in front of us.

It takes a half hour, but finally, the traffic slides by, every car swerving by one abandoned in the center of the road.

"Do you know that's the fifth car just there in the middle of the road?" Gerard says as he jerks the wheel hard to re-center us from grass back onto pavement. I look back at the large gutted area the tires left off the side of the road. I had not noticed. We were still an hour outside Baltimore and my mind was elsewhere. Black and empty and red.

"Six!" Gerard yells as we swerve around another car. "Some people! Is this town full of idiots?" Gerard honks the horn before pulling onto the grass again.

As we neared the city, the parked cars only grew, creating a traffic jam around I-95. Our three-hour car ride turned into twelve. We abandoned the car and walked the last two miles on Key Highway, up three flights of stairs to our apartment. The elevator broke down last week and still no one had come to fix it. "Great. Perfect," Gerard says with a wheeze as he carries the heavier of the two bags up the stairs. "Never take me to the boonies again. Never."

"It was your idea, remember," I say absently, spying around the corner. Apartment 203's main door is cracked open.

"Yeah. Yeah, at least you got some sleep!"

"Right."

"I'm about as tired as a dead donkey." Gerard sighs as we make it to our landing. He stretches his back. "You got the key?"

Inside, I drop my purse and overnight bag on the floor and open the fridge. There's beer. Thank god, there's beer. I chug one, then another, and I remind myself that fasts and nature and health are not all they are cracked up to be. A little voice in my head says to drink water or risk the consequences tomorrow. I grab another beer.

"Jesus, you have to come look at this!" Gerard yells from our living room. He's standing instead of his normal position spread-eagle across the couch—a far too large number that he insisted on purchasing for our tiny one bedroom apartment.

"What?"

"No, come here, really."

I squint. I'm on beer three after thirty minutes of being home and I'm unsure if Gerard is up to his old tricks.

"I'm serious. I'm pausing it, but come quick!"

I sit down on the couch. Gerard does not. The beer finds its way to the coffee table as I realize too late that I should have gotten water instead. My stomach churns.

"Here, let me rewind."

"Is that Rome? What are you watching? Is this the History Channel?"

"Here." Gerard turns up the volume. He takes a step back. He does not sit next to me. He does not laugh. Gerard *never* does not laugh. And my stomach expands now, whirling the air up my esophagus. A bit of car snack—Cheetos and peanuts—regurgitate. And my body grows cold.

The woman on the screen is speaking loudly, but it takes me a moment to digest her first few words. I take a sip of my drink, slowly this time, not daring to ask Gerard to rewind again. I've never seen Gerard not laugh. "That's right," the reporter says when my ears begin to tune to her instead of just the pictures on screen. "The whole Vatican vanished over night."

"Well, that's not entirely accurate." Gerard paused the video again as the great columns that wrap around St. Peter's close into view. The church and Michelangelo's dome are still intact. There are even people walking around, but fewer than my mind tells me there should be. The modern metal gates around the columns are covered in yellow tape.

"What do you think? Aliens? It's gotta be aliens."

I am no longer listening. I grab my phone from my purse and dial the third number down. It rings. It keeps ringing. I press the second number in my phone and close my eyes. The red cavern is still there. Open and waiting for me, yawning.

"Mom?" I say when the receiver clicks. I open my eyes and I'm back in my own apartment. Gerard is staring at me.

"What are you doing?"

"Shh!" I hold my hand up and Gerard goes into the kitchen. I hear a beer crack.

"Mom?" I repeat.

"Hmm?" my mother answers drowsily on the other line. It is nearly midnight, I remind myself. That shouldn't matter. Mom usually is still watching trash TV at midnight.

"Mom, have you watched the news?"

"No, why?" There's a pause. "Oh god, we aren't being nuked are we? Damn that lunatic. Frank," I hear her call my father. "Are we being nuked?" My father's voice grumbles back a response I cannot decipher.

"No! Mom, Mom!" The indecipherable voice continues on the other side of the line. "Have you talked to Nana?"

214

"Oh, Mags, you're still here?"

"Mom, have you talked to Nan today?"

"No, why?" My mother yawns.

"What about dad's parents?"

"No, why?" she parrots, the same words becoming more critical, tense with yet another pause. "You know, if you're going to guilt trip me again, I'm hanging up."

"No, Mom, I think something's wrong." I can feel Gerard staring at me now. He's back from the kitchen with two beers in hand. He offers me one and I shake my head. "Have you seen the news?" I repeat.

"If I turn it on will you let me sleep?"

I push the mute button on my end and put it on speaker. "Call your parents," I instruct Gerard.

"What? Why?"

"I don't know. I've just had this feeling all day. I don't know how to describe it. It's-it's like..."

"Okay, okay! Let me find my phone."

"Christ in a hand basket," my mom's voice comes through the line moments later and I nearly drop my cell. "Half of Congress is gone!" And I know now that she is flipping channels just as Gerard is. He still hasn't called his mom. "Fox News is a blank screen—for once. What is going on?"

I fumble to unmute myself.

"You know, you'd think the rapture would take the good people? Right?" Gerard says.

"Oh, is that Gerard?" my mom answers back.

"What did you say?" I can't keep the two conversations straight.

Gerard flips to another channel, CNN. There is a reporter there, at least. "Probably Jewish," Gerard mumbles. "Nope," he later confirms, "Look at Jerusalem, took them and all the Muslims too."

"What are you talking about?" The yawning mouth inside of my head is closing. Inside the red lips, I realize that too is pitch black.

215

"Well, look who's gone — Fox News, the Pope, just about everyone who attends any kind of church or temple or mosque or anything to do with the Abrahamic religions, *whewf*, the president? Really? Didn't think he actually believed in anything. Lord," Gerard says, "took all the religious folk and left us non-believers behind."

"The rapture?" I shake my head. "You can't be serious—"

Besides abandoned cars and some wreckage on the roads, there was no fire and brimstone, no looting, no scourge of the Earth attacking one another. I get up and look outside the window and though there are hardly the amount of lights I was used to seeing in Baltimore, nothing else seemed out of place. There was possible even less yelling and horn-honking than usual. It was all, relatively, quiet.

Gerard flips the channel to the BBC. The woman on the TV is speaking in a British accent. Now, I truly cannot digest the words. My mind is swirling.

"The world is missing more than 60% of its population. Governments have fallen and crumbled over the course of the day. The people are on their own for now. For now, we must be diligent. We must be smart...."

The news all say the same thing. There is no other news. There is no shoplifting or terrorist attack or war. *Only the rapture.*

"It will be hard figuring out just who is gone, but we must overcome," some politician says, at least my mind says it's a politician, probably one who lied about their faith. Who else would say such a thing at such a time? I stare out the window. The sky is dark.

I feel the pair of black eyes behind my own slowly shutting. The mouth is closing. The landlady's voice reverberates out of the now small opening. It's the voice of my grandmother, of her pastor, my extended family, the little old couple down the hall and the loudest voices that once graced my television screen. They all call out to me. *You can still be saved,* they say. *You can still depart.* I just have to walk blindly into the cave. Walk blindly into the mouth of the Lord.

But I am not Zeus. And we can't all be Cronus' children.

I open my eyes and God's cavernous mouth shuts over my brothers and sisters. The shouting and cursing and lamenting rises and falls with a snap. *They are gone*, my mind says. *They're all gone.*

"What do we do now?" I say absently.

Gerard shrugs and finally sits down on the couch. He signals for me to follow and I slide in next to him. Even with me on it, there is plenty of room for him to spread eagle with ease. That was the whole point of it — one less thing to fight about. A far too large couch lets us both sit however, which way we wanted, after all. The weight of the whole world lifts as I curl up next to Gerard, head on his chest.

Gerard laughs and ruffs up my hair. "So, I'm starving. What's for dinner?"

THE END

Biographical Information

Christy Brown is an author living in the Hampton Roads area of Virginia. She was born and raised in Southern California. Christy lived in Los Angeles and Santa Barbara until she was an adult, at which point she joined the Navy and relocated to Norfolk, Virginia. She has lived in the Hampton Roads Area of Virginia for twenty years, where she attended Old Dominion University and is currently a high school English teacher.

Christy majored in English literature and education at Old Dominion. Although Christy always loved to read, college is where she started growing a passion for writing. Once Christy earned her degree, she became a high school English teacher in Suffolk. Christy married and went on to build a large family of seven children, and she's currently expecting an eighth child.

Christy has had multiple short stories published through Black Hare Press and in *The Bear Creek Gazette*.

Joseph Cooper grew up in Baltimore, and he "did what he loved" by earning his bachelor of arts degree in history from the University of Maryland Baltimore County. After realizing that his degree lacked a clear path to a paycheck, Joseph claims to have doubled down on questionable life choices: He attended to law school at University of Baltimore. He spends time seeing every live theater show he can find in the Baltimore area—over 100 shows in 2019. He also practices insurance law in Baltimore.

Zoe Copeman grew up not only listening to folktales about but also exploring the haunted locations around her hometown of Historic Ellicott City, Maryland. She graduated summa cum laude from the University of Maryland College Park with a dual degree in psychology and art history, which included a focus on abnormal behavior and constructions of identity. Zoe served as an associate therapist in the Baltimore area before moving to the United Kingdom to complete her masters in the history of art at the University College London, where she received distinction for her MA dissertation entitled "Deviating from Monstrosity: The paradox of the normal in *Les Ecarts de la Nature.*"

Currently, Zoe is based at the University of Maryland, pursuing her doctorate in eighteenth-century European print culture.

Devon K. Hardy was born in Miami, Florida, and spent her childhood in Northern Virginia, daydreaming about being a marine biologist and talking about sharks to anyone who would listen. Devon currently lives in Fairfax, Virginia with her beloved dog Benney and her rambunctious kitten Spock.

She obtained degrees from Loyola University Chicago, George Mason University, and Johns Hopkins University. She is currently working on her first novel about a graduate history student who stumbles across the century-old murder of a female lighthouse keeper in a fictional town in Chesapeake Bay, Maryland. She plans to write a series of novels about maritime themes, including roles women played in maritime history (and yes, that includes pirates).

Devon's writing continues to be inspired by all the genres she grew up reading. Her short stories, including "The Perfect Flight," tend to be tales of horror. However, her longer stories fall under the genre of mystery/thriller (with a bit of dark, sarcastic humor sprinkled in).

Frank E Hopkins has lived most of his life in Maryland, Delaware, and New York. After teaching, he returned to Maryland where he lived for 30 years working as a government contracting consultant. He spent the last two decades living and writing in Ocean View, Delaware.

Frank is active in the Rehoboth Bay Writers Guild, the Eastern Shore Writers Association, and the Berlin chapter of the Maryland Writers Association.

Edward M. Lukacs was born in Elizabeth, New Jersey in 1943, and he lived in Point Pleasant and Manasquan until moving to Homestead, Florida in 1983.

After spending more than 12 years in Florida, at the US Naval Obsevatory, he was transferred to Washington, DC in 1996. Edward lived in Georgetown, DC, behind the Russian Embassy until retiring. He retired early due to his wife suffering a severe stroke at the end of 2000. The couple moved to Georgetown, Delaware where they lived together until her passing in 2006, and he still lives there. While in DC, they travelled extensively in northern Virginia, eastern West Virginia, and Maryland, but after moving to Delaware, his wife's condition limited their travels to day trips on the Delmarva Peninsula.

Dereck Mangus (guest editor) is a Baltimore-based visual artist and writer. His work has been exhibited in select galleries throughout Charm City. His writing has appeared in *Artblog, frieze*, and *Full Bleed*, the annual journal of art and design at the Maryland Institute College of Art.

Jeff Markowitz is the author of five mysteries, including three books in the *Cassie O'Malley Mystery* series. *Who is Killing Doah's Deer*, published in 2004, introduced readers to the tabloid reporter and amateur sleuth who serves as the main character. Cassie returned two years later in *A Minor Case of Murder* and again in 2009 in *It's Beginning to Look a Lot like Murder*. In 2015, his standalone black comedy *Death* *and White Diamonds* won a Lovey Award and a David Award. His latest book, *Hit or Miss*, follows a murder set against the backdrop of the Vietnam War.

Jeff grew up in Valley Stream, New York. He moved to New Jersey in 1970 to earned his degree in psychology at Princeton University. Although he lived in the Princeton area for more than 50 years, Jeff currently makes his home in Monmouth Junction, New Jersey with his wife Carol and two cats, Vergil and Aeneas. Jeff is Past President of the New York Chapter of Mystery Writers of America.

Morgan McClure grew up in Columbia, Maryland and went on to attend the University of Maryland Baltimore County to complete a mechanical engineering degree. She became interested in reading and writing thriller and mystery stories. Following her undergraduate degree, where her lone writing class was overshadowed by math and physics, she studied legal writing in law school at George Mason University. Upon passing the bar, Morgan was able to start devoting more time to creative writing.

In the fall of 2020, Morgan was a finalist at Old Town Book's Spooky Story contest, in Alexandria, Virginia. During the day, Morgan hones her writing skills by corresponding with applicants as a patent examiner for the government.

Savannah S. Miller is a playwright, storyteller, actor, and artist currently based out of the Carolinas. Miller graduated summa cum laude from Dartmouth College. As strong believer in the power of words, she writes one-act and full-length plays, as well as a handful of short stories.

For her writing, she has been awarded the Eleanor Frost Playwriting Contest Award twice, the Robert H. Nutt '49 Award, the Benjamin & Edna Ehrlich Prize in the Dramatic Arts, and the Warner Bentley & Henry B. Williams Fellowship. Her full-length play *The House* was also selected by Young Playwrights' Theater to be work-shopped for future performances.

In addition to writing, Miller has acted in productions at the Women's Theatre Festival, Dartmouth College, and with a diverse artist collective called CRASH Theater Co. She has developed works with the New York Theatre Workshop and CRASH Theater Co. As an arts educator and arts advocate, Miller has fulfilled positions with the Smithsonian's Discovery Theater, the Stratford Festival, and the Virginia Theatre Association.

Shane Moritz arrived in the Mid-Atlantic (Baltimore, specifically) in 2016 behind the wheel of a Nissan he purchased with loan money he hadn't spent from an MFA in Creative Writing he earned in the Southern Gothic outpost known as Georgia College & State University.

After spending time writing poetry, Shane returned to teaching creative writing: first for Johns Hopkins Odyssey Program, then at Jessup as part of the Goucher College Prison Partnership. Today, he teaches English Composition at University of Maryland Baltimore County (UMBC) and works in the writing studio at Maryland Institute and College of Art (MICA).

Benjamin Robb resides in Orefield, Pennsylvania. He calls Quakertown, Pennsylvania his hometown. Robb attended Columbia College Chicago for screenwriting. His stories have been featured on The No Sleep Podcast, which played a large role in getting him into the short horror fiction genre in the first place.

His work in screenwriting includes credit for the story for *The Eighth Commandment* and writing the screenplay for *Broken Bond*. In his free-time, he reads, enjoys prestige television and all manner of film, and plays with his dogs and cat.

Bud Scott has lived in Maryland nearly all his life. He was born and raised in Berlin, Maryland and now resides in Salisbury. He is a member of The Maryland Writers'

Association. Bud has won several flash fiction contests in the UK and the US. His book *Dead People From the Attic* was published in 2018

Shaun Vain (managing editor) connects with writers and editors and enjoys working with literary journals, academic admissions committees, and state arts councils. Over 10 years into his career, Shaun has written as much fiction as possible of a man in his station in life.

He writes all types of written work that people are asked to come up with (and some work that people haven't asked for), like whitepapers that businesses pay him to write and cover letters to find more clients in need of whitepapers (and deeply imaginative fiction). He creates short, snappy lines. But he loves to write long pieces of fiction. Although he has a passion for novel writing, he's spending more time working in publishing the work of his peers and some time perfecting the short story.

Mark Willen was born, raised, and educated in New England, but within days of his graduation from Dartmouth College in 1969, he moved to the Washington, D.C., metropolitan area to begin a career in journalism. He has lived in the Mid-Atlantic region ever since.

Over the next four decades, he worked as a reporter, columnist, blogger, producer, and editor at The Voice of America, National Public Radio, Congressional Quarterly, Bloomberg News, The Federalist Paper, and Kiplinger. Though based primarily in Washington, he has reported from datelines as varied as New York, Moscow, Cairo, Beijing, London, Paris, Buenos Aires, Nairobi, and Johannesburg.

For his work in providing programs to assist aspiring young authors, Mark was awarded the Friends of the Library Charles W. Gilchrist award in 2016 and the Montgomery County Executive Award for Excellence in the Arts and Humanities in 2018. Mark lives in Silver Spring, Maryland, with his wife, Janet.

Index of Subgenres

Acknowledgments

This project was made possible through group collaboration and participation of guest artists and reviewers, including a review committee and support from local literary arts groups.

To select the stories for the book you're reading, a group of 10 volunteers, artists and scholars, focused on writing quality and genre. For assistance with reviewing, discussing, and choosing submissions for this project, FPH acknowledges Jessica Ruth Baker, Barbara Bryan, John Joseph Enright, Julia Golonka, Kenny Leon Horning, Emma S. Rund, Alexander Scally, Denise T. Smolarek, and Frank Wisniewski. Additionally, FPH acknowledges Emma for her assistance with drafting the land acknowledgement statement; Barbara for her creative consultations and feedback; Alexander, Frank, Jessica, John, and Julia for in-depth discussions and meetings in support of the project. FPH acknowledges support from staff members at arts councils and arts collectives who work directly with the writing community, especially Laura Weiss, Tammy Oppel, Dana Parsons, CityLit, and Carla Du Pree. Special thanks go out to Canadian author Melodie Campbell for her wisdom and insight.

The interior of this book was edited with assistance from reviewers, writers, and those involved in creating work for this project, including formatting and design notes from Kiirstn Pagan and Dereck Stafford Mangus.

This project is supported in part by the Maryland State Arts Council (msac.org).

In closing, FPH acknowledges the authors who wrote the stories bound within the book you're holding for their patience, comradery, and creativity.